Copyright

Widow's Lace
By Lelita Baldock

ISBN 978-1-71697-459-5 (Lulu Paperback Edition)
ISBN B086BK5CTF (Amazon Kindle Edition)
ISBN 9798630704184 (Amazon Paperback Edition)

Disclaimer
The characters in this book are entirely fictional. Any resemblance to actual persons living or dead is entirely coincidental.

Editing by Lelita Baldock
Cover Art by Ryan Hewitt

First published March 2020
Visit: lelitabaldock.com

Author's Acknowledgement

I would like to acknowledge the Ngarrindjeri people of the Lower Lakes region in South Australia, on whose land much of *Widow's Lace* is set.

References to the culture of the Ngarrindjeri have been made with the aim of creating an accurate description of the region during the times of this novel. All research as been conducted by me and any errors are solely my own.

My intention has been to acknowledge and share all the cultures of the Lower Lakes Region.

Sincerely,

Lelita Baldock - Author of Widow's Lace

Map of the Lower Lakes, South Australia

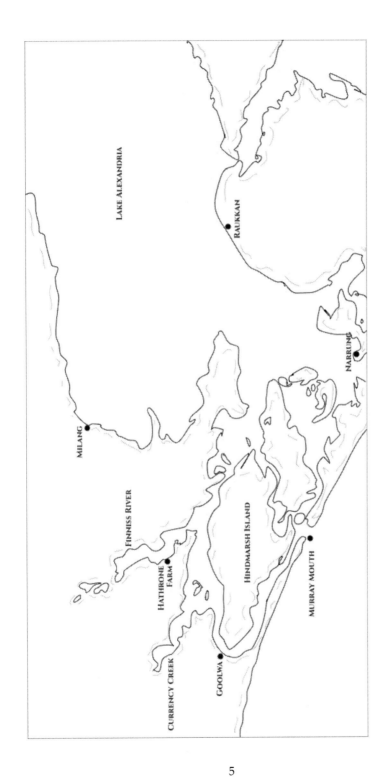

LAKE ALEXANDRIA

RAUKKAN

NARRUNG

MILANG

FINNISS RIVER

HINDMARSH ISLAND

HATHRONE FARM

MURRAY MOUTH

CURRENCY CREEK

GOOLWA

Prologue

Before

Sunlight glints through the brown murky water, spreading warmth. Small fish dart where the green reeds break the surface, swaying in the gentle current. Suddenly, bubbles spill forth and the surface begins to move further away. The light above darkens. A white hand reaches up to the few remaining shards of light still penetrating the murky depths. The hand is not fast or alarmed, it does not clutch. Buffeted by the swirling water it drifts in an arch through the gentle current. Riverbed mud rises up like bellows of smoke in the brown water. The reeds close in, thicker at their base, twining around the hand as it floats back down to the river bed. All dark now. Still. Not even the current moves.

Ellie

1

Silence. Cold. Dry and brittle.
Adrift in an ocean of darkness.

Sydney, Australia 2018

I've always loved the sight of water, cooling, calming, the shades of blue, green, brown, all natural and peaceful. I hugged my handbag to my chest and gazed out towards Sydney Quay, the harbour waters rolling gently beneath me. Dusk kissed the currents in orange and pink. The breeze, though warm, carried the promise of winter at its edge. Another ferry crossed our path, it's wake rocking us side to side, forcing me to admit that perhaps that last pint at the Four Pines was a pint too many.

My friends and I had spent the morning hours in the waters off Manly, swimming, splashing, laughing, the warmth of the sun soaking into our skin, before retiring to the micro-brewery by the ferry station to eat and drink away the sunshine hours. Golden light had bathed our smiles, glinting off our auburn and rose coloured drinks, shading us in the hues of summer. Chasing away the sound of tomorrow morning's 6 a.m. alarm and the grey of weekdays ahead.

Crowded trains, blaring car horns, shoulder to shoulder in black suits, carrying briefcases, sucking down the last ash of a cigarette before the office doors, thoughts of my father… all pushed firmly aside as another slice of fruit cheese, dried apricot popping from the pale flesh, was gathered up in greasy fingers, wrapped in bright pink salami and passed through wine stained lips.

My mobile bleeped. I rummaged through my bag, pushing aside lip balm, tissues, beer change and a barrage of crumpled receipts from the bar.

Message from Caleb: 'Happy studying. See you Wednesday?'

A heavy sigh escaped me as I returned the phone to my bag, message unanswered. I'd told my boyfriend I needed tonight to prepare for my tutorials, ready to launch into the new term. And to work on my thesis, if in fact I could find the time around the marking and lesson planning. *Truth*. But another truth was that I would stop at the little grocery store on the corner of my street in Darlinghurst. That I would buy a bottle of sav blanc - or rosé? *Both*. I would climb the stairs to my student apartment under the dim light of the automatic fluros: five lights, three broken. I would sit on my tiny balcony, just wide enough for my bum, legs stretched out before me, the view of the concrete apartments of next door rising up, gum trees silhouetted against the last of the suns rays. And, wine in one hand, ice blocks clicking in the glass to cool the room temperature liquid (that mattered for the first one), cigarette in the other, I would rest my head against the concrete panel behind me and toast the night. A cloud of smoke rising from my lips to mix with the cooling autumn air. Open wine bottle wedged between my legs, I would watch the darkness swallow the sky, the ambient light of the city and gathering winter clouds hiding the stars.

And I would drink, and smoke, and drink some more. Until I finished both bottles - why stop at one? And finished my cigarettes - because I would quit tomorrow and these shouldn't go to waste. And finally, sometime around 1 a.m, exhaustion would creep into the haze of boredom tinged with nothingness that sat inside me. Not heavy, not light, not anything really, just there. And I would stagger to bed, bottles and butts left on the balcony and collapse onto my mattress, not even bothering to pull back the sheets, definitely not brushing my teeth. But remembering last minute to set my alarm, because tomorrow… tomorrow, I had to show up.

'Good Easter break Ellie?'

I looked up from the essay before me, red pen hovering over yet another correction and smiled warmly at Tessa.

'Wonderful, thank you.' I said, reaching for my coffee – third one since arriving at my office, 'You?'

'Yes, went down to Bondi with the family. Lots of niece cuddles. Can you believe she's almost two already?'

'Two! Wow, time flies huh?'

'I can't wait to have my own. But thesis first. Did you find any time for good ol' EB over the break?'

EB - Edward Barrington, author of the poem I was analysing for my PhD thesis. I suppressed a cringe. No, no I hadn't. Truth be told, I hadn't 'found time' for my thesis in weeks...

'Some,' I said, 'but mostly I had to catch up on these papers. And planning for the term.' *Lie.*

'I hear you. The extra money is nice, but taking tutes and working on a PhD is tough. Still, better than the 'real world', am I right?'

I smiled in response and, slurping down a large mouthful of coffee, returned to my marking. I still had half of this class and all of the third to get through before the end of the day. Tessa settled down at the desk opposite me and soon the only sound around us was the scrape of my correction pen and the click of her typing... probably finishing another chapter of her thesis.

I liked Tessa. Her thesis was in history, specifically definitions of genocide, which still surprised me every time she gifted me one of her smiles. Straight black hair, shimmering glory unlike my dull ash brown; bright eyes behind purple rimmed glasses, mine bloodshot hazel; pearl white teeth, Tessa seemed totally at odds with, well, the horrors of war. When we'd first met as new PhD candidates two years ago I had thought her crazy for taking on such a complex topic. I had chosen *The Fall*, a poem by a famous and revered English Poet who had also lived in Australia. An unfashionable poem sure, but with the fame of Edward Barrington, and the connection to Australia, it would be easy... *should* have been easy.

Yet here we sat, entering our last 18 months of scholarship, and she was almost finished her core chapters. I was... not there yet. Not even close.

I had started well. My opening chapters covering his life, fame, and his move to a property just outside of Goolwa in South Australia, drew from his personal history to shape and support my interpretation of *The Fall*. I'd even won a grant to visit the UK to research on Barrington's home soil (I hadn't used it). From my own structured life I could indulge in the wretched sense of loss that leaked from the words: someone else's pain, someone else's cage.

It made me feel closer to my dad; how I miss him.

He found the good in things. Always said, 'Even in shadow, there will always be hope.' I still liked that.

I applied it to my research and study of *The Fall*. But as I learned of Barrington's life, I came to see the poem's paradox. A sense of loss and hopelessness ached from the words, a return to the dark poems that had made him famous, though it was written at a time of peace in Barrington's life. My pace had slowed.

Then I visited my mum, and the foundation of my life was torn away. Her words plunged me into my own dungeon and *The Fall* became too personal, too real. No longer could I indulge in the emotions of the poem, safely distanced. Now it seemed to speak to my own heart and soul.

I'd decided I needed a break from study and had taken a few days off to brunch with friends, say yes to a few date invites. I'd met Caleb and, sucked into the vortex of a new relationship, I was happy to drown my thoughts, my feelings in his warm tanned body and ready fingers. My few days had become a few weeks, then months. And now, now...

I sighed and reached for my coffee cup. Empty. Restless, I rose from my desk, pen falling from my fingers. 'I'm going for a refill, can I get you anything?'

'Hmmm...' Tessa held up a quick finger and, brow creased in concentration, finished off a thought before, 'Sorry, you asked? Coffee! Right. Um, no thank you, I am fine for now.' And returned to her typing.

I nodded and headed for the door, the sound of Tessa's focus taping on the keyboard behind me. As I pulled our office door closed I wondered: had I been engrossed in my thesis like that too? At the start? Had I felt that passion and lost it? Was it somewhere still, inside?

I squared my shoulders and lifted my chin, fixing an amiable but vacant smile on my face, ready to run the gauntlet of staff and students between my office and the cafeteria. The picture of professional calm, studious and focused; the PhD candidate nearing the end of her tenure, looking forward to a career in academia as a professor and lecturer. I smiled at a group of passing students, they nodded to me in acknowledgement. I knew I looked the part, in my blue shirt and black heals, hair neatly tied back. And I knew it for what it was. Felt it. I was on the precipice of failure. If I got past my upcoming review with my supervisor without being stripped of my scholarship, it would be a miracle. Because I was a fraud. Pretty packaging wrapped over an empty box. Nothing inside, nothing to show for the years of funding, research grants, time. I had taken my scholarship. I was expected to give back to the academic community, to advance knowledge… but I couldn't even get through a class worth of tute marking. Not the problem. Not really.

The cafeteria loomed before me. I made a snap decision. Rather than enter and get that longed for coffee, I turned and headed out. Out across the campus, through the front gates and down the street. A walk, some fresh air, that's what I needed to clear my head. To find some focus. *Liar*. The word leapt up at me but I pushed it down and headed for the park, for the chair by the lake I knew was waiting for me. Waiting like it did most days lately, to keep my bottom off the dry grass as I gazed at the water and felt nothing inside me. Nothing at all.

2

I reach for colour, bright and warm.
Rejection another shade of black.

The rosé slipped coolly down my throat. The Vanguard bar was dimly lit but the conversation around me sparkled and shimmered. Wednesday evening. Mid-week drinks. Not as raucous as Friday night cocktails, but still lively and buzzing. Caleb slipped his arm around my waist and I leaned into him, hoping to feel – something. He smiled down at me happily before continuing his conversation with Tessa and Paul across the table.

'Personally, when I finished my accounting degree, I couldn't wait to be out the door. I don't know how you and Ellie do it… further study. I feel ill just thinking about a library these days.'

'No!' Tessa exclaimed, eyes gleaming, bright. 'Surely you are exaggerating.'

'He's not,' Paul chimed in. 'That Caleb even got into his degree still amazes me. We were the boys who weren't meant to finish year 12, let alone get a degree.'

'What do you mean?' Tessa asked.

Leaning in close to her, voice hushed, Paul said, 'Too busy with the ladies to get our homework done.' Tessa reddened prettily. 'Some habits die hard.'

'Now, now,' Caleb said, 'I'm a changed man since I met Ellie. You just have to find the right girl Paul, that's all.'

'I wonder if I'll know her when I meet her,' Paul breathed in Tessa's direction.

I felt ill.

Inviting Tessa had been Caleb's idea. Thinking the shy, slight woman might be 'the one' for his perpetually single mate from high school. From what I could see, Paul had no desire to 'settle' for anyone for more than a night.

I poured the last of my wine down my throat and reached for the bottle to refill.

'Well, Ellie and I are just different from you both I suppose,' Tessa said.

'So what are you studying? Is it something, intimate...' Paul leaned closer, Tessa shifted uncomfortably.

'Genocide,' she announced like a shield, 'but that's not really drinks talk. Ellie's thesis is far more interesting anyway. Famous poet, mysterious death, romantic love story... won't you tell us a bit about where you are up to in your research Ellie?' Tessa turned a pair of too wide, startled eyes to me and I read the request, clear and pleading: talk, shift the focus.

Caleb turned, an eyebrow cocked in my direction. 'You know, I would like that too Ellie.' He addressed the table, Paul now leaning back into his chair, 'six months in and Tessa just told me more about your thesis topic than you have...'

Tessa laughed a little too high and reached for her glass, barely touched. 'It's truly a fascinating story... And so sad. Edward Barrington was famous beyond reason in England, but his wife was ill. So he risked everything to bring her here to Australia to get better. And she did. But then, less than two years later, he disappeared. All very mysterious. His wife remained in Australia until just before the First World War, when a young academic came over from England to learn about Barrington's life here. He took her home...'

'Dirty little bugger,' Paul interrupted. 'Getting off with the widow.'

Tessa slid an irritated glance at him before continuing, 'Not at all! She was an old woman by then and he young and engaged. But he took her home to England, and then he died in the War. It's a very sad story on all sides. She brought back Barrington's poems from those few months in Australia. A plethora of work, all when everyone thought he produced nothing.'

'And what is your angle on the story then Ellie?' Caleb asked, eyes searching.

I tried for a brief overview, 'I'm looking at a poem he wrote, one of his last, from when he was here in Australia. One that his widow brought back. It's not well known, probably not his best work...'

'But there is just *something* about it… isn't there Ellie? Some question unanswered.'

Paul scoffed. 'A poem? What's the point of that…'

A glare from Tessa. 'It's personal. It was her father's favourite poem. Wasn't it Ellie?'

Shit.

'So, you are looking to interpret the sadness?' Caleb prompted me.

Sadness? The word took me by surprise. 'Sad' just wasn't strong enough to describe the darkness and longing of *The Fall*. It was desperate and resigned and hopeless.

I glanced up at Tessa. Her passion breathed out across the table. It was like Barrington and his poem were her thesis. I felt my own interest responding, a glimmer of my former self. Uncomfortable, I shoved it down. I didn't want to talk about this. I didn't want to admit…

'Well, what are the odds?' Paul drawled from across the table. Bored of the conversation, he'd been scrolling on his iPhone.

'What?' Caleb said, irritation in his voice. Probably at being interrupted by his friend.

'Your poet's on the news,' Paul said, turning up the volume on his mobile and placing it on the table, oriented for me to see.

We all hunched forward watching the device broadcast its tinny news report from channel Nine's Facebook stream. A young reporter with short bobbed, brown hair and thick-rimmed glasses was speaking to the screen.

'The bones were discovered yesterday, on a property just outside the town of Goolwa in South Australia. At this stage it's too early to say, but there are high hopes that they may be those of the famous English poet Edward Barrington, who lived on the property until his mysterious disappearance in 1888. I spoke with the current owner, Deborah Jenkins, earlier today.'

The vision cut to a shot of a large verandah-rimmed home nestled on a green lawn. Beyond the house shone a waterway edged by reeds shifting in the breeze. Then a middle aged woman, dark haired, face lined with wrinkles creased in a smile, stood by the reporter saying, '… the workmen found the bones. You know the rules here, with the Aboriginal history of the area. We contacted the council immediately.'

'They could be aboriginal bones?'

'Well, they say it's not likely…'

'So, this could be the missing body of Edward Barrington?'

'Well, yes, yes indeed. It's certainly a possibility. I'd never really thought much about the history of this place before. But as soon as I heard about the bones, Barrington was the first thought that popped into my head.'

'How long until the bones are processed and dated?'

'They say a couple of weeks, and then we will know. Such an amazing find. And on our little property...'

I turned to Tessa, our eyes meeting across the table. 'Ellie,' she breathed, 'they've found your poet!'

'They've found some bones.' I said flatly.

'How can you say that? It's obvious! Amazing. This will put Barrington back into conversation, just as you are finishing your thesis on his work from Australia. The timing couldn't be better for you Ellie.'

Oh it could. It really, really could. Yet despite myself something within me stirred.

'This calls for a toast,' Caleb said, beaming at me, something like pride in his eyes. 'Cheers to Ellie, and her good fortune. To those with talent who deserve good luck. None more so than my girl.'

'Cheers,' Tessa echoed. I smiled lamely and gulped my wine. From across the table Paul's dark eyes watched me. A small, knowing smirk on his face.

Conversation ebbed and flowed between us for a few more hours before we all decided it was time to head home. Waving to Tessa and Paul as they headed for the bus stop, Caleb looped an arm around me and pulled me into an embrace. I fought the cringe at the contact and allowed the hug. He pulled back, looking into my eyes. 'Back to mine?'

Panic gripped my heart, how to say no? 'I'd love to but...'

'You have to work on your thesis. I understand, Ellie. Well, I do now anyway. I never really got it, a thesis on a poem. What does that matter? But seeing your guy on the news... people care about his works, his history. And the connection to your dad... Study might not be my thing. But I support you, Ellie. I do.'

Study might not be my thing either, I wanted to scream. *I can't focus, I can't see the point. I feel trapped, caught between expectations. And I can't do it. I can't do it. I'm not enough.*

But I smiled and nodded. Caleb pulled me close, brushing a kiss to my lips. I willed the rush of desire, the flood of lust that had had me gasping for him in those first few heady months. But nothing came.

We parted and I walked to my train, a stone in my belly. And I stopped at the corner store and stared at the window, stared and stared. And then I went in, and I bought the sav blanc and the rosé and a fresh packet of cigarettes and returned to my apartment, my balcony, glass in hand. The news report buzzing through my mind.

My fingers interlaced in my lap, curling together, then apart. I twisted my hands to thread my digits the other way, then back to curling. Fidgeting. I was fidgeting. *Stop it.* I clasped my hands together and faced my supervisor.

Peter Tuft was a round man, robust and vibrant, but slowing down as he neared retirement, his grey moustache drooping over swollen lips. A deep frown of irritation (or was that disappointment?) marked his brow. Presently, he dropped the stack of papers in his hand, my latest chapter, and leaned back in his chair heavily. Folding his hands over his rounded belly, he fixed me with his milky blue eyes. Silent. Staring. I held his stare as long as I could. Then, shame flushing my cheeks, looked down and away. I knew. He breathed in. I braced myself: for my reprimand, for dismissal from my scholarship, for what I deserved.

'When did you last see your mother?'

Shocked, I looked up sharply. His eyes remained on my face, but softness had replaced the irritation of before.

'We spoke… last month.'

'Not over the holiday?'

'Easter was never something she was into.'

'We all need family, Ellie.'

I looked away, mouth set in a grim line.

Peter huffed loudly and leaned forward, bracing his elbows on the desk. 'So, are you going to ask me? For the time off?'

Confused, I cocked my head at him. 'To go to SA? To see the burial site, speak to the locals? The discovery of the bones is all over the news. People are talking about Barrington again, the town is alive with the memory. It would be ripe with inspiration for your thesis.'

He glanced pointedly at the pages before him, 'Inspiration seems just what you need. And perhaps, family.'

'Phone calls with her are plenty. I live here now, not in Adelaide,' I said, purposely avoiding his real point.

'Ellie Cannon,' Peter said, straightening, 'I've never known you to be a fool.'

I frowned at him. Where was this going?

'This,' he flicked his wrist at my pages before him, voice hardening, 'is not a chapter. It's not even a collection of thoughts. It's just words, repeating your first chapters, but in new phrases. You haven't brought me anything new in months.'

Six months.

'Something has to change. *You*, have to change. What happened to the passionate girl who first walked into my office and announced her thesis topic? Who had already written the outline plan and argued confidently against my suggestions? What happened to the girl who would be a professor? Because she is not here now Ellie. She's not been here for a while.'

'You know what happened.'

A frown. 'Yes, Ellie, yes I do. But you can't let it best you. I told you to take time off, to reset. But you haven't. It won't just heal, Ellie, you have to work at it.'

'There's nothing to work on. What's done is done.'

'So act like it!' I cringed back at his sharp tone and looked at him through hooded eyes.

"Ellie, this cannot continue. I have given you all the leeway I can. All the time I can. But if this... *phase* doesn't correct itself, well, you know what I have to do.'

I did. I would have to leave my thesis, abandon my PhD, my academic goals. Was that what I wanted?

Into my silence Peter sighed. 'Go to Goolwa, Ellie. Speak to the people, walk the land that Barrington called home. And visit your mother. In person. You two need to talk this out. You need to find closure.'

'I can study well enough from here. And my tutes...'

'Tessa will take your tutes. They will learn more from her anyway and the parental complaints will wash over...'

Shame burned my cheeks. I was struggling, but that didn't make it right to let down the first years. I hadn't known parents had complained, but I wasn't surprised. I had given them so little lately, I hadn't even marked the last semester papers.

'... Ellie, this is not a choice. You will go to South Australia, on research leave for the next four weeks. Don't object. You will go. And you will deal with what has happened to you, to your family. And when you come back you will present to me a *new* core chapter. One with the fire of your first and we will never speak of this time again. You will go, or you leave me no option. Have I made myself clear?'

I nodded, sullen. Fingers twitching for a cigarette.

'Your study leave starts now. Go. Pack a bag and go *home*. Bring back that sparkle. Bring back yourself. You are dismissed.'

I stood up stiffly, gathering my satchel and headed for the door.

'Ellie,' I paused on the threshold. 'I understand Ellie. I do. But you have to rise above it. You cannot let this take you down. Not any longer.'

I pulled the door shut behind me, harder than I needed and walked out of the university. Irritated, but for the first time in a long time, energy bubbled in my core.

3

I create escape. In browns and greys and maroons.

The Finniss River, Australia 2018

A cup of coffee warmed my hands as I gazed down an expanse of green grass that coursed in a gentle slope to the riverbank. The sound of the reeds rustling in the cold breeze and the tweeting of birds filled the silence. Barrington's estate, Hathrone Farm, was just as beautiful as I had imagined from his poems. The homestead at my back was of the old style, with a low ceiling and thick sandstone walls. The verandah on which I sat was polished wood, almost certainly a replacement of the original.

I'd flown down from Sydney that morning, hired a car in Adelaide and driven the hour and bit from the city to the coastal town of Goolwa, just outside of which, along the Finniss river, lay Barrington's former home. Despite growing up in suburban Adelaide, I'd never been to this holiday and farming region. So far, it looked to be a beautiful place.

'Mum said you are welcome in now, she's done with the builders.' I turned and nodded my thanks to the tall, fair skinned youth. 'Thank you, Alison.'

'Just head to the kitchen,' she shrugged, walking past me down the steps and, moving with the loping stride of a teenager newly grown out of childhood, headed to a shed on the side of the property. I watched as she hauled out a kayak and pushed it into the water, paddling out through the reeds onto the Finniss River. I rose, downed the last dregs of my coffee, cold now from the autumn chill, South

21

Australia was always colder than Sydney, and headed inside.

The hallway was dark and empty, a weathered looking rug running down its length. But finding the kitchen proved to be no issue. Voices, speaking rapidly over and around each other, floated down the hall from an open doorway, bright lights shining within. I entered cagily, feeling very much an intruder. Within stood three workmen, a teenager (boy, probably brother to Alison) and Deborah Jenkins, the owner. We had spoken briefly twice now: over the phone when I asked to speak to her about the discovery of the bones, and then again this morning, when I arrived to the chaos of her home renovations and, plied with coffee, was asked to wait outside.

Tall and lean, despite being the mother of teenagers, Deborah radiated elegance. Dark hair pulled back in a high ponytail, a few grey hairs fuzzing from the sweep to catch the light from the window in a soft glow about her forehead.

Waving her manicured hands expressively, she addressed one of the workmen. 'I understand Brett. We are happy to accept the delay. But it would be better for us if the time could be used on the shed extension, then come back to the lounge. What do you think?'

'We can do it. No drama. But we will need to get the supplies. We'd have to invoice for them ahead of time…'

'Of course! No worries at all. Just send it through and I'll get on it. Then you and the boys can get back to work.'

The three workmen, clad in light green shorts and t-shirts, boots crusted with dirt, stood comfortably around the central kitchen bench, a bowl of cookies in the centre, a mug of coffee in each man's hands. Despite their bulk filling the pristine kitchen with the musty scent of dirt and sweat, they seemed not at all uncomfortable. Like mates hanging out.

'Mum, I have to go…'

'Oh, yes, Billy. Hang on.' Deborah reached into her purse and proffered the boy a 50 dollar note. 'Have a great day in town,' she called as he slunk past the workmen and me, heading for the front door.

It was then that Deborah saw me. 'Oh, Ellie! Alison got you. Excellent. We are just about finished here. Thank you for your patience.'

'No trouble at all,' I gave her my nicest smile as a wall of male faces, browned from the sun, turned and took me in. I couldn't help but notice the strong muscles moving beneath their shirts and fought the blush that threatened to redden my cheeks.

'Take a seat over here, dear,' Deborah indicated a bench stool to her left as she turned back to the men. 'Anything else, just give me a call. But we are happy for you to move on to the next stage while the lounge is paused. I'll get that invoice paid ASAP.'

'Cheers, Deborah,' Brett, who seemed the boss said. 'I'll be in touch in the next few days with a start date.'

'Thanks Brett. Have a good day lads.'

As they shuffled out, dropping their mugs in the sink on the way, Deborah returned to the coffee peculator bubbling in the corner. 'Fresh cup?'

'No thank you, I am fine.'

'Help yourself to some cookies love.' She poured herself another mug, all coffee, no milk or sugar and came to sit on the stool opposite me, 'Righto, now I am all yours.' She offered me a welcoming smile.

'Thank you for seeing me.'

'No trouble at all. I mean, reporters...,' she rolled her eyes theatrically and grinned, 'but a young lady studying. For you I will always have time.'

'You are having renovations done? You look to be very busy.'

'Yes, sorry about the mess. That's how we found the bones. The hold up with the lounge is causing no shortage of drama. We wanted the works done by November – it's my 50th. But the bones have thrown a spanner in that plan!'

'So they were found quite close to the house?'

'Yes, yes,' Deborah said, slurping her coffee down between sentences, 'just out on the side. Would you like to see?'

Surprised, I nodded. 'Yes, yes please.'

'Follow me,' Deborah stood, plucking up a cookie as she led me out of the kitchen to the opposite side of the house. We walked through a large lounge room. It had been gutted. Walls stripped back to the frame, bare board beneath my feet. 'We are knocking out this wall,' Deborah pointed to the wall that would be the outside of the house, a small door stood in its centre. 'We want to open it up more – have a larger room and then a deck that heads out to the far garden. Great spot to sit outside and enjoy the river views with a glass of vino.'

'Sounds delightful.'

'Wait til you see the side views.'

Pushing the small door open, Deborah led me down some makeshift scaffold stairs. 'Mind your step. They had already removed the verandah here before we had to pause.'

Before me was a large rectangle of cleared dirt, perfectly flattened. Around it were deep cuts in the soil, orange plastic sticking up and out of the cuts.

'So this is where the extension will be?' I asked, showing an interest.

'Yep, those are the footings,' she indicated the orange plastic rim, 'and then beyond will be the deck.' We stepped over the footings and walked across yet more flattened ground until we came to a rough edge of turned earth. It sat on the verge of the bushland that surrounded the property. Looking up towards the river I realised this angle afforded a more sweeping view around the river's natural curve, allowing us to see further down it's passage, the birds swimming over the currents, the reeds poking through. For a moment, I lost myself in those shimmering waters.

'Beautiful, isn't it?' Deborah smiled. 'And there,' she pointed to the upturned earth, 'is where they found the bones.' I glanced down. I don't know what I had expected to feel. Something. I took a moment. It was a beautiful resting place. Lined by trees, the water not far away.

'What was here before?' I waved my hand back over the flattened outline of the extensions.

'Just grass. When we bought the place last year, Andrew's retirement gift to himself, my husband's a little older than me, it was all overgrown shrub. We've had gardeners in to clear the area for grass, and give the bush some shape. Found a patch of old woody rose bushes, they had to go. Then Andy had the idea of the deck. Summer parties. We honestly never thought there would be any traditional owners here. And the poet! Well, that was just completely out of mind.'

'When will you know the age of the bones? Does the dating take long?'

'Around a week or two they said, so we are just waiting. But we know they're not aboriginal.'

'You do? I thought that was still in doubt…'

She waved a hand. 'No, that was just for the news. The Ngarrindjeri elders were here the very day they were found… and they know. Their ancestors were smaller in stature and buried standing up. This was a white man's body for sure…'

A thrill of excitement raced through me. 'So, it really could be Edward Barrington?'

'Umm,' Deborah mumbled distractedly, 'Barrington. Oh, well I hope so! At first I thought them being aboriginal would be the biggest issue,' she heaved a sigh. 'Don't get me wrong, I get it. The importance of culture. But I now realise an unknown body is a far greater hold up. Police, forensics, I tell you, even I really hope it's your man.'

She grinned at me and I found myself smiling.

'It would have been a lovely place for him to rest. It would have made her happy.' I said.

'Who's that then?'

'His widow, Rosalind. They originally moved here for her health. She was older than him by some 12 years, and a divorcée, quite the topic for gossip when they were wed. She had a lung illness, probably TB. The climate here cured her. But then she outlived him, by about 40 years. He was not 30 yet when he died.'

'Oh, that's tragic! To overcome societies pressures, sickness and then to lose him anyway. I can understand that, to some extent. When Andy and I were first seeing each other my friends didn't like it. But you know what? It's not about them. It's about us. Tell me they at least had some happy years before he passed?' she begged dramatically.

'By all accounts they were a devoted couple, utterly in love. And very happy here.'

'How romantic. Tragic, but romantic. Why is it that the best love stories always end in grief?'

'I think it gives them more substance. To love is one thing, but to love over adversity...'

'Wise words young lady,' Deborah smiled at me wryly and I felt myself blush. 'Did they have any children?'

'Sadly no. It is assumed Rosalind was too ill or too old to conceive...'

'Sounds like they had a lot of pain in their lives.'

We stood in silence regarding the empty hole in the ground.

'So...' I began, ready to break the moment, but the crush of footsteps interrupted us.

'Hey Mrs J,' a light friendly voice called from behind us. We turned. There stood a young man of around my years, tall and lean, moving with an easy grace that suggested a wiry strength to his limbs. Tanned skin peaked out from his arm length brown shirt, his hair a mess of brown curls atop his head. He smiled at me easily, hazel eyes shining. I didn't think I'd ever seen such an open, warm smile. I blinked.

'Taj! Oh, I'd forgotten it was your day. The garden needs it. Things here have been such a mess since, well, you know.'

'No problem Mrs J. I know what needs doing. Just wanted to let you know I was here. Didn't want to startle you.'

'That's very thoughtful Taj. This is Ellie, I was just showing her the gravesite. She is doing a thesis on the poet they might belong to. Now we know they are not Kaurna or Ngarrindjeri.'

Deborah bobbed her head respectfully, and I wondered at her polite diffidence with this youth.

'Pleased to meet you Ellie,' Taj gifted me another of those smiles, and I felt a welcome warmth spread through my belly.

'And you.'

'In town for a while?'

'Around a week, initially at least.'

'Make sure you get down to the Coorong. Best first thing in the morning.'

'You mean where the mouth of the Murray is? Can I drive there?'

'You can, but it's better from the water. You wanna see if you can get on a boat. Plenty of us have them around here.'

'Thank you, I will keep that in mind. Local pro-tip!'

Taj grinned at my lame attempt at humour. 'Well, have a great stay. Mrs J, I'll just get to it now. Won't be in your way.'

Deborah was wearing a private smile I couldn't interpret as she waved Taj off and returned her attention to me.

'For while you are on dry land,' she smirked, 'I think it might be worth your time to check out the local library. They've been doing a whole heap of electronic archiving, things like newspaper articles, birth records. Could be you find something about your poet, local info. If he was as famous as they say on the news, I am sure little old Goolwa would have wanted to write about him at the time.'

'Thank you, yes, I will do that. Is the library in the town centre?'

'Right on the main street. Nice quiet space too. Well, I have to leave it there. Alison is due at a job interview in an hour and I haven't seen her return from her kayaking yet. Teenagers!' Deborah rolled her eyes, but an indulgent smile gave away her lie.

'It was nice to meet you Ellie.'

'And you Deborah. Thank you for seeing me, and for the coffee.'

'The pleasure was all mine. And hey, if you find anything interesting before you leave, about the poet I mean, be sure to pop past. All this bone stuff has stirred up my interest in our famous former resident.'

'I would be happy to, though I wouldn't hold your breath that there is much new to find.'

'Well, perhaps pop round anyway. It would be nice to see you again before you go. You can tell Taj and I about Barrington over a coffee and some more cookies.'

Again, that secretive smile. My hands twitched, wanting to fidget. I clamped them into fists. 'You are very kind. I will call if I have anything new to share.'

'You do that,' Deborah smiled. 'You can see yourself out? Good girl. Enjoy Goolwa, Ellie dear. It really is an inspiring place to be.'

4

But black returns. Always returns.
Dark waters swirling.

After checking in at my accommodation at the Marine Cove Resort on the lakeside in Goolwa, I took a walk along the water, enjoying the sweeping views of Hindmarsh Island floating in the centre of the lagoon. Fresh ocean air blew over the sand dunes that separated the town from the beach; the ocean's roar clearly audible on the wind. Overhead a pelican flew, so elegant in the skies, in complete contrast to their cumbersome waddle on land. As I breathed the salt tinged air my hair whipped back from my face in the breeze and a sense of resolve started to settle in my stomach.

I was here, where Edward Barrington had lived the happiest years of his life, where he wrote *The Fall*. This sleepy town, filled with more weekend holidaymakers than locals, was beautiful. And it was peaceful, surrounded by water. 'Dad, you would have loved it here.' I breathed to the winds.

Something had awoken inside me. Despite my reluctance to come, now I felt invigorated. The determination to know was flaring. I would find out more about Barrington's life here. Surely there would be information to discover.

After a quick lunch at the local fish and chip shop on the corner of the main street (schnitzel sandwich and a coke, I was treating myself) I walked down Cadell Street, heading for the library. It was a surprisingly modern space. Automatic doors whispered open in greeting as I walked into a high ceilinged open area, lined on all sides with shelves of books. I made my way straight to the large central space, populated by a circular shaped desk and an array of librarians of various ages over 50. I chose a lady with hair dyed deep auburn, cropped close to her head, her oversized red fingernails clicking audibly on the keyboard as she typed. Large golden hoop earrings caught the sun from the skylight above us as she turned to me and smiled. 'Beverly,' her name badge read.

'Can I help you?' Beverly asked.

'I think so. Um, I am here researching about the poet Edward Barrington. He lived here in the 1880s. A friend told me that newspaper articles and other data from that period had been recently digitally archived? Is that something I can access?'

'You most certainly can love. Just take any free terminal over by the windows and follow the search prompts. Anything in the system will come up. I hope you find lots of information.'

'Thank you,' I said and she turned back to her screen.

I picked a terminal as far as possible from the other users and settled down. The wall went up higher here, meaning the window was above my head, keeping the light down for the screens I supposed, but still offering a glimpse of the clear pale blue sky outside.

I opened the browser and typed in my search, keeping it simple: Edward Barrington. The browser chugged, loading line creeping in a small circle in the centre of my screen. Then a list popped up. It was arranged by title, with a sub-note beside each for it's source: newspaper article, council letter, magazine, book.

The third listing down caught my eye: 'Local poet visits Point McLeay Mission in education coop for administrator Phillip Merryweather.'

I clicked. A black and white scan of an old newspaper article flicked up. And there he was, Edward Barrington, posing for a photo, face solemn, eyes forward, surrounded by a group of smiling aboriginal children dressed in white shirts, trousers or dresses. He stood stiff, hands clasped behind his back, dark curls ringing a gentle face; the very picture of an English gentleman. The children looked relaxed and happy, all toothy grins and wind blown hair.

'Edward Barrington, esteemed poet from England, made the trek to the McLeay Mission orphanage this week to talk with the children about words and meanings.' I read.

'In what can only be seen as a master stroke, current administrator, Phillip Merryweather, asked the poet if he would spare some time with the class and he readily agreed. By all accounts his lessons were well received, the children polite and engaged. Barrington showed no nerves around the natives, despite *their obviously rudimentary manners and social skills. Another testament to the teachings of the Mission and the wonderful volunteers who govern there...'*

I read on, more praise for the Mission and staff, but little information on Barrington and his classes. I moved on to the next article: Barrington and Rosalind attending a writing society meeting, and sharing a reading of his famous poem *Of earth and wind*. This time the picture was of Barrington in a fine cut suit, top hat perched upon his brow. Rosalind stood beside him in a long, lace trimmed dress that flowed to the floor. Despite the grainy image, her beauty leapt from the screen, dark flowing curls, open round eyes, full lips. She must have been in her mid-forties when this photo was taken, but she looked younger than Barrington. Such a beautiful woman.

I adjusted my search, specifically looking for information on the Mission and Barrington's involvement. Turned out he had strong connections to the place, even taking on two young boys as farm hands.

On I scanned, newspaper clippings, magazine extracts, and then, the mystery: *'Esteemed poet and local man. Missing'*. They hadn't even needed to use his name in the title. The article was brief, but to the point, detailing his disappearance and the efforts of police and local men to search and rescue. I already knew that they never succeeded. It was one of the most famous disappearances in South Australian history. And this was a state of some horrid crimes...

Light footfall behind me turned my head.

'Sorry to interrupt love,' my red-haired librarian stood before me. 'My daughter is part of a local online group here. Through Facebook. I was thinking, if you are after local knowledge about Edward Barrington, perhaps I could ask her to post if anyone has any information? Might get you a different angle. What do you think?'

'Oh, thank you, I would appreciate that greatly. If that's ok? Not too much trouble?'

'Not at all, it may take a while though. Can I take a number?'

I scratched it down on a scrap of paper and Beverly promised to contact me should she hear anything. I thanked her and then found myself at a bit of a loss. The newspaper clippings had been interesting, especially those about the Mission. The Barringtons had never been gifted the child they longed for. I hoped he found some joy being around the orphans. More to look into there for sure, but for now, the sky above was darkening. I had been out and about all day, fatigue from my early flight from Sydney was starting to seep into my bones. As was the need for a cigarette.

I had intended to walk back to my motel, but the route took me past a beautiful sandstone hotel, the Corio. It sat on the corner of the main street of the town, old and proud, rimmed with a green painted balcony. Deciding I should eat, I headed in and ordered a prawn stuffed chicken breast and Imperial pint of beer. Taking my table number on a stick, I headed to the outside seating area at the front of the hotel and claimed a seat in the smoking section. Table secured, I lit a cigarette and leaned against one of the green balcony supports, watching the dusk colours paint the sky. The wind was chill; only myself and another group of smokers braved the outside. But I didn't mind. The quiet was welcome. I watched the darkening silhouette of a cluster of pine trees across the way and breathed the warmth of smoke into my lungs.

'Been on the water yet?' a smooth, deep voice cut into my daydreaming. I snapped my head around. Standing off to the side, calmly watching my face, was Taj. He was still dressed in his brown shirt and shorts, but it looked as though he had tidied his hair, maybe just with his hands as a brush. He held out a pint glass, half empty, towards me. 'Cheers,' he smiled.

'Cheers,' I returned, clinking my glass to his. He stepped up beside me, closer.

'So, how did your first day of research go?' he asked. I sucked in the last of my cigarette and dropped the butt on the ground to stub it out.

'Don't worry,' I said, 'I always pick them up after.' Taj only nodded, waiting silently. 'It went well, I think. I checked out the library. Found some interesting articles about Barrington working with orphans at a local Mission. It's not something I'd read about before, so that was cool. And Beverly, a librarian, said she would ask the locals, see if anyone has any information. Could be something, probably nothing. That tends to be how these things go.'

'If Bev is looking into it, you will have all there is to know,' Taj paused. 'Do you know where Raukkan is?'

'Raukkan?'

'That's the Mission's name.'

'I read Point McLeay...'

'Was renamed when the Ngarrindjeri took charge. Raukkan means *Meeting place*.'

'Oh. No, I'd never heard of it before today.'

'It was up on Lake Alexandrina, near Narrung, round the river bend. Intended to be self sustaining for the aboriginal community, but the land was too barren. The State gave it to the Ngarrindjeri people to run themselves, back in the 70s. Now it's really just a small township.'

'How do you know so much? Local knowledge?'

'Nah, my grandma was there as a kid, before the orphanage part was shut down.'

'Your grandma…?'

'Prawn stuffed chicken breast,' I turned. A diminutive waitress stood by my table with my dinner.

'That's me, thanks.' I headed over to my meal. Taj followed, relaxed and at ease, slipping into the seat opposite me. Mildly surprised, I took up my cutlery. 'You don't mind if I eat?'

'Not at all, go ahead. So, any plans for tomorrow?'

I bit into my chicken, covered in a garlicky creamy sauce. 'Oh, that's good! Um, yes, well, sort of. I guess I will head back to the library…'

'Don't want to spend too much time inside. I have tomorrow off, how about I take you down the Coorong, show you the dunes and the Murray Mouth? I reckon everyone needs a break from work, from time to time. And you are in a holiday town.'

I chewed my mouthful thoroughly, giving myself time to think. Truth was I really didn't need a break from researching, I had been doing bugger-all for months and had only just started to feel it's lure again… Across the table Taj's dark eyes watched me as he drained his pint. I decided.

'You know what? I'd love that. If you are sure you have the time?'

Taj grinned. 'It would be my honour. I'm getting another, can I grab you one too? Pale Ale was it?'

I looked at my empty glass. 'Yes please, thank you.'

And so we talked, and drank and talked, the evening turning to night around us. When the hotel switched off it's lights at 9 p.m, Taj and I walked slowly along the water front to my accommodation, the stars sparkling above our heads and dancing over the gentle ripples on the water. At my door Taj pecked me on the cheek and grinned. 'Home safe. I'll pick you up tomorrow at seven.'

'Seven?' I exclaimed.

'You gotta see the water early, it'll be like glass tomorrow. Bring a warm jacket. I'll see you then.' And with that he turned and ambled away, leaving me to my apartment. I crashed into bed, and for the first time in a long time sleep found me, and kept me right through until my alarm blazed at 6 a.m the next morning.

5

White, wet snow reveals a light. Anchor.
A gleaming emerald of green and fawn.

Taj was right. As we motored over the lake towards the barrage that separated this freshwater basin from the briny passage to the sea, the water all around us was smooth like glass. Our boat cut a line through the placid waters, round waves, milky blue from the pale morning light, rippling out from us and fading again into stillness. I sat at the front of the tinny, Taj at the back steering.

As we neared the middle of the lake Taj slowed the motor so we were almost stopped in the waterway. He lifted a finger and pointed back around the curve of the river.

'See how it bends?'

I nodded. He killed the motor and we sat, floating in the centre of the lake, drifting.

'That's where the name 'Goolwa' comes from. It means *elbow* in Ngarrindjeri.'

'Really?' I felt my eyebrows rise and a broad smile form on my lips. 'I like that.'

He smiled. 'Where we are going today is called the Coorong, starts just after the river mouth. 'Coorong' means *long neck*.'

He pointed back to a row of affluent houses wrapped along the lakeside. 'The green area there? That's *Stranger's Ground*. Back when aboriginal groups traded along the river, other groups could come here to camp. It was the place they could set up and show they were there for trade and not for trouble.'

'I never knew they had such rules,' I said, and grimaced to myself at the ignorance of the words. Nodding, Taj fired up the motor again.

As we neared the barrage Taj waved to the operator. Soon enough the large gates opened and we motored into the channel between the waterways. Taj roped up the boat in silence as the gate shut behind us. The water rushed away, exposing barnacles and drooping lichen as we sank to the water level of the Goolwa Channel on the other side. Then the gates opened and we were away again.

The view was spectacular. Before me stretched a long, narrow waterway, lined on my right by tall, proud sand dunes crusted with saltbush and spinifex, to my left, the coast of Hindmarsh Island. Both sides were lined with narrow sandy beaches. The water here had a current, no doubt from the ocean tides. This early we were the only souls on the water, though Taj assured me there would be fisherman up ahead. Slick, black water birds sailed overhead, or rode the currents, ducking under the water chasing their breakfast. We passed a tumbling channel of water: the Murray Mouth, where the river meets the sea. Taj slowed the boat as I took in the churning waves, the glimpse of ocean beyond. I settled down inside the boat, pulling my jacket tight against the brisk winds that coursed down the natural alleyway of the Coorong National Park and simply existed.

At some point on our journey Taj passed me a fruit muffin from the backpack he carried, and poured me a cup of hot coffee from a flask. I accepted both gratefully as we carried on our way, the silence between us comfortable and companionable.

Eventually Taj slowed the motor, this time turning into the sandy bank that lead to the sand dunes. He motored the boat part way up onto the shore before jumping over board, feet bare, jeans rolled to his knees and pulled the boat up a bit further onto the beach. I jumped out and taking up a spot beside him, helped to finish the beaching. He slung his backpack over his shoulder and then led me up the beach and onto the sand dunes. Around me the spinifex rustled, the rising sun glinting off their sharp edged leaves. Underfoot saltbush crunched, their green and red fronds plump and juice heavy. We crested the dune and came to a flat expanse of sand between the first dune and the next, the ground covered in cockle shells.

'My ancestors ate pipis, left the shells.' Taj said by way of explanation. The shells crunched under my sneakers. I wondered at Taj's still bare feet but said nothing. We topped two more dunes, the sound of the ocean growing louder and louder as we approached. Finally, we broke over the last dune and there before me was the ocean.

Wild, powerful, full of storm, the waves crashed against the long sandy beach that stretched undisturbed as far as the eye could see. The clouds were grey, but high overhead. Seagulls and small black birds littered the skies and the beach. A sensation welled up inside me. It felt like my chest expanded, opened up, released.

Taj headed down the slope of the dune and I followed. At its base he squatted down and drew a towel from his backpack for us to sit on. We settled and he passed me a sandwich of ham and cheese, wax paper wrapped. Again I smiled in silent thanks. When my alarm woke me that morning, the challenge of getting out of bed had been all encompassing. It had not even occurred to me to bring food or drink.

'I told you to only bring a jacket,' Taj said, as if he had heard my thoughts, or perhaps read my face. He passed me another cup of coffee, not as blisteringly hot now, but still steaming. We ate and drank in silence, watching the waves break over the coastline, churning up the sand in a frothy wave along the shore: the Cappuccino Coast.

'My grandma's people are part of a coastal group, this was their place. The white settlers called them all 'Ngarrindjeri'. It's a collective word they used for the aboriginal people of this area, but really we are a series of separate groups. Grandma tries to keep the old traditions alive, pass them on. But you can't be truly traditional these days. And why would you anyway? We all like TV.' He gave me a cheeky grin.

'I'm sorry,' I started, not sure if I was being rude, 'I just... I didn't realise... You don't look...'

'Ngarrindjeri? What would one look like?' he asked, stone faced. 'What does an Australian look like?'

What have I said?

Taj grinned. 'Don't worry. I don't look it, not really. Too many white ancestors mixed in. And in this country we all look, however we look.' He shrugged. 'But they are still my people, my mob. I am proud of where I come from, on both sides.'

'So your grandma married a 'white man'?' I cringed at the term. Taj gave me another grin.   'She did indeed, and my dad was white too, though I never met him. Or my grandfather, he died before I was born. Heart attack. Mum raised me alone. And grandma did her fair share of babysitting. So I guess the Ngarrindjeri way was how I was raised. Even if I don't really look the part.'

'I suspect that doesn't matter. Not really.'

'No, you're right. It doesn't. We are still one people.'

We fell into that gentle silence again, munching our sandwiches and watching the waves. Taj fished into his backpack and pulled out two cans of cider, passing one to me.

I smiled. 'You thought of everything.'

He laughed, cracked his can and leaned back, stretching out his long legs before him, arm behind his head, sipping his drink and watching the sky.

I followed suit, enjoying the feel of the cool sand beneath my hand, the kiss of the salt air, the fizz of cider on my tongue.

'My dad died 2 years ago, just as I was finishing my under grad. I picked *The Fall* as my thesis topic because of him. It was his favourite poem… It's a really depressing poem, but I felt able to work on it because of dad. Because he loved it.' I stared out before me, surprised at myself for what I had just shared so openly.

Taj lay next to me, chewing the last of his sandwich.

'So, are you going to tell me about it?' he asked.

Lazily, I flopped my head to face him. 'It?'

'Your thesis, your poet – Edward Barrington. I have heard of him. We did one of his poems at school. I think Mrs Anderson hoped we would 'connect with poetry' because he had lived here. Same reason we studied *Storm Boy*, I guess. Bet the teachers had a field day with the new film this year. Didn't work though, not for me.'

I huffed a laugh. 'I think that's why my teachers chose Peter Goldsworthy and Les Murray.'

We grinned together in shared experience. I took another sip of cider.

'Barrington moved here in the 1880s, from England. We know so much from before then. He kept extensive journals. But then he came to Australia to heal his wife, she was sick, and the trail goes cold.'

Taj rolled over, rising up on an elbow, head on his hand. 'That's a big move, especially back then. But he was already famous?'

'Oh yes, very much so. From a young age.'

'So he gave that up, for her.'

'I don't think he saw it that way, but yes, I suppose that's true. His writing took off while he was at university, very unusual. I think his fame had a bit of old school 'sex appeal' to it. But he was really talented, not just a pretty face… When he married his success slowed. His works weren't as dark. But the 'lost poems' discovered after his death, *The Fall* is one of those, they were definitely his old style. The mystery of his death and his wife staying out here, it all increased his fame anyway. The story really is a bit unknown, there is more to it definitely.'

'Tell me, Ellie.' Taj said quietly, intensely.

So I did.

Edward

6

I approach. Hesitant step.
Head too high to see horizon's future. Gently glowing golden aura.

Port of London, England 1886

The long, loud wail of the ship's horn blew a second time. Edward, sat in his carriage on the dock, took a deep steadying breath. It was time. Gripping the carriage handle, he straightened his shoulders and swung out of his seat landing lightly on the dockside. Before him the docks teamed with activity; families of steerage passengers trying to navigate the crowded space while keeping together and managing their luggage; cargo boys hauling barrels and steering groups of pigs and lambs, presumably water and food for the journey; baggage men carting the belongings of the wealthy. Several boats were in port. Large bails of what Edward supposed was wool and barrels of wine were being hauled by dirty, hefty workers. Smoke rose from large chimneys on the deck of one of the cargo ships, creating a hazy shimmer over the dock, its heat and smell permeating the air and mixing unpleasantly with the slimy scent of the fish some men were catching further downstream.

Despite all the bustling distractions of the port, it was their passenger vessel that dominated the scene. The Orient, her dark steel sides glistening in the morning sun, rose up from the water like a leviathan. Long and sleek, her body would house some 500 hundred souls on her voyage to Australia. She was a combined design, powered by steam on the run through the Suez Canal, then by sail as they surged across the empty oceans of the Southern Hemisphere.

Currently, her decks were awash with sailors checking ropes and packing sails or having a final cigarette before official duty began. Edward closed his eyes a moment, gathering himself. *You can do this,* he told himself firmly. His thundering heart beat a silent retort he resolved to ignore.

Edward scanned the docks for a luggage worker to manage his belongings.

'Excuse me, sir,' a young man clad in tailored trousers and an Orient jacket stood before Edward. 'Mr Barrington I presume? I'm Mr Davids, here to arrange your luggage, sir.'

'I am Mr Barrington. Thank you. There is quite a lot I'm afraid, you may need to get some help…'

'Don't be worrying yourself, sir,' the young man grinned up at Edward as he moved towards the luggage strapped to the back and top of the carriage. 'Cabin 34, am I correct? '

'Yes, thank you.'

'Course, sir. Leave it to me.' Mr Davids turned calling out to a group of lads standing off to the side dressed in brown slacks and shirts, not an Orient colour among them. The boys came running over, all pimples and fuzzy beards and began loading themselves up with more bags and boxes than seemed feasible before heading for the ship. Mr Davids swung a smile at Edward and joined them, leaving him adrift in the sea of activity. He strode to the carriage and opened the door once more, 'Darling, if you are ready to board?'

A white gloved hand appeared from the carriage to grip his own and he gently guided his wife, Rosalind Barrington, down the carriage steps to the dockside.'

'Oh!' The soft sound escaped her lips, but not his notice. Edward gripped her waist quickly, steadying her against the pull of gravity that threatened as her knees wobbled beneath her.

'I am sorry my love,' Rosalind breathed, 'I must have risen too fast from my seat.'

Edward stared hard into her deep green eyes. Grey smudged the hollows beneath them, her skin waxy and pale. 'Of course,' he lied and gave her his most reassuring smile.

Rosalind smiled back, transforming her features to those of the healthy woman he married, offering a glimpse of why they were here, his hope and promise. If only for a moment.

They'd met three years ago at his poetry recital in Manchester's neo-gothic town hall. Dressed in green silk trimmed with black lace, hair gathered in large cascades, eyes bright with copper tinge, Rosalind had turned every head in the room. Edward could not look away. Showing an uncharacteristic confidence, he'd approached her, dared to touch her arm, invited her to Hathrone to take tea. She accepted. A week later they stood beneath the apple trees, red with winter's promise and declared their hearts.

'I love you,' he had whispered.

'I love you too. But, I must warn you. I am to be a divorced woman. I will… damage your reputation.'

Edward had laughed. Rosalind's brutish husband was well known in society, loudly decrying his wife for the absence of an heir, while escorting a series of young women about town.

'I am overjoyed that you are to be divorced. I do not wish to have you as a mistress. I wish to make you all mine. Now and always.'

Overcome, tears limned Rosalind's eyes.

Gently Edward wiped them away. 'Don't cry my love, not ever again. Until my last breath I will protect you. We will never know loneliness and sorrow again.'

They fell into each other and on a bed of leaves sealed their love, skin to skin, forever.

Straightening her sun hat, Rosalind turned to take in the docks. 'This harbour is much larger than I expected, there are boats lining the water out as far as I can see.'

Edward leaned in close to her ear and whispered, 'Follow the inlet with your eyes, where it seems to meet the sky? That is the start of our journey to Australia!'

Rosalind turned to face him, bringing their eyes, their lips closer. He felt a huff of breath as she laughed lightly, 'What an adventure we are to begin.'

Edward's heart tightened at the bravery of her words. Throwing social etiquette to the winds, he pecked her on the cheek, her skin warmer than it should be beneath his lips.

'Come Mary, it is time we boarded,' he called back to the carriage.

The older lady, well into her 60s, stepped gingerly from the carriage, the swelling of her ankles and lower legs had been troubling her more as the days cooled into autumn. Her right hand clutched a single satchel, all her worldly possessions. She had been with Rosalind since his wife was a child, it would have been cruel to take a younger maid. Mary had earned this. She looked up at him and nodded stoically. They turned as one and walked to the Orient, their transport to another country, almost another world. And hopefully a new life.

7

Red. Billows of red surround me. Beneath the red tinge we vow.
Offered honestly. Freely.

The sickness was intolerable. Edward languished on his bed, feeling every bit as green as the country pine curtains and furnishings that decorated the cabin. Through the thin wall beside him he heard retching. The exhaustion in the cough told him it was Rosalind. The travel from their home estate, Hathrone, had exacerbated her symptoms terribly, and the constant pitching of the waves was doing nothing to help. When his own stomach allowed, he tended to her every need, pulling more blankets over her when she shivered at night, feeding her broth, helping her to dress in the mornings and pretending not to notice the blood that stained her pillow; a halo of red splattered about her head. Her condition had advanced, they both knew it. But acknowledging this new development would do nothing to help either of them. So he praised her resilience and she batted his fussing away. All a rouse to disguise the fear that hovered around them.

Mary, whose constitution somehow overcame the constant roll of the sea, watched on frowning. Edward could see the rebuke in her eyes; he was taking over her role. Today, however, she would have Rosalind all to herself. Edward was too ill to move. He had thought his symptoms to be easing, but a wild storm the night before had thrashed the boat for what seemed like hours. And now, in the soft light of morning, the smell of Rosalind's vomit drifting through the rooms threatened to set him gagging.

He rolled onto his side, curling into a ball, quietly groaning to himself.

'You need to get some exercise, and you need some distraction.' Mary's authoritative tone broke through the malaise of illness that cocooned Edward.

The sheet was thrown from his body. He looked up at his round maid, ready to give her a firm piece of his mind. But the words died on his tongue as he took in her pale face, the dark circles under her eyes, wrinkles etched in deeper along her mouth and cheeks. She had not slept, not all night. How selfish of him to lie here in self pity while she carried the burden of caring for his wife.

Edward sat up. 'Get some rest Mary. I will tend to Mrs Barrington.'

'Miss Rosalind,' Mary began, she still used the diminutive for her long time charge,'is finally at rest. And I plan to catch a few minutes myself. But you need to get outside. Fresh air is the only cure for the seas, everyone knows that. It's so musty in here it's no wonder you are ill. I can't imagine what the poor people in steerage are dealing with.' She paused, huffed and planted fists on ample hips. 'Miss Rosalind, she can't be moved. But you have no excuse. Now get to the decks and take a walk. Get some colour back in your cheeks. And when Miss Rosalind is more rested you can take her for a turn through the halls. What do you say?'

Irritated he began to rise, but his stomach rebelled. He barely made it to the chamber pot beside his bed before retching. The spasms gripped his stomach, his cough tearing his tender throat raw. Only a few drops of liquid came up. He was empty. Retching from illness alone with nothing left to pass. Next door he heard Rosalind murmur fitfully. He tried his best to be quiet as he cleaned himself up, Mary watching his every move. She did not offer to help.

Grudgingly, he admitted that Mary was probably right. He was far better off than his wife, and he should get some air. Mary would take care of her. Standing stiffly he reached for his cloak. Allowing himself to check briefly on Rosalind, he pressed a butterfly kiss to her forehead then strode from their rooms.

He wandered along the hall from their rooms, stepping gingerly, one hand clutching his stomach. Light was shinning through the portholes positioned along the roof, shards capturing the dust motes that danced up from the rich red carpet lining the floor. Mounting the stairs to the top deck Edward stubbed his toe against the wooden stoop.

'Dash it!' he exclaimed, slamming his fist into the handrail before continuing to climb the stairs.

The despair that had been coursing through his veins these past months was transforming into an indignant fury. His vision went red, then deepest black as his mind followed an all too familiar path down into a spiral of hopelessness. Everything he tried went wrong. Australia was meant to be the answer to Rosalind' sickness, and yet here they were, emptying their stomachs of all nourishment, surrounded by nothing but waves and wind.

His head broke free of the lower deck and into the bright sunshine. A wash of icy wind traveling off the open ocean smacked into his face. Above his head two large expanses of white flapped and caught its power, blowing Edward from his homeland. Bracing against the cold, Edward lurched himself onto the deck. His temper was so enraged he didn't notice the drastic change in temperature. He stumbled to the left heading for the front of the boat, his balance unsure on the open deck where he became suddenly and acutely aware of the waves buffering the vessel from side to side, front to back. Edward pitched forward with the boat, catching his feet on each other, yet his frustration propelled him on. Coming to the boat's bow Edward threw himself against its railing.

Clutching the cold steal barrier that held back the sea, or rather his body from the sea, Edward screamed as violently as his lungs would allow. As if in time the boat pitched back, wrenching Edward's grip from the rail, heaving him onto his back. He hit the deck with a loud thud, a sharp pain shooting up his spine. Edward screamed his anger out again, punching his fist against the wood. The boat leaned forward once more, Edward felt his weight move with it and he slid forward again. Gripping tight to the rails, he looked out before him.

There was nothing to be seen.

Blue water so deep as to appear almost black stretched on for miles, ending only at the line of the sky. The heaving of his chest began to slow and his breathing deepened, filling his lungs with the cold wet air of the ocean. The nausea that had tormented his nights began to ease.

Pulling himself into a tight ball, still clutching the rail, Edward bent his head down and wept. Wept for Rosalind, for his passion to write; so linked with his love for his wife that its place in his heart was also dying. Wept for the open sea; too alike the echoing halls of his childhood abandonment. Wept for the wide world and the pitiful nothingness his life, and his tribulations, were to it. Against the black of the depths, Edward felt even more alone than he had ever before.

8

Slithering, slippery mud peeks between the auburn.
Reveals the lie.

The Indian Ocean, 1886

Tick-tock, tick-tock, clicked gently against his consciousness. Edward rolled away from the sound, clinging to unconsciousness. Sleep his only sanctuary from the endless expanse of the Indian Ocean.

Tick-tock.

Travelling through the Suez Canal had provided some distraction, to see with one's own eyes the immensity of the endeavour to carve out a passage between continents was truly breathtaking. But the knowledge that soon his horizons would widen again as they crossed the seemingly inexhaustible ocean, caused his skin to prickle. As the sails were hauled up for the run south across the Indian Ocean, that prickle had grown into a buzz of invisible pressure that enveloped his limbs.

Tick-tock.

Restlessness had overtaken his body. His nights spent tossing and turning, his days tense and tight. Even the daily walks Mary insisted he take around the ship provided no release. Other passengers seemed to have found a stride that simply eluded him; groups of young men set up cricket matches on the deck or played cards in the sunshine, lounging calmly. Edward felt he might snap.

Tick-tock.

He longed for the oblivion of sleep. Hours where the boat sailed on and he was floating in the dark, thoughtless, senseless, nothing.

Tick-tock.

It knocked against his mind more firmly this time, and he felt it, the shift between sleep and consciousness. It was subtle, but it was there. He threw the sheet off of his torso, seeking a cooling breeze to relieve his clammy body. But there was no fresh air to be had, the porthole windows firmly closed against the waves. Twisting about, his legs became entangled in the sheet, forcing him to kick and wiggle to free his feet, bringing himself fully awake in the process. He lay still for a moment, taking deep breaths, willing his eyelids to grow heavy, his mind dim.

Tick-tock.

No use. He tore the remaining entangled sheets from his legs and sat up on the bed. Lighting a candle, he checked the insistent clock beside the bed. 11pm, he had not even managed an hour of rest since he had come to bed. Edward sighed. It was a silly time of night, one made only for rest. But his body and mind were not going to comply. He needed distraction.

He considered his options. He could light his desk lamp and work on his travel journal, or perhaps read. Both were heavy with effort. A hacking cough sounded from the next room. Even through the walls he could hear the solid wetness of the sound; death made manifest and soggy. He listened as Mary rose and shuffled over to his wife, the soft murmur of her soothing croon drifting to his ears. He longed to go in and care for his wife himself, but he knew Rosalind would only turn him away. Their pretence that all was well had been wearing thin this last few weeks.

He had to get out, to move. Hastily he dressed. Perhaps the saloon would still be open and he could enjoy a whiskey to dull his restless mind. Grabbing up his journal and pencil, he quietly exited the room.

The lights were still on in the saloon casting the ornate brass finishings of the room in a comfortingly warm glow. Strolling in he found the bar unattended. He waited a moment, hoping that the waiter had simply popped out briefly. In truth Edward had no idea of the schedule of the boat at large. When they first set out he had taken lunch in the restaurant with the other first class guests, but the constant enquiries after his wife had taken on the tone of gossip, driving him back to his rooms. The excuse of seasickness could only work for so long.

After waiting a moment more Edward sighed, he was clearly too late to be served. Surprised at the disappointment he felt at missing out on a drink, he turned to leave.

'Ah, excuse me, Mr. Barrington?' a gentle voice came from the side of the lounge. Edward glanced over. A man, younger than himself by a few years, sat in a plush armchair, book in hand. Edward swept his eyes over the youth, almond coloured hair and eyes glittered in the soft light as he crossed the space between them. He looked familiar, though Edward could not recall his name.

'George Harbot,' the young man supplied, smiling warmly, 'we were at the same table the night before the Canal.' He held his hand out in greeting. Edward took it, the warmth of the contact surprising him.

'Of course,' he replied.

George stood before him, awkwardly silent. The moment stretched and Edward, damning himself for leaving his rooms on this foolish quest, was about to wish him goodnight when, 'You only just missed the waiter. 11pm is close. But, I've most of a bottle of wine left. You would be welcome to join me.'

'That's very kind…' Edward began.

'The company would be most welcome,' George smiled again. An urgency came over his face as he did, giving his round, open features a sense of desperation. Despite himself, Edward found himself nodding his acceptance of George's offer and made his way over to the table.

George poured them both a wine. 'Don't worry, I wiped the glass,' he said, handing Edward a generously filled glass of deep red liquid. 'To your health.'

Edward nodded, repeating ,'Your health,' and took a deep drink. The wine was both sweet and bold, its warming tannins sliding down his throat and spreading tendrils through his chest. He felt his body start to relax.

'A nice vintage,' Edward ventured.

George gave him a wry smile, 'There I will have to take your word for it. I'm not really one for the taste so much as the effects. Takes the edge off after a long day on the water.'

Edward eyed him, looking for any clue that the young man was fishing for gossip, or information. George returned his gaze with one of simple friendship.

'I've not seen you down here this late before. To be honest, it's normally just me at this hour. I've not been sleeping very well on this trip. Everything feels too close and too spacious, all at once. That probably sounds rather silly…'

Surprised at hearing his own feelings of unease voiced back to him,

Edward almost agreed, but stopped himself.

'What brings you to this journey?' he asked to cover his pause.

'Recklessness, if you asked my father,' George gave a short, indulgent laugh. 'Avoiding responsibility would be my mother's take. She can't wait for grandchildren.' He winked at Edward as if the two were in on the same joke. Edward longed for children, but with Rosalind's health…

'But really, adventure.' George continued. 'I'm a doctor, newly trained. While I was studying I read so much about the impact of our diseases, colds, the flu, on the Aborigines in Australia, when we first settled. And then about the challenges the settlers have faced getting care in the more remote parts of the country. I wanted to go see it all for myself. See what help I can give,' George paused, taking a sip of his wine. 'What about you?'

Determined to enjoy this moment of companionship, Edward pushed aside the fleeting sense of panic at hearing George was a doctor. 'Much like you,' he lied. 'Before I was married I loved to travel. Italy, France, Greece. I left all that behind, for my wife.' He paused, realising for the first time just how true that was. 'But an opportunity came up to work in South Australia and I couldn't pass it up.'

'To work? A commission?'

'Yes, I am a poet of some note,' he swallowed uncomfortably, he hated talking about his success. 'Fortunately for me, there is a man in South Australia, Mr Alistair Harbinger, who wishes me to describe his part of the continent. And so another adventure, but this time, not alone.'

'I envy you that,' George said, eyes softening, 'I have always travelled alone. It's never bothered me so much before, but this trip…' A quiet loneliness in the man's voice spoke to the same need inside of Edward. He felt comfortable with this man.

'Thank you,' Edward blurted, surprising himself as he spoke, 'for the wine and company. While I am not travelling alone, it is nice to have someone else to talk to, for an evening.'

'Thank you for joining me. It is good to talk with someone who listens, and understands. As a fellow traveller. I have been to Italy and France. But not Greece. Will you tell me of your time there?'

Edward sucked in a swift breath, shoulders tensing. Missing nothing, George's eyes went wide, 'I do apologise. I did not mean to pry.'

Edward stretched his neck, aiming to shake the nerves that had hit him so suddenly.

'Not at all. I mentioned the trip. And it was quite extraordinary. But it coincided with a very difficult time in my life. Some of my memories of Greece are not so pleasant.'

'I am sorry to hear that. It must have been difficult, being so far from home?'

George's eyes were gentle, enquiring without demanding. Edward suppressed a rueful grin at how successful his bedside manner would be as a doctor. With that quiet, calm invitation to speak, his patients would be confessing their sins. Without consciously intending to, Edward found himself accepting a re-fill of wine and opening up.

'My father passed away while I was in Athens,' he began, 'it was a long journey home, so I was absent for his funeral.'

'That must have been terribly hard. I would be devastated should I suffer a similar fate.'

'To be honest, we were never close. My father worked in business, travelling all over the Continent to meet with contacts. My mother died when I was born and father, well, I don't think he really knew what to do with me.'

George took in this intensely private information in silence. His face revealed no judgement, no pity, only openness.

So Edward continued.

9

Black start. Black Heart.

Derbyshire, England 1871

'Come lad. Away from the wall, you appear too short in that light. Walk about, and look happy. Anyone would think you were starving hungry with that long face. Smile lad!'

The small Edward raised a nervous head. Dark blonde curls gently cupped his pixie face, his pale white skin reflecting the glow of the candles that hung over head. About him buzzed the sounds of society: the murmuring of gossip, the higher cadence of excitement, the hush of boasting and the freedom of laughter. Voices of the elite, pinning him back against the polished wooden walls of his father's entertainment hall. In a room filled with people, Edward was alone. He watched his father, Walter Barrington, a man born into money, mingle comfortably with his guests, savouring the banter of the rich chorus.

Looking up Edward observed the solid chandelier that hung lifelessly from the high domed ceiling.

'Come on now, I don't have all day.'

Edward looked at his father, so comfortable with these strangers of business and enterprise, completely awkward with his own flesh and blood. Timidly, Edward ventured forward, stick thin legs shaking his knocked knees ever closer together.

Walking through the medley of silk dresses and pressed dress pants, Edward breathed the scent of femininity: perfume and powders. Standing still in the centre of the room his tiny chest filled with the promise of comfort and the sharp pain of absence. A whisper of longing.

The only son of a factory owner, Walter had made his wealth on the back of the newly mechanised textile industry in Derbyshire, taking his father's business legacy and making it his own grand success. On the back of changing times he consolidated his position, using his wealth to buy shares in the right industry and that wealth to buy his way into society, eventually even moving his family into the well regarded country estate known as Hathrone. But the jewel in his crown had been his marriage to Lady Elizabeth Usinet. At the time of her presentation, Lady Elizabeth had been the most eligible lady in Derbyshire society. And despite his less than traditional history, Walter won her heart. Cynics said he married her only for her good name; an enhancement to his list of assets, no more than a conquest in his drive to gain position and respect in the upper reaches of society.

But the servants of Hathrone, who saw him after Lady Elizabeth's untimely death, knew beyond doubt that theirs had been a love match. She passed on Edward's birth bed, leaving her only child alone and motherless and her new husband inconsolable.

After Edward's unfortunate arrival into the world his father found numerous reasons to be absent. The tiny babe left in the care of nannies and parlour maids. Whether it was the emptiness of the house without his wife, the two storeys, the cold stonework, the high looming ceilings, or the reminder of loss that the child embodied, only Walter knew, but something drove him away from the success and the home he had so avidly sought. Rooms were mothballed, windows closed, fireplaces left unlit, and Walter travelled. The emptiness of being a small boy, standing alone, a mammoth house surrounding him as he eagerly awaited the return of his absent father, only to be brushed aside with bare acknowledgment, would never fully be erased from Edward's heart.

Upon reaching the tender age of four, Edward was sent to boarding school 500 miles away in London, separated from Nannie Mabel, the only source of warmth and love his young heart had known. Unlike the other boys, he spent most of his holidays at the school, returning to Hathrone only in the summers and for important events. Arriving home that first summer, Edward had raced down the drive, bursting through the door calling for Mabel, only to find the house dark and cold. Walter, seeing no further need for a nanny, had let Mabel go. Edward would now be responsible for himself at boarding school and at home.

This cold and detached upbringing shaped the man Edward would become; the shy child grew into a solitary teenager. Outcast at school by his sensitive nature, invisible at home, his world became the four walls of his bedroom chambers and the two covers of a book, within which he could not be touched, overlooked, unwanted. There was no one else to judge. Rain or shine he kept to himself, reading and studying and writing an extensive journal. He longed to speak with his father, to hear of his mother, but even on the rare occasions that Walter was in residence at Hathrone, the thick oak door to Walter's study formed an impenetrable barrier, keeping his sorrow- filled son away. Edward came to see these as the black years. Pain and darkness a never ending well sucking him down into its core.

It wasn't until Edward started at university that he learned to put his father's wealth to good use, using his summers to travel Europe, rather than visit the cold and empty manor house in the North. Walter was happy to oblige.

****

'I didn't visit,' Edward said, staring into the firelight. 'My father asked me to come home for Christmas before I went to Athens. I wrote to him from the boat, promising to see him when I returned in three months. He was ill, dying, but I didn't know. I'd just returned from the Parthenon when the news arrived.'

'You could not have known your father was ill. He didn't give you the information to make a proper choice.'

'Perhaps. But I think a part of me did know, or at least suspected. He had always placed such importance on my role as keeper of the estate. But Hathrone, it wasn't home to me, not really. It was a role I didn't want. The pressure and challenge of the position. When he called me home, that's what I heard. And so I ran.' *I felt the darkness creeping back,* Edward thought. Adjusting his cuffs to make use of his hands, he did not voice the thought.

'That's a lot of pressure to put onto anyone, especially a young man,' George said, a small frown between his eyes. 'No wonder you enjoyed the freedom of travelling.'

'I did need to learn from him though, the business and estate has not faired well in my hands. But, in the end it has all worked out for the best. I came home, and met my wife. I wouldn't change that for the world.'

'You are very resilient.'

Edward felt a warm blush of embarrassment colour his cheeks, but again, George showed no indication that he realised how open and personal he had been. Calm settled over Edward, a lightness spreading along his limbs. It had felt good to talk.

'Well,' George said, 'seems we have finished the wine, and it is getting late. I might turn in.'

'Yes,' Edward agreed, rising and shaking George's hand. 'Thank you again for the wine and company.'

'And you. I am here most evenings. Please come and join me, anytime.'

Edward paused, 'Yes, thank you. Yes, I will.' And returned to his cabin and his wife.

10

But then: pinks and pearls. Copper and light, sun.
Blues hues and greens and violets.

Bursting into their day room, Edward brought with him a rush of clean air that radiated from him like ecstasy. Rosalind, reclining on the sofa, looked up, startled by his obvious excitement. Before her Edward strode to the calendar and counted the crosses... just over a month, not long enough by half. And yet he was sure his eyes had not deceived him, he had seen the continent of their destination

'Rosalind!' he cried, turning about to face her, arms extended in joy. 'I have seen it. I have seen Australia.'

Rosalind felt her own heavy mood lift, the hope from months before returning to surge through her limbs, making her numbed head feel almost normal once more.

'... it is still very distant, and as we were told we must travel along the coast for some miles before we reach our port... But my love, there is land in the distance.'

Rosalind let out a light laugh, like a huff of air, at her husband's enthusiasm. *He is so young,* she thought smiling to herself, *he makes me feel young.* For 'childlike' was exactly the word to describe Edward's wonder at seeing land. This joyous passion revealed to her just how depressed he had become over this journey. She had been so wrapped up in her own illness and guilt she had not fully appreciated the burden her husband toiled beneath. Resolve flowed through her body and she sat up with purpose.

The sudden movement made blood rush to her head, making her feel nauseated and dizzy. Normally this sensation would have sent her back lying down, but not today. Rosalind was determined. She closed her eyes to steady herself then stood up. Pulling herself tall and strong, or at least she hoped she looked strong, she walked to her room. She was rummaging around in a small closet when Edward entered, still glowing from his sighting. 'What are you doing?' he asked, gently. Sighting what she had been looking for Rosalind produced her thickest coat. Pulling it on she turned to Edward.

'This is a momentous occasion,' she said firmly, 'and its coming has made me feel quite invigorated. You must take me up to see this country, Australia, which is to be our home and our salvation.'

She fastened the last of the buttons on the coat and moved to the mirror to fix her face, there would certainly be people on deck if land had been sighted. While she plied blush and shadow to her drawn skin, Edward fussed.

'My dearest love,' he began, 'it is an astoundingly exciting day, but your health is, to me, far more important. I want you to share it with me of course, but I fear it will prove too much for you and... '

Rosalind interrupted his placation with a swift jerk of her hand.

'I have been resting for months. The fresh air will do me good. I wish to be seen on deck to welcome the coast with my husband, as every good wife should do. I wish to celebrate this with you.' She turned her eyes to Edward. Within them he read her plea for normalcy, if only for a few hours. Edward softened and took her in his arms.

'You look beautiful,' he smiled and kissed her gently. 'How I have been looking forward to escorting you on deck. And today there is sure to be many to show you off to...'

'Then you had best let me finish preparing,' Rosalind pushed at his chest playfully, implying he was in her way. Edward stepped back, his joy brimming over. Two miracles in one day, the sight of the coast and Rosalind out of bed. He left her to finish her preparations.

In the sitting room Mary waited, her face disapproving and stern. He looked away, not wanting to see his own concerns mirrored in her eyes. When Rosalind appeared she looked like another woman. She had pulled her hair back off her face into a high pile, revealing her slender, pale neck line, and two emerald earrings that dangled down to enhance her eyes. Her face was bright. Knowing her as he did, the signs of fatigue were still there. But he doubted anyone else would notice. Regardless, she was beautiful. Beaming, he wrapped a protective arm about her waist; how much thinner she had become over their journey, even through her thickest coat. Shaking the unwelcome thought away, he led her out into the passage.

On deck Edward held her close and they walked in step along the side rail of the vessel. Rosalind's eyes scanned the view. Wrapped up in their rooms she'd contented herself imagining seaside trips to Brighton as a child, assuming the ocean would be much the same. How wrong she had been! On the deck a mass of blues and greens met her eyes, reflecting soft sunshine onto her face. Its brightness shocked her eyes, she took a moment to adjust. Then the water-filled air hit her face. It was cold from the ocean but fresh and exhilarating. Rosalind dared, and breathed in deeply, holding the freshness in her lungs for as long as she could muster. Breathing out hard she felt renewed.

Edward looked at her sharply. 'My love?' he asked.

'It's just too beautiful,' she sighed looking out to sea. Edward wondered at her, all one could see was water on this side of the boat, like a wall of nothingness.

'This way,' he whispered, guiding her gently around the deck.

Up on the port side other couples and children were now gathering. Word of land had spread fast and all the passengers, after weeks at sea, were excited to see their destination emerging before them. Edward and Rosalind nodded at passers-by, stopping occasionally to say a few words to fellow travellers Edward had come to know on his walking rounds. Pride at having his wife by his side radiated from Edward, warming her with his joy. Behind his back however the gossip swirled. While her beauty was unmistakable, it was clear that Rosalind was deeply unwell. Some less polite passengers murmured of his selfishness, taking her out in the cold when she was so sick. Other, more perceptive folks, understood that even this ill health must be an improvement and quietly prayed for their future.

Gracefully the couple walked, arm in arm. Coming to the port rail, Edward positioned his wife in front of him looking out to the sea. Arms on either side of her small frame, her hands on the rail, his on hers, the couple stood scanning the horizon. Rosalind stared out, taking in the view slowly, more interested in the whole than the brown of land. And then she saw it. Off to the left of the bow was a high brown peak, jutting out from the blue. *Most out of place*, Rosalind thought whimsically. She felt her face crack into a wide grin and looked at Edward with surprise.

'Yes,' he whispered into her ear, 'that is Australia.'

What had been an idea for so many months was suddenly real. Rosalind felt light with relief. Leaning into Edward's arms, she rested her head back on his shoulder. Cheek to cheek they stood in the early morning sunshine, eyes fixed on the brown tip surrounded by blue, fighting for its place; they knew it would win.

'Not quite record time, but pretty swift,' Edward said. Rosalind looked up at him, tears limning her eyes. But her smile was radiant. It was like the years of illness had been washed from her face, leaving her well again. Overcome by passion Edward pressed his lips to hers, then let go of the railing and still holding Rosalind's hands folded his arms around her body. They swayed gently with the boat, but Edward's practiced sea legs held them secure. And together they watched, as the distant land seemed to bob a welcome to them from across the sea.

'My good man,' someone spoke. Edward turned from his routine walk on the decks, and seeing George coming towards him smiled deeply at the man he now considered a friend.

'George, how are you?'

'Well, I think. Thank you. I believe at this rate we will disembark tomorrow, what are your thoughts?'

Edward looked out at the land lit by the fading sunlight, its hills reflecting red across the ocean, so unlike the green countryside of home. He nodded firmly. They would be in dock within 24 hours. George took a deep breath and looked at Edward. Sensing his friend's unease, Edward cocked his head to one side.

'What is it George?' he asked. 'I can see there is something you wish to say. Surely after all our time together we have an understanding. You can say it, whatever it is. To me.' As he said it, he realised just how true those words were. The two men had spent many an evening talking in the saloon and Edward rather felt the younger man had been the reason he had survived the dastardly journey at all.

George twisted his hands together, visibly tense. Edward gave his most reassuring smile and waited. It was the least he could do.

'Forgive me. But as you know I am a doctor,' he began nervously, scratching his chin absentmindedly, 'And I could not help but notice your wife's condition. She is not well...'

'I told you... the sea...'

'It's more than that Edward, any fool can tell. But as a doctor I can judge its cause. I know it to be of the lungs.'

Edward's face went blank.George paused, waiting for Edward to respond. Edward gave him nothing.

He forged ahead. 'As I told you, I have been studying my profession in Germany, a wonderful place for medical research. We have had some great breakthroughs in the last two years in understanding consumption, and other lung infections, owing to the bacteria we discovered...' George heard the sharp intake of air Edward seized as he spoke the word 'consumption', felt him struggle to master an anger long suppressed. He rushed on.

'As I was saying, because of the large number of cases we see, much like your wife's, in some cases even further advanced, I have learned a great deal about treatment options. Your move to Australia is a wonderful step. But you must know, it is not enough. She needs proper treatment. There are facilities, even here on the new continent. If you would permit me I...'

'What?' Edward interrupted, voice low and hard. 'You would what? Examine my wife? Tell me your professional opinion?' Barely contained rage clipped his words. Then they crystallised, each syllable like chips of ice cracking. 'You would take her away from me?'

'Take her away... no! But she needs treatment. And there are places she could go.'

'She stays with me. Always.'

'As you say. But at least allow me to examine her. I may be able to offer some further insight.'

'I know what is wrong with my wife. I don't need to see another doctor's eyes gloss over. I cannot bear to read their thoughts again. 'Such beauty, such a waste...' Do you imagine I am strong enough to withstand even your lack of hope?'

He raised a hand to his hair, taking a deep breath, head shaking side to side. 'No. We are on the verge of setting to land. This country is our final chance.' He turned back to George, eyes like flint. 'I will not have you take that from us, not now. Hope is the last thing we have left between us.'

Edward turned sharply away.

George stood in silence. Frozen. He had never seen Edward show so much emotion, so much pain. He had suspected his friend's unhappiness, sensed it coursing just below the surface. But this? With such force? He opened his mouth to speak, to explain, but he knew it was no use.

'I am sorry...' he whispered, resigned. Then walked quietly away, heavy with regret.

Edward remained on deck watching the dark waters churning

below. At length he took a deep breath and rolled his neck. Standing tall he adjusted his jacket and assembled his features, a calm smile settling on his lips, before walking back to his rooms.

The sound of voices shouting and movement on the deck brought Edward from his slumber. Instantly he knew. They had docked. He rolled out of bed and, still in his night clothes, padded to Rosalind's room. For a moment he waited, watching her peacefully sleeping face before bringing her awake with a gentle caress of his hand across her forehead.

'We are here,' he whispered. 'Take your time to prepare, I will go above and find helpers to carry our things. You will not be disturbed before nine.'

Pecking her cheek, he went to leave but Rosalind clutched his arm to hold him back. She brought his face in line with hers, opened her mouth to say something, but had no words.

'I feel the same my love,' he whispered, before squeezing her hand and leaving the room.

He woke Mary and gave her orders for the assembly of their things. Stepping out of their rooms he nearly slipped on a piece of paper. Looking down he realised it was an envelop addressed to him. He opened the note. It was from George, an apology, and request for forgiveness. For a moment Edward could not move, caught in the moment between emotions. Not wanting to face the guilt, hard and cold, that had settled in his gut, he pushed the envelop into his pocket and continued with his preparations.

When he returned to help Rosalind depart she gave him a small frown. 'What is it my darling? You seem, distressed.'

'Nothing at all my dear. Just a silly misunderstanding.'

'That's not like you,' she pressed. 'What happened?'

'I fear I have made a mistake and offended someone I respect, very deeply.'

'Well, I am sure it is nothing that cannot be resolved. Once we are settled you can write to this person and explain. That will fix it. Communication always does. Don't you agree?'

A calm washed through Edward, she was right. 'Yes, I do.'

'Wonderful. Now put it from your mind. We are about to meet our new home.'

Edward nodded, gratitude for his beautiful wife sweeping the guilt away. Together they walked out onto the deck, leaving behind a past of pain and fear and into a future of hope.

11

Tipping the currents in every shade. Emotion filled.
Black concealed.

Goolwa, Australia 1887

His white dress shirt was transparent where it clung to his sweaty body. Even inside the Australiasian hotel, where Alistair Harbinger had arranged their accommodation, the heat of this country was oppressive. Edward pulled on his dinner jacket, frowning at the tight fit, the pull of his sweat-wet shirt against its silk lining. After the long few days of travel they had endured since stepping off The Orient Liner he wanted nothing more than his bed, and being close to Rosalind. But he was a guest here and Mr Harbinger, his benefactor, had arranged a diner party to greet them.

As he descended the stairs from their rooms, his first glimpse of Australia framed by his carriage window, swirled in his mind. Never had he seen such vast tracts of untamed land. Browns and muted greens crowding in beside the carriage, ghostly white trees standing silent in the stifling heat. And such heat! Within the hour he had been forced to loosen his cravat and as the sun rose he had abandoned it entirely, mopping a prodigious amount of sweat from his brow. Rosalind had faired far worse, the heat thickening the air, forcing her lungs work even harder. By the time they had arrived at their hotel she was white as a sheet. Edward had longed to carry her to their rooms, but propriety would not allow it. He would never willingly embarrass his wife.

He smiled to himself, remembering her faint jest when, finally, he had been able to take her into his arms and carry her to their shared bedroom, 'Now, now my dear, we've no time for that,' she'd said, smiling weakly. Even in the face of her discomfort it had made him smile.

Pausing on the landing, Edward gazed out at the little town, glowing in the light of the moon. Percy, Harbinger's driver and the largest youth Edward had ever seen, had met them in Port Victor a larger town to the west set along the coast. They'd changed carriages and been driven along a track adjacent to the beach, the setting sun spraying the horizon with bright pinks and oranges, purple glints dancing across the turquoise currents as they washed against the shore. It was like nothing Edward had ever seen before.

They then cut inland following a local train line through the gums, flashes of red breaking through the tall white trunks. Soon they came to the main street of Goolwa. The journey had taken them from the lengthening shadows of afternoon into the pastels of evening. The Australiasian stood proud at the street's end, two storeys of stone with red brick edging and a neat wooden balcony on the second floor, an echo of England. As their carriage rocked long the road, dust kicking up from the unsealed track, a discomfort began to form in Edward's gut. Set against the lengthening dusk, Goolwa seemed no more than a few sand coloured cottages huddled against the curve of the river. This was nothing like the towns of home.

On the ground floor the young driver waited for him. 'This way, Mr Barrington,' the youth said and began to lead the way. Edward was once again surprised at the sheer size of the lad and the floating grace with which he moved across the wooden floors. Arriving in the dining room, a large open space, sparsely but well furnished, a stout, red faced man barrelled over to him.

'Mr Barrington,' he exclaimed, thrusting out his hand in greeting. Edward took it. 'I'm Alistair, Alistair Harbinger. I am so glad to finally meet you.' Introduced, Harbinger lead Edward to a circle of men standing at the centre of the room, dressed in distinguished black jackets and white sleeves, drinks in hand. A glass of brown liquor of some sort appeared in his hand.

'Brandy, just what you need after the heat of the day,' Alistair explained.

'Yes, it is rather warm,' Edward agreed, 'Please forgive my wife. She is much exhausted from the heat and travel.'

A snigger went through the gathering. Unsettled, Edward turned his attention to Alistair, who smiled at him warmly. With his bulbous belly, stocky frame and the ruddy sheen of drink already showing on his brow, Alistair was not the patron Edward had expected.

A short woman dressed in fine yellow lace plodded over and beamed at Edward. 'Well,' she began, glancing at Alistair, 'this is him, then? I can't tell you how excited we have been to meet you, Mr Barrington.' She placed a gentle hand on his arm, a gesture of familiarity and welcome.

She smiled and Alistair did the introductions. His wife, Clementine. 'Lady of the outpost' she proclaimed, patting Edward's arm to punctuate the words. *The title suits her*, Edward thought, her heavy face, sun stained and wrinkled.

'I was so longing to meet Mrs Barrington, these gatherings of men can be a frightful bore. But Alistair tells me she has taken ill, from the heat.'

His stomach clenched, but he forced a smile, 'It has been a long day of travel.'

'Don't I know it. I remember when we first arrived. I told Alistair to wait a day or two before having this dinner, but, well, you will come to understand, where my husband is concerned there is no changing his mind. I look forward to meeting her, once she is recovered.' And with that Clementine strolled away.

There followed a cascade of introductions, smiling faces and warm welcomes. Most of the gathered were farmers, come in from their respective acres to welcome him to their country. Conversation was rapid. The men spoke of places and people Edward knew nothing of, but they always paused to fill him in on particulars.

Despite their apparent good will, Edward could not shake the terror settling in his bowels. The scent of liquor, the craw of robust laughter, the shifting glances between guests; suddenly Edward was five years old again, and at his father's call, the men blurring from landowners of Australia into aristocrats and politicians of England seeking favour and power. He took a large gulp of his brandy to steady his nerves. Alistair clapped him on the back. 'There you are, that will take the edge off,' he grinned, returning his attention to the tall gentleman beside him, Mr... Tailor?

'Well I won't be going. It's a spectacle. It's not decent.' A crisp high voice cut through the deeper murmur of conversation that was swallowing him.

Edward looked across the room to where a smaller group of men stood talking beside an empty fireplace, rimed in marble. The man was tall, in a bony way. His jacket, though clearly well made, hung from his shoulders. His thin face was twisted in distaste.

'What is all my work for, if only to be undone by such displays?'

'Come now, Mr Merryweather,' Mr Hallow, one of the farmers beside Edward, called from their circle. The two groups opened and merged like waves. 'It's tradition. What harm can really come from it?'

'Harm? You ask about harm? It sets them back. Encourages the brute in them. It's not decent and I would expect people of your station to be more thoughtful!'

Edward's mind was racing, the air in the room had changed so rapidly he'd had no time to prepare his senses, and nerves. What were they talking about?

He did not wonder long. 'Mr. Barrington,' Alistair began, 'you must think us rude to discuss politics on your first night here. Please allow me to explain.'

The room fell silent. Tension prickled along Edward's spine.

'Mr Merryweather is the director of the Point Mcleay Mission. Have you heard of it? No? Well no, of course. It's an Aboriginal Mission, on Lake Alexandrina. It's there to help the natives learn about civilisation, about proper conduct and what not. As you can see, Mr. Merryweather is rather passionate about his role…'

'I am indeed,' Mr Merryweather took up the baton. 'I feel distinctly that you all have no understanding of the difficulty of the task.' He turned and faced Edward directly, 'Did you know that most of them still live in the bush like savages? They refuse to acknowledge the benefits and advantages of our society. The children who come to me, come from that! It is a task, a *task* to put them right.'

'And we all respect that, Mr Merryweather,' Mr Hallow interrupted smoothly, 'I just can't see the harm in a little canoe race, that's all.'

'It's a spectacle,' Mr Merryweather repeated, again turning to Edward, 'Once a year they are allowed to race their traditional boats, canoes they are called, long, carved from a tree…'

'Masterful engineering.'

'Yes, thank you Mr Hallow. As I was saying, they are allowed to race their canoes. And what do we do? We watch. We stand on the river bank and revel in their backwardness. I don't care what you say Mr Hallow, but it shows their barbarian, it sets them apart and encourages racial difference.'

The image of a black man in a suit he saw on the train flashed into

Edward's mind and before he could think better of it he blurted, 'I saw one, an aboriginal man. On the docks in Adelaide. He appeared well dressed, clean, just like one of us...'

That comment was met with a scoff from the room, at which Mr Merryweather bristled even more.

'Thank you, Mr Barrington. There are some indeed who are very civilised. I am pleased you had the privilege of seeing the good of the work I do...'

'Oh, come now Mr Merryweather, we all see the good you do, and we respect it,' Alistair declared. 'Now who would like another brandy?' And with that, his patron shifted the focus of the room and brought calm back to the gathering.

As the evening progressed, Edward watched a shift in Alistair's manner. Somehow, he managed to become even louder, and more crude as the imported wine was passed around. Edward kept his drinking to a minimum, he always had, disliking the after effects from which he suffered greatly, particularly in the heat. Sometime around midnight, when Edward was past ready to head back to his room and check on Rosalind, Alistair slouched down into the couch beside him.

The men had retired to the lounge for brandy and cigars. Alistair smelled of smoke and booze, any semblance of a refined demeanour well drowned in the bottom of the glass of claret he clutched tightly. He wrapped an arm around Edward's neck and began a long recount of his property and his love for 'this great land, Australia,' to which he raised his glass at every utterance. Some of his phrases were mildly poetic and Edward soon realised the man was quoting to him from his own poetic attempts. Mild annoyance threatened to show on his face. The one thing in life worse than people critiquing your poetry was others asking you to critique theirs. He suppressed a frown, working to keep his face and manner neutral '....and over yonder hill I see the top of my own eucalyptus tree.' What do you think, old sport?' Alistair grinned drunkenly into Edward's face.

'Quite elegant, sir, 'Edward stammered. 'Did you study literature?'

Alistair laughed aloud and slapped Edward hard on the back. 'That I did,' he cried. 'And that is why I know it...well...leaves a lot to be desired. Why'd you think I brought you here if I thought I myself could actually write? Haha! No, no, I love the word. But have not its gift. You, on the other hand, do.'

The tension that had been building inside Edward evaporated. Once again, with just a casual phrase, Alistair had settled the moment.

Edward felt himself relax.

'No, no' Alistair continued, 'I love this land. But nothing that's good has been written about our part of it. There's Patterson's 'Snowy River' for the East and that's a marvel. But I want Goolwa on the literary map. You are the one for it. Barrington's 'River Port'. Must say it surprised me when I received your agreement letter. Always thought it was an unlikely coup I was chasing.'

Edward felt the older man watching his face. Sensing his probing, he shifted uncomfortably.

'But listen, it matters not. You are here now. Plenty of time to get to know her...'

Time to help Rosalind heal, Edward thought.

'Formed the impression when you entered that the country was more you than the city, though our small settlement is hardly much to what you have come from... Anyway, I am keeping you. Please be at your leave. Give my best wishes to your wife. Be sure to bring her down tomorrow and my Clementine can show her around the town. She will probably welcome the distraction of the shops here in the coming months. I will take you on a tour myself, after morning business. Until lunch tomorrow.'

Alistair thrust himself to his feet and waddled away unsteadily.

Pausing suddenly, he turned back and called to Edward, 'Oh, and take no heed of Merryweather, the natives are fine, placid and gentle. You've nothing to fear from them.'

Edward smiled his thanks and watched Alistair walking from him, laughing loudly and slapping other men on the back. So boisterous and loud, yet underneath it all sat the soul of a poet.

12

Cracking bright golden light shatters emerald mists.

Rosalind did not make it down the next morning. Edward, noting her need to rest, took his breakfast in their rooms and settled himself in for a day of quiet reading and reflection, content to be in her presence, perhaps also putting off facing just how small an outpost he had moved them across the oceans to call home. Alistair however, had other plans.

A loud knock sounded on Edward's door just before midday. Percy stood in the hallway. 'Mr. Harbinger wishes to show you the town and requests your presence.'

His message delivered, the looming young man glided away. Irritated, Edward turned back into the room. Rosalind smiled to herself, observing the set of his face.

'My love,' she whispered from her couch by the window. 'He is playing host. One would expect no less.' Edward smiled at her and nodded his acceptance. He knew she was right but the knowledge did little to curb his annoyance. Dressed in traveling clothes, Edward headed down the stairs to meet his host.

'Mr. Harbinger,' he greeted the ageing gentleman, alert and seemingly unaffected by the heavy drinking of the previous evening. 'Nice day for a tour, I expect.'

'Perfect,' Alistair replied. 'Glad you could spare me the time.'

'Of course,' Edward lied. Alistair smiled knowingly.

'I am a man of action,' Alistair began, 'I love this place, this beautiful place. I want that passion to be described. For that you need to know the passion. You too need to live it. I thought I would take you on a tour, show you the township, the place we call home. So that you are well situated. I like to know my guests are comfortable.'

'Of course,' Edward repeated, 'I am delighted and honoured that you have found the time for such a personal excursion.' With that the two men set off towards the river, Alistair setting a brisk pace.

Almost immediately the smells of the night before, mud and water, filled Edward's nose. The track on which they walked was of simple dirt, dug out from nature. Unlike the same roads from home, in which wheels became regularly bogged, here the earth seemed perpetually dry. Coming out from behind a small rise, the waterway opened before him. A small group of cottages nestled above the water wore a sandy sheen that emphasised the cream stone of their construction. Green only really began at the waterfront. Overlooked by the squat stone Customs House, the banks of the river were lush with grasses coloured a yellowish hue but thick and wild, giving way to reeds before the brown of murky water emerged. Located on the bend of the river, where it turned to sweep inland, was the port dock. Heavy, blackened timber formed the wharf, a train line right beside it.

Alistair pointed, 'That line runs all the way to Victor Harbor, a short journey. First railway in South Australia. The business here is to transport the wool and grains of the farms up the river to the cities and townships. The Mighty Murray River,' he announced proudly. 'She's a special river. Runs all the way to New South Wales and links in with the Darling river system up there. Powerful and beautiful. But temperamental.'

They came to the water and the dark grey wood of the dock. It was short when compared to those at home, but its construction was sound. Around him workers buzzed, stacking bales of wool and grain into large storage sheds that lined the wharf. Off to the side stood more large sheds, their open doors revealing what appeared to be ships in various states of construction and repair.

'We are the leading port for ship repair,' Alistair said, noting the direction of Edward's attention. 'Been a growing industry for some years now, and one we are mighty proud of.'

Suddenly, a loud horn sounded in the distance, its dull boom reflecting off the water and up into Edward's unaccustomed ears. He jumped slightly and looked out towards the inland bend of the river.

'We run one major paddle steamer out of here. Used to be more but now days there isn't the same need, or volume of work. She ferries wool mostly, up to a port at Mannum, that's where it's really the river…here she's a mixture of fresh water and the ocean.'

Edward looked at him, confusion on his face.

Alistair smiled, 'Around that bend, to the right and up, is what we call the Mouth of the Murray. Where the river flows to the sea. The river water and the ocean mix, so along here its quite salty.'

Edward watched as a large, flat bottomed vessel paddled into view. Black smoke puffed from the Florence Annie's large central chimney as it slowly rounded the river curve. Its design was very different from the boats back home. Thick like the floor of a homestead, its deck, empty on the return voyage, would soon be stacked with supplies for the upper river township trade. The vision was impressive. The Florence Annie's slow progress created a majestic air of timelessness that seemed out of place in the world Edward knew yet in this place was entirely correct.

'Now sir, if you will indulge me,' Alistair smiled, gesturing to a small steamboat tied to the far end of the wharf. It was perhaps ten metres long, with almost the whole front half filled with an outside steam engine. Because of the tidal nature of the river system, the dock was built high, so that it would still be operational at any point in the river's routine. At this time that meant that the water was low, the large greying pylons which supported the blackened deck standing proudly out of the water. Edward would have to navigate a ladder down to the small steamboat. Following Alistair's lead, Edward tried to step down onto the boat with grace. The unstable rocking of the water beneath him however, was determined to undermine him and pitched the small boat to the side. Edward stumbled, but Alistair was there to catch and support his inexperienced footing. Unsteady, Edward pushed his body onto the panel seats that ran along the sides of the vessel, hands gripping the edges. His mind decided, he disliked water travel.

An old man dressed in light cotton pants and a shirt, with a thick woollen beanie pushed down low over his eyebrows, fired the steam engine. It spluttered to life and pulled stutteringly away from the wharf that now loomed over Edward's head, almost in time with the arrival of the paddle steamer. The size of the paddle boat from water level was unsettling, its large paddles frothing the river water and splashing salty droplets all over Edward's well groomed jacket and pants. Edward filled his eyes with the water that lapped against the wooden pylons holding the dock up high, the mark of high tide etched across their tips. On the steamer deck workers scurried, hauling a large bridge over to act as a link between the lowered paddle steamer and themselves for loading. He was pleased as distance was placed between them and himself in the small steamer.

Out on the river the water reflected the intense sunlight directly into Edward's pale, English face. The winds seemed to whip around him, scolding his skin, but as they went further into the middle of the waterway, the waters cooled the heat until there was almost a chill. Welcome relief from the relentless heat of this new country.

A small island sat still and close before him, within swimming distance, its sides brown rolling hills. Again the desert of merely metres inland was clearly visible.

Edward stared at the muddy waters. The steamer came up along side the sandy hills that formed the edge of the township, Edward could now see they were covered with short, tattered looking spiky bushes, long thin fingers of foliage spread low along the sand, as if trying to hold their roots in place. Salty winds whipped at the small plants and filled Edward's nose with a sharp reminder of the proximity of the sea. They traveled on, the noise of crashing waves rising around them.

'Slow here,' Alistair called to the old captain, before pointing to a gap in the dunes.

Between them Edward could see the ocean. Luminous and expansive, the water stretched uninterrupted to the horizon. Alistair pointed to the river of water that swept from the ocean through a channel into the river system along which they now bobbed. The Mouth of the Murray.

Edward felt the breath taken from his lungs. The air of the ocean slapped against his chest and arms, forcing his eyes to squint. Where the fresh and salt waters mixed the force of the ocean currents bubbled and churned, Edward could almost feel himself being dragged into its depths.

'It changes constantly,' Alistair was saying, though Edward was only half listening, 'The original plan was to traffic all South Australia's supplies through here, but the channel keeps shifting. Too unreliable. That's why we focus on the river trade now. Immense isn't it?'

Edward did not turn to look at him, his eyes were captured by the power of the sea. On The Orient he had witnessed this kind of expanse, but somehow, in juxtaposition with land so vast and remote, it felt even more unstable and awesome.

Edward glanced back towards the peaceful town of Goolwa. Safe in the curve of a river, protected from the spiteful sea by hills of sand. The port town seemed almost sleepy, as if it rested, unaware of the power which resided so close to its shores. A sense of fear, perhaps natural in the face of such unrestrained power, tugged at Edward's insides. This country, so vast, so unrefined, represented thrilling possibility and terrifying challenge; it held none of the safe calm synonymous with the English hills and cultivated gardens of his memory. Here, everything was wild and untamed, even the ocean at the end of this land seemed more dangerous, more ready to threaten, than the pebble lined coasts of home. Edward felt his hands begin to shake, adrenaline coursing through his limbs, exciting an unknown passion. It was as if in the face of the threat, when you realise just how small you are, anything becomes possible. The terror was enlivening; it set Edward free, unleashing his inner self, his craving to explore.

'I hear Mrs. Barrington is still not well,' Alistair said, interrupting Edward's reverie. 'I would say, this must be the worst case of heat stroke I have ever seen.' He paused, raising his eyebrows. Edward felt his bowels turn to water. He opened his mouth to try and explain.

Before he could speak, Alistair continued, 'I feel I must offer my finest carriage for the last leg of your journey. It is quite large and rides smoothly, far better transport for someone overcoming illness. I've decided to set you up on a small farm of mine, just out of town. Beautiful spot, and, private. It would be best to move soon, I feel. The quiet will probably do her some good. The hotel is so loud. Send word and the carriage can be ready within the hour.'

Edward stared at the man, overcome with gratitude. It was obvious that Rosalind was sick with more than heat stroke, but rather than press or accuse, Alistair simply offered a solution, support.

'Soon would be fine, I feel she is quite recovered. I thank you for your kindness and for this gesture.'

'Humph,' Alistair nodded stiffly, uncomfortable with the compliment and, turning away, ordered the captain back to town.

Breathing deeply Edward kept his eyes fixed on the sea, the white wash of ocean breaks calling to his nature. Beneath him the steamboat began its journey back to port.

13

Dark and cold seeps. Slowly, slowly.
Silently creeping.

They stood straight and proud all around him, rows of natural fencing. Sunlight glinted through their bows, throwing striped shadows across the carriage path. The gap between the ground and the foliage of their high placed canopies allowed you to see into the depths of their forest, emitting an eerie aura; one could easily become lost in a thicket such as that. Edward breathed deeply the scent of eucalypts so foreign to his senses and gripped Rosalind's tiny hands. Excitement flushed his cheeks.

Percy slowed the carriage and Alistair moved to sit on the edge of his seat as they turned carefully down a smaller but well cleared pathway. Suddenly, rising as if from the dust before them, a flock of bright pink-bellied parrots flew up and over ahead, their flight mythical against the greys and dull hues of the landscape. Focused on the wildlife, Edward's attention was distracted as the homestead came into view.

Alistair brought his attention back, 'And my lady, my good fellow, this is the country house. I hope it will please you both.'

Edward looked forward as the carriage pulled up alongside the majestic riverside home. Built from sandstone like most of the buildings in this area, it stood at the apex of a small hill that rolled down to a modest tributary river, the Finniss. The house itself was of ample size, single storied, but sprawling. Surrounding it was a large wooden verandah made from pine, the edges of which ran into a green and succulent lawn that fell from the house, right to the water's edge. Lining the bank were reeds of brown and green whispering softly in the river breeze. The home stood still, powerful, its sharp edges framed by the encroaching bush, but seemingly holding it back. Edward was stunned. It was not that the house drew a more distinguished picture than the country estates from home, nor that its site was particularly remarkable. But the poise with which it stood, a sole bastion of civilisation set against such harsh and scrappy flora, left Edward in awe.

He stepped from the carriage, pausing to aid Rosalind's decent before wrapping a supportive arm around her frail waist. Together they strolled around the outside of the home, the afternoon light turning the gum trees golden, framing the house in a glow of warmth and security. He looked out from the house towards the river, gentle and still; a protected waterway, safe from the ravages of the ocean and its tides. Above his head one of the small black and white birds cried its supernatural warble. Edward glanced up to see the little creature spread its wings and take flight, soaring over the roof of the homestead into the bushland behind. Down to the right of the home was a small set of matching stables, like miniatures of the home itself. Beside them grew a quaint vegetable patch and beyond that Edward could see the fences of paddocks.

Alistair came up beside them. Rosalind moved knowingly a slight distance away, to give the men their privacy.

'Further down that way is the farming land, wheat mostly. Percy runs that land, you won't need to think on it. All I want you to do is feel the place and write her.'

Edward nodded and gazed out over the small river. On the far bank was simple bushland, small hills covered in gums and grasses. The house stood alone in an ocean of nature. The smell of oxygen and eucalyptus permeated the air, it felt fresh and clean but without the soaking moisture of home. Edward's nostrils were already feeling the drying effects of the climate; he hoped it was the same for his wife's lungs.

Standing there, surrounded by foreign landscape and unknown air, Edward felt his chest expand. This land, so dangerously invigorating, could it be the answer to his hopes, the solution to his search? He returned to Rosalind's side. Together they stood, framed by the homestead their hopes had chosen, only time would tell if this gamble was the right choice.

Time passed slowly, eking its way across the reddened sky. Rosalind, still poorly from the heat and travel, passed her days in their bedroom deep inside the house, the stonewalls providing a welcomed insulation from the scorched landscape. Gaslight had not made it to the bush home, nor piped water, so Mary returned to lighting candles and collecting water from the large tanks situated down a side path, busy always with these tasks and tending to Rosalind. Boxes of their belongings lined the halls waiting for Edward to unpack. He took his time, languid in the striking heat.

One particularly oppressive day he spied a rowboat resting alongside the outhouses. Seeking relief from the suffocating weight of the air, Edward hauled the wooden craft to the tributary's edge. Stepping carefully into the small boat he took hold of the oars. The wood was rough under his hands, pealing paint threatening splinters, but Edward was determined. Leaning backwards, he pulled the oars through the water with all of his strength. The boat glided out onto the river, gently parting the muddy currents. Edward looked back to the homestead. Quiet and still the house stood. No motion or signs of life inside. Rosalind would still be sleeping, he thought and he decided he had a good two hours before he would be missed. This brought an unexpected sense of freedom to his limbs, which cried out to be worked harder, to pull through the river and flex their unused strength.

Edward set off, aimlessly. The sun beat down sharply upon him, the still water reflecting its rays up into his pale face. Soon, Edward's arms and lower back, eager only moments before, began to complain and stiffen. His academic hands, small for a man and used only to pencils and quills, felt raw from gripping the oars. Edward paused his rowing and allowed the currents to drift him slowly back towards his home. Around him the water rippled softly, reed beds brushed the air in whispers. There was not a soul in sight. Edward lay back in his boat, dangling a hand over the edge of the boat into the cool of the stream and closed his heavy eyes. Subtly, without aplomb, visions of Australia began to move through his mind: the white of the trees, the greyed wood cylinders of the docks, the frame of bush around his home. Momentarily, Edward's fingers tensed, muscles twitching in time with his eyes beneath his lids, words forming and twisting around each other in his mind.

But only for a moment.

Then, there was peace. Edward heard the soft warble of a magpie, distracting his focus before his mind was flooded with emptiness. Edward's boat floated down the river and he drifted off to sleep.

Some time later he was awoken by Percy's voice, calling him from the riverbank. Edward's rowboat had lodged itself in a large bed of reeds opposite the farmhouse. Sitting up, rubbing his sleepy eyes, Edward grinned over to Percy and waved gently before organising the oars and rowing inexpertly into the bank. His limbs, heavy from unaccustomed exercise, groaned and Edward's head felt groggy. Percy helped him to tie the boat against the small jetty that jutted from the property before Edward walked dreamily up to the homestead and fell into another slumber on the couch of his library.

That was the beginning; a shift within him. Days later when a horse's neigh announced the arrival of Percy for the bi-weekly farm toil, Edward left the mess of boxes and wrapping to join him working the earth.Percy greeted him with a smile, broad and without judgment, passed him a shovel in silence. Then together, under the cooling sun of autumn the men dug a trench for seedlings, which would in time produce wheat. The earth was dry on the surface. As Edward pushed the shovel down it almost skimmed across the light powdery consistency. But pushing harder, deeper, tilled up a rich, dark brown, full of goodness. Edward bent his back to the task, ignored the friction of the handle against his palms and wiped the sweat of his brow against his sleeve. The actions felt uncomfortable at first, jarring and coarse, against the normal flow of his body. However, as the sun slipped down the other side of the sky, his limbs found a new rhythm. Lift, push, shuffle, dump. Edward mouthed the motions, keeping time with the earth's movements. His mind was emptied, focused. Time was meaningless.

As the last of the suns rays dipped below the horizon, Edward packed away the remaining tools and, grinning broadly, escorted Percy in for dinner with the family. Percy washed outside in a trough, Edward took the main bathroom. Staring at his dirt streaked face in the mirror Edward felt a laugh rise in his throat. Shaking his bemused head, he washed the grime as well as he could from his fingers, finding his nails to be the most resistant. Clean and dressed for dinner he again observed his reflection, now transformed, now English once again. An odd disappointment settled in his heart. Confused, he turned from his image and headed for dinner. Underneath his bow tie however, the top button of his shirt remained loose. He felt an excited anticipation brew in his stomach thinking of the next day he could till the land with his new friend.

Edward sat sipping his tea as three riders approached down the drive. He rose slowly and strolled to the edge of the verandah. Mr Merryweather came first, black priest dress distinguishing him from his companions, who as they came closer Edward realised were not white. He raised an eyebrow and waited patiently. Merryweather rode right up to the house before stopping his horse and disembarking. Two aboriginal youths held back, waiting a few paces from the house.

'Mr. Merryweather,' Edward began, 'What a pleasure to see you. Would you care for some tea? It's freshly steeped.'

'Why thank you, yes,' Mr Merryweather replied.

'And for your men?' Edward indicated the two youths with a calm gesture.

'That is very kind of you, yes, I am sure they would enjoy some tea. Peter, Paul tie up your horses and join us for tea,' he called to them before following Edward to the verandah table.

Rosalind, having heard the arrival, called to Mary for extra teacups and now stood waiting to greet their guests, and pour their refreshment.

'Mr. Merryweather, please meet my wife, Rosalind.'

Merryweather doffed his riding hat and bowed politely to Rosalind, 'A pleasure madam. I hope you are finding our humble region to your liking?'

'Quite, I assure you,' she smiled. Catching sight of Peter and Paul, her eyes widened but only briefly before continuing with tea.

The boys paused at the verandah steps, waiting to be invited to the table. Edward gestured them up into the remaining seats and Rosalind inquired as to their tea preferences (both white with two sugars) before the unusual group sat to talk.

'Well, my good man. What brings you here this morning? Business in Clayton?' Edward's farm lay between Goolwa and the next large town in the area.

'Why, no. My business is rather more local,' Merryweather smiled. 'Peter, Paul, sit straight,' he chided, then, 'These are two of my finest pupils, both of working age and highly skilled. I was hoping you might have need of some farm hands? I understand you are here to write, not work, all the more reason to have more help. Give you free time.'

Edward regarded Merryweather for a moment, before turning to the two young men. They sat well, but were clearly ill at ease on the verandah. Peter was the slightly larger of the two, though both would be considered slender. Their skin was dark, but a lighter milky brown then that of the man Edward had seen on the train, their hair brown and frizzy. Both were immaculately clean, as though they'd just come from church.

'I know they appear small,' Merryweather was saying, 'But they are bushmen, and surprisingly strong. They will work for meals and board, perhaps in the outhouse I see down the way?'

'You are certainly a business man,' Edward spoke straight, looking directly at Merryweather once again.

'Forgive me, sir. I do not mean to be insistent. Too many people in these parts forget their Christian duty...'

Edward took a moment, though looking at the two adolescents, his mind was already decided. 'They can start on Monday. That will give me time put things in order. But they will have to bring bedding and be prepared to clean out their accommodation. Both stables are currently for horses, one can be spared. I have big plans for this farm, their expertise and manpower will be advantageous.'

He turned to Peter and Paul. 'It will be a pleasure to hire you.'

And it was settled.

The two moved into the stable the following week. Initially they brought animal furs to sleep on, but Rosalind was appalled and shortly Percy brought two cots from town. They worked hard and kept mostly to themselves, seeming to believe their role was to keep out of the way as much as possible.

It took weeks to coax them from this silence. Both would answer 'yes sir, or no, sir' with all proper respect, but declined the invite to extrapolate on their opinions or backgrounds.

But Edward, seeing something of his childhood self in their shyness, worked to make them feel at ease, comfortable on his land.

The breakthrough came with Paul. Always more prone to smiling, he had finally warmed to Edward's constant questioning about his culture and background.

'My mother calls me Allambee, he is Balun'

'Your Aboriginal names? And where do you come from, your people I mean?'

'We are Ngarrindjeri people, we fish Karangka, the ocean and collect from the land.'

'Karrrenka?'

Allambee smiled at Edward's clumsy pronunciation.

'Karangka, is like the water's neck, where it joins the ocean.'

'You mean the mouth? The Murray, the river mouth?' Edward smiled at the memory of the wild ocean beyond the sand dunes. Allambee nodded, his eyes misting over as he spoke of hunting.

'Sometimes there, sometimes other places. We move to the food, but not far.'

The conversation was a turning point for both Allambee and Edward, Allambee gradually became more and more open about his culture, Edward increasingly intrigued by the way of life the boy described. He liked Allambee's view of the land, harsh and unrelenting but also giving and sustaining. Initially, Balun remained distant, unsure about this white man wanting to know of his people's traditions; such talk was banned at the Mission. It was Rosalind who brought him from his shell. All it took was the offer of cake. Munching through the crusty icing Balun offered her the first real grin Edward had seen on the boy's face. He and Rosalind glanced at each other, longing in their eyes. It felt good to guide and care for these boys. One day they hoped to do the same with a child of their very own.

14

Faster, faster. Pressing out the forest and gold and fawn, white.
The hope.

Finniss River, Australia 1887

George pulled hard on the rope, dragging himself and his raft to the side of the river. The raft hit the muddy bank harder than he intended, rocking it violently backwards. He heard several of his boxes of medical supplies shake and cursed his impatience. He had been traveling the river in this manner for some eight and a half months now, tending to the many families and small communities along its banks. Thus far, the horror stories of men gone crazy from isolation or roaming natives on the war path, had proved just that, stories, though George had come across many unhappy farmers, and even more unhappy farmer's wives.

Unfortunately, there was nothing his profession could do for them but be a listening ear. This night, George had come from one such depressive homestead. The rains had failed the previous winter and their crops were down. George had tended their sickly infant, whose golden curls were not made for this oppressive heat and allowed his parents to vent their frustrations at the ways of this harsh land.

At least the river still ran strong, and now, with the coming of spring, even more flow pushed him along. Someone had told him it was the melting snow from the Colonies upstream; George found it hard to believe any place in this hot and dry land could generate the conditions required for snow.

Tying up his raft, anchored by a tree stump, George set about making his campsite, pitching his tent, collecting firewood and lighting the fire that would keep the cold at bay while he slept. As he did, a smile formed on his lips. It had been a lonely time tending to the remote families of the river. Though always welcoming, George was still an outsider here. But tomorrow, almost ten months since they parted on such prickly terms, George would get to see his friend Edward Barrington again.

He washed extra well that morning, using the last of his soap, brushed his hair and donned his best suit. The sail was gentle, a light breeze pushing him down the river towards his friend. Banks, lined with reeds, green and lush from the winter cool, rustling gently in the breeze that transported him so calmly down the tributary. As the waterway narrowed, its paths split by islands of sand covered in reeds, George lowered his sail, the wind too fickle whistling through the surrounding hills, and rowed the last few miles

Nearing midday a square of land cleared of reeds and scrub appeared before him. Grass ran up the gentle slope of the hill atop of which stood a colonial style stone house, full verandah across its front. To the left of the homestead were a set of stone stables, out from which three horses, two brown and one stunningly black, grazed peacefully in the shade of the eucalypts. Jutting out from the grassy bank was a small jetty, a sign stuck to its side reading: 'Barrington'.

George pulled in his oars and looped a rope around the jetty pole. He paused a moment to allow the spring sun to shine on his face, its rays soft and soothing. It was time to make things right.

Edward was sat on the verandah writing a list of supplies in his notebook as George approached. Seeing his friend walking up his hill, arms loaded with belongings, brought Edward to his feet.

'Rosalind, George is here!' he called inside before swiftly walking down to meet and greet his sailing companion.

'I see you still prefer water travel?' Edward joked, nodding his head at George's small boat.

'Only way to get to my patients with ease.'

George smiled and the two men embraced. Rosalind walked out on to the deck, dishcloth in hand. She was dressed in a light green dress, hair swept back gracefully from her neckline. While still remarkably small, she had gained good weight around her hips and a fullness of cheek. When she smiled, George saw new dimples. The effect was stunning. Rosalind was much, much better.

After settling in his rooms, George joined his hosts for a cold lunch on the verandah table. The view was amazing, sweeping down on both sides. George looked out at the tributary and rolling hills, stuffed full of bushland, wild and free. But around this house was order, grass and paddocks for horses and some crops around the back, sheep grazing by the river. The muddy water reflected green in the midday sun. George kept thinking about Rosalind's shinning eyes.

'So,' he began as he stuffed another piece of preserved pork into is mouth, as common as ham was in Australia, this one tasted especially nice to him, 'Things appear to be well?'

Edward beamed at George. 'Yes, I think my wife is almost fully recovered. She has gone from strength to strength. The summer here, though terrible to bear, seemed to dry out her infection and with the milder winter she has done wonderfully.'

George started. In all their months of friendship upon The Orient, Edward had never once openly acknowledged Rosalind's condition.

A gentle smile came over Edward's face. He took Rosalind's hand, as if for strength, and took a deep breath.

'My friend,' he began, 'I owe you an apology.'

George opened his mouth to disagree but Edward held up a hand for silence. George sat still.

Edward's soft brown eyes glistened with unshed tears. George saw Rosalind squeeze his hand tighter.

'When your letter came, asking to visit, it was the opportunity I feared and longed for. When we parted I was… rash. Rude even. I believe fear of losing my wife caused me to lash out.' His voice caught in his throat, a single tear tracking down his cheek. He did not wipe it away. 'It's no excuse for my appalling behaviour. But perhaps it can be an explanation of something forgivable?'

George was speechless. Where had this new found freedom to express his emotions come from?

'I have also longed to make amends,' George began. 'I knew your pain and I pushed. No really, I believe… I believe there was fault on both sides. I hold no anger towards you. If you can forgive me too.'

'There is nothing to forgive.'

Both men sat, staring, unsure of what to say or do now all was resolved. Rosalind released a joyous laugh, breaking the moment. 'You see husband,' she exclaimed, 'I told you all would be well. And now, Dr Harbot can examine me and prove what we already know. That this country has healed me, and we can start our plans to return home.'

'Not today,' Edward cut in. 'Today I thought a trip to the beach, if you would agree? It is not an hour's ride from here and will be wonderful exertion for us both. Then tomorrow, once you're settled in, we can think on these things. I have far too much to show you!'

After months of the tug of sail force, the power of the horses felt good under George's legs. Edward rode fast, with seeming abandon, shouting out to George the occasional landmark.

'That far hill is the edge of my boundary. There is the road to the town of Goolwa and here... is the turn off to the beach.'

They rode for a solid hour before they hit sand but it had been exhilarating and wild and had passed swiftly. George felt transported by the freedom and wondered at its affect on Edward.

At the beach they cantered down the sand dunes, the loose ground forcing them to slow their pace. The horses, hot from the exertion, headed straight for the water's edge, settling into a slow trot through the shallows.

George could not believe his eyes. Never in his life had he witnessed such a beach! The strip of sand was thick and wide, stretching in both directions as far as his eyes could see. Off shore waves crashed with all the might of the ocean, but at his horse's hooves whimpered to a calm wash of tide. Its colour was grey, like the coming of a storm, melding beautifully with the afternoon sky. Behind him sand dunes rose, covered in spinifex, shinning gold in the sunlight, their sharp leaves reflecting its rays in a spectrum of colours.

'We ride here often,' Edward said by way of explanation.

'You and Rosalind?' George asked alarmed. While it was clear she was well improved this kind of exertion would never do.

'No, no. Mr. Harbinger, Alistair, and myself. You are riding his horse. Don't worry, he won't mind. We have become quite close. He says I have a natural gift with his land. Strange how talents you never realised you had can come to you when you least expect them.'

'One could fall in love with this freedom,' George heard himself say.

'I think I quite have.' Edward smiled, 'I can be how I want here. I can farm. Imagine that? Me using his hands. My father would most like not approve.'

George laughed at Edward's clear enthusiasm and they cantered on a while.

'This land is harsh,' Edward continued after a time, 'So harsh for the first few months, I thought I had brought my wife to her death. The initial thrill I had felt at her beauty vanished in sweat and fear.' Edward paused, shook his head. 'It was hard, but then things began to change. *She*, began to change. And while not everything was healed, what was not was replaced by something else, by something new. This land has given her back to me George, and I love her for it.'

Edward turned from George and looked out to sea, his eyes tracing the far off horizon, savouring the vastness. George gazed out as well, heart full of joy. The coastline swept forever before him, curving beautifully, wide and inexhaustible. Looking straight out he knew there was nothing between himself and the end of the earth; he was at the very bottom of the world. Or was it the top? The thought was exhilarating. He regarded Edward and felt he could understand all that his friend was saying. Where pain had laced his features, joy now shone.

'Come on,' Edward cried, 'I will race you home!'

And with that he was off, pushing his horse hard as it charged the sand dunes. George laughed again, amazed at the man he was meeting now, as if for the first time; an Edward more changed than he had ever expected to find. Together they raced across the plains, freedom wrapped around them.

Just outside the fences of his home, Edward slowed his horse. George piped up, 'I hear there are some interesting herbs out here… native plants that heal. I had hoped to come across some of the natives for myself, but it seems they are not among us much any more. Do you know where I could find some information?'

'Yes. In fact, I do. We have two young aborigines from the mission working with us. They know much about their native ways, despite Mr Merryweather's most ardent efforts to the contrary,' Edward smirked. 'They have taught Mary much, she has even begun her own herb garden. They are probably out in the field. Go gather them from their task. There is still a good hour or so before dinner. They can take you on a tour of our herbs, and then Rosalind and I can call you in for dinner.'

George was surprised, and excited headed off to find Allambee and Balun at the other side of the property. Such strange names.

Edward continued on to his home, savouring the moment he rounded the trees and could see his house, standing atop the small hill. *Or what will soon be my house,* he pondered the thought, testing its shape. Releasing his horse into its paddock, he wiped off his trousers and washed his hands in a nearby trough. Mounting the stairs he came to the entranceway. Instead of calling for Rosalind, as he often did, he crept towards the back room. She was putting flowers from her rose garden into vases in the sunroom; her 'Piece of England'.

Silently, he stood in the doorway and watched her graceful movements. The late afternoon sun still shone softly through the windows, catching the wisps of hair that had worked loose from her clasp, shining through them, turning her deep brown hair to a golden blonde. His eyes traced down her waist, still so slender, and back up to her hands, so elegant and small. Passion rose in his throat, all he could do to stop from crying out was move towards her. Two steps were all it took and he had her in his arms. She turned to him, surprised, but pleased, and beamed into his eyes. He looked into hers and was lost, everything but this moment gone in a sweep of love and gratitude to the world. To this country for giving her back to him. She sensed his intensity and looking down at the part of his chest that covered his heart, placed her hand upon it. Gently, he took her chin and brought her mouth to his. Their kisses waves of ocean surging together. Edward swept her up into his arms, grown larger from farm work, and carried her to their room. There he abandoned all else, losing himself in her as the last of the sun's rays licked through their window.

15

Cobalt water flows, toward the future.

'Breathe in, now out. In again. Hold. Now out. Good.' George pulled the stethoscope from this ears and nodded encouragingly to Rosalind seated before him. She pulled her shawl back over her thin shoulders and waited. George turned to Edward. 'Shall we step next door?' he invited his friend, as was customary.

Edward frowned, 'Speak freely, George. We are both keen to hear your analysis.' He stepped across the room, placing himself at Rosalind's side, hand on her shoulder in solidarity. She smiled at George, an invite to continue.

'Well, erm...' George began awkwardly, unused to consulting to an audience, 'I am amazed at the improvement. Her lungs are nearly healed. Though there is still weakness, some of which I doubt will ever repair and some more time is needed, she is well out of danger and I feel, set for a full and happy life.'

Edward clapped his hands together and let out a hoot. Rosalind lowered her head demurely, but her smile of relief was clear to see.

'But...' George cautioned. 'She still needs time. At least another summer here before she can return to England for any length of time.'

He felt Edward wince. Unsure why he hurried on to the next point, 'And, I am sorry to say, no children. Not yet anyway. Her body is not yet strong enough. But within the year I feel it will be.'

He stopped, sensing the mood in the room shift.

'Yes,' he said, eyes flicking between the two lovers, 'She will be able to try for children. Just not yet.'

Rosalind seemed to physically relax. Edward gripped her in a tight embrace.

'Oh,' Rosalind let out the long sob of a lifetime of failure and buried her head in Edward's chest. George turned away to hide the emotion that played across his own face.

After a moment Rosalind pulled herself up, 'Well, I must go see to Mary. I think a special dinner is only fitting for this evening.' She pushed up onto her tip toes and kissed Edward's cheek before turning and walking out, a lightness in her step George had never before seen.

Edward came to George and enfolded him in a huge hug. Unsure of what to do, George stood still, arms at his side. 'Thank you my friend. Thank you,' Edward whispered.

'It is yourself you should thank,' George said, pulling out of Edward's grip. 'It was your decision to bring her here that made the difference. The hot, the dry, it keeps the rot at bay.'

Edward turned to him sharply. 'At bay? Meaning it is still there.'

'Yes, consumpt…' he caught himself, 'illness of the lungs is rarely fully healed. The cold and damp will bring it out again in the weakened tissues. It is a good thing you have decided to stay.'

'Who told you that?' Edward shot him a look of alarm.

'Why, Harbinger said you had discussed the possibility of purchasing this land. I was speaking with him last week, I am thinking of opening up a practice here and wondered if he would be interested in sponsoring me. At first, I didn't believe him. I remember how you and Rosalind talked of England on our trip here. But now, seeing you here. Well, it quite becomes you.'

Edward shifted uncomfortably. 'It is a possibility. But by no means decided. George, I would appreciate it if you didn't mention this to Rosalind. Her health, it can be fragile. Though she is so much better. But I rather prefer not to burden her with financial details unnecessarily. You understand?'

He didn't, but he smiled amiably and nodded anyway, 'Of course Edward. Your business is your business. But I am sure she will be delighted when you tell her. This is the place that saved her life, after all.'

'Indeed,' Edward said, but he seemed distracted. 'It's sometime before dinner, shall we take a ride before the sun is down?'

'Yes, that sounds very agreeable,' George said, smiling through his confusion, soon forgotten in the joy of riding with his friend across the sands of South Australia.

* * *

The sun was high overhead. Edward rolled up his sleeves and plunged the shovel back into the earth. His hands, now hardened and accustomed to farming, no longer complained as they rubbed the rough wood, little calluses protected his once aristocratic flesh. His browned face, burnt often enough by the sun to have developed a protective shade, creased with the effort of the work. His body stretched and groaned and the earth gave way as he expertly moved it to the side. Toiling beside him were the ever present Balun and Allambee. Merryweather had been right, the two were ardent workers, always keen to please.

Now as sweat gleamed from their bare skin, Allambee caught Edward's eye and flashed him a broad grin, Edward nodded, they both loved to work the soil. Edward had decided to plant a new crop here, some orange trees to match with the lemons by the house. It was a new venture he had been planning for some months now, alongside other ideas. The traditional crops of the farm, corn and wheat, were profitable and effective, especially in this climate, and the sheep had added a whole new dimension, but Edward was looking for more self-sufficiency, for everyday foods, hardy and reliable. These thoughts teased his waking moments. A new challenge. An exciting one.

Satisfied with the hole they had dug, Edward paused to observe his new field. Bringing a small notebook from his pocket, Edward scrawled a few plant varieties in a list of plans. He would need extra fertiliser to make this venture work, he decided. His elegant writing caressed the page, his hands, for a moment their old selves, writing beautifully, gracefully, before he plunged the book back deep in his pocket and resumed the manual labour of his task. Hands transformed into the instruments of action.

Rosalind appeared on the balcony, a broad smile on her lips. So many joys had come to them of late, she had too much to be happy for. Resting her hands on her stomach, she watched her husband toil, amusement brightening her face. Working with the natives! What would his father have thought? She could not understand his love of farm work, but it gave him joy and kept him happy. She would not contend it, after all it was only a symptom of this place; Hathrone would soon right any impropriety when they returned home to England.

Edward stood tall and stretched his back. Spying Rosalind, he raised a hand to wave before wiping his dusty face, dismissing Allambee and Balun for the day and heading up for lunch. Washing in the tough by the out houses, he mused to himself over the beauty of this moment, this day. The sun was hard, but a gentle breeze made its way from the cooling river. The earth was rich and ready for crops, the air smelt of the coming rains. It was the time for planting. He splashed the cold water over his face and savoured its texture as it coursed down his neck and spilled onto his chest. Breathing deeply, he dried his hands on his shirt, pausing to watch the bush around him quiver in the heavy air. Contentment swelled within him, the scent of food wafting from Mary's kitchen adding to his calm. How good those oranges would taste. How succulent. The thought reminded him of his parched throat and drew him from his reverie, back to his wife who waited, smiling their joy, at the verandah table.

They would lunch together and then Edward could use the afternoon to plan his farming acquisitions at the coming Saturday market. Rosalind liked to listen to his ideas and the afternoon would pass nicely together this way, before an evening of quiet reading. The cool verandah was their favourite haunt in this season. Maybe he would take Rosalind out in the rowboat? It now sported a freshly painted sheen, she seemed to enjoy bobbing with him on the river. No need to decide, Edward could allow the afternoon to take them as it wished. He felt calm, not having to actively plan the order of events, but knowing subconsciously how his day would play out, with nothing to distract or stress him, only the surrounding nature and his wife's lilting voice to enjoy.

And so it came to be that Rosalind remained on the farm one morning, content to water the roses and help Mary with the dinner herbs, not wishing to see the ladies in Goolwa, while Edward ventured in. He traveled past the town, stopping only once he had reached the oceanside.

Sitting atop a vast sand dune, fingers sifting white sand and pulling at spinifex, Edward gazed out to sea. *This place has taken me over,* he thought to himself. *It's all I can see, all I can feel. Here I can be me.* Edward had been transformed by this remote continent. It had gifted him Rosalind's health. But it had not brought all he had thought he wanted; it had not returned his passion for poetry. In its place was something new. For the first time in his life, Edward did not need words, books or poems. There was nothing in his world to escape from, no role to be played, no expectations. The pain of his childhood, from which he had been running for so long, had dissolved under the high Australian sun.

Here Edward Barrington was free.

The bright sunlight shined on the white sand bottomed ocean, reflecting back to Edward's eyes a turquoise so rich he had to blink to ensure it was real. Like the colour of thick blown glass, it swam through his mind. He wanted to take the colour and wrap it around Rosalind; her deep brown hair cascading beside it would bring out the full richness of her new glowing beauty. Edward leaned back into the sand, the sun kissed ocean calm beneath him. *Everywhere I look there is Rosalind: her eyes, her skin, her voice, all a part of this landscape.* Edward realised it had never been England that made him feel safe, it had been his wife. Hathrone was just a house, she made it their home. Open windows, vases of roses. A place of love, until the warning echo of her coughing stole it all away. And now, the farm that had been just a tool to save her, had through her health become a sanctuary. Where she was safe and well, was where he himself needed to be. *This is her place,* he realised, *this is our place.* And George's warning... He would not risk losing her. Could not go back to being alone. A decision cemented itself in his mind.

Edward rose to his feet, collected his black steed and rode into town. There he sat, alone at Mr Harbinger's desk and signed over ownership of his father's estate in Derbyshire to Alistair, as the older man signed over ownership of the small farm by the waterside to Edward; there after to be known as Hathrone Farm, Australia.

Six months later, he would be dead.

Ellie

16

Life bringer, sustainer, hope returner.

Sydney, Australia 2018

Soft morning light filtered through my curtains, staining my doona cover in shades of green and pink. I rolled lazily onto my back. These past weeks since returning to Sydney, I'd taken to sleeping in. Late. I had not realised just how much sleep I seemed to need. After months of barely making 5 hours, these 10 hours stretches were, for want of a better word, decedent. I rubbed my eyes sleepily and snuggled down into my pillows. The clock read 10am, no need to move yet. I was feeling healthier than I had in years, lighter in myself.

I had loved my time in Goolwa, passing my days on the river or along the beach with Taj. He even took me out to Raukkan. We'd walked the streets of the town, small and quiet. Peaceful. The old stone church of the Mission still stood. I pictured Barrington visiting this remote place, teaching the children of poetry, and found a smile on my lips. There'd also been coffee and cake in town with Deborah, and fishing trips with her kids, until I really couldn't justify staying in Goolwa any longer. Deborah had thrown me a goodbye dinner at her house, her husband Andy had even been down from Adelaide that night. Taj was invited too. The dinner had been delicious, roast lamb and all the trimmings; wine flowed freely from Andy's impressive cellar. When I finally headed for the door to taxi back to my motel, the sun was already rising. Deborah, pulling me into a tight embrace, had made me promise to visit again soon. Taj accompanied me home. We'd parted with a languid hug, both either too sleepy to pull away, or just too relaxed to care. When he finally stepped back he'd cocked his head and grinned at me.

'I'll ring. Be sure you answer.' I'd confided in him that I had been screening Caleb's calls all visit. I didn't know why.

'And find that poet, Ellie. Find out what happened to him.' And with that he walked away into the rising sunlight that spilled over the lake.

Taj had been true to his word. Most evenings since coming home were passed not with cigarettes and wine, but on the phone with him, talking about everything and nothing and sometimes just existing over the line.

I'd talked to Caleb too. I'd had too. Called him when I landed at Sydney airport and apologised, 'I was just so caught up with the research.' He'd sounded hurt, unsure, but had asked to see me that weekend, dinner and a movie. We'd seen the new Avengers one. I couldn't tell you the plot. I was there, but not there. When Caleb kissed me after dinner, Taj's face had flashed before my eyes. But the guilt that sunk my stomach had faded quickly. Pushed down by my insistence that it was just a weird brain thing and nothing to worry about. I hadn't agreed to stay the night at Caleb's though.

Snuggling in bed that morning thoughts of Caleb, and what I did and didn't want to do with him, were far from my mind. My leave was nearing an end and though I felt much rested and, dare I say it, inspired to get back into my thesis work, I still hadn't resolved the other problem I was facing. My mother.

I hadn't visited her during my time in SA. Hadn't even called to tell her I was in town. And that was just fine with me. But an off the cuff question from Taj last night while we chatted, 'you said once your dad loved the water. Does that go for your mum too? You should bring her down next time you visit, ' had thrown me.

I had never spoken to Taj about my mother – other than to say she was in Adelaide. He didn't know that we weren't... close. Or even talking really. And he didn't need to know why. No one needed to know that. I'd lightly deflected the offer, thanking him but saying we'd have to see, 'she's very busy.'

Taj hadn't pressed, but I'd felt a shift between us. He knew I was avoiding something. *That* guilt hadn't faded. Though I'd only known Taj for a month, I felt completely safe with him, could tell him anything: my thoughts, dreams, fears. Though it seemed that didn't extend to the situation with my mother.

My mobile bleeped to life. I cringed, hoping it wasn't Caleb and reached for the hand piece. Deborah's number filled the screen. My heart skipped a beat in anticipation. She was expecting the results of the bone testing this week. Could they have come through? I answered.

'Hi Deborah, how are you?'

'Ellie, dear. It's lovely to hear your voice.'

I knew. It was in her tone. The bones didn't belong to Edward Barrington.

'You've the results. But they aren't what either of us wanted hey?'

'I have the results yes. But they aren't what anyone expected really. Ellie, the bones are the right age – well as close as they can tell. Definitely not aboriginal bones. But they can't be Edward Barrington. They belong to a woman.'

'A woman?'

'From what they can tell she would have died around the time Barrington lived there, give or take a few years. You know how loose dating is. I took the liberty of looking up the previous owners. Only a wealthy man named Alistair Harbinger was listed, but his wife is buried at the Goolwa Cemetery. So it can't be her. Unless you know of any other women who lived on the estate, I fear she may remain a mystery.'

'There was Rosalind's maid, Mary Smith. But she is in the cemetery as well. What about before you moved in?'

'We acquired the property of a descendent of Harbinger's. But according to the records it had been uninhabited since the early 1980s.'

'So someone lived there after Rosalind Barrington returned to England?'

'Not until after her death. She never sold it. But when she passed, Harbinger bought the property back from her estate. His son and their family lived here for years, then it was empty until Andy bought it last year and we moved in. Unless there were some unregistered tenants, which I guess is highly probable, I really don't know what else to think.'

'What does this mean for your renovations? Do the police need to investigate?'

'Fortunately, we are free to move forward. The bones are over a century old and the police are satisfied that they don't match with any known missing person record, so they are putting it down as a mystery. They'll keep an ear out, but there is no active investigation.'

'So strange. It fit so well.'

'I know love, but don't fret. His bones are still out there somewhere. It's kind of lovely that they remain undisturbed. *Rest in Peace* proper, you know?'

'I guess so. I'm glad you can move ahead at least. Be able to finish things in time for your 50th.'

'Which I am hoping you will be in town to celebrate with us? Your invite will be in the mail as soon as I set a date.'

'Thanks Deborah. And thank you for ringing to tell me. I'm disappointed, but I can see the positives. Talk again soon.'

'Yes, take care love. Bye for now.'

I stayed sitting in bed for a few more moments, brain whirring. Then, possessed by an unusual energy, leaped up and headed to my study table across the room. Shuffling through my books and notes I found the text I sought. A volume of the *Great poets of the 1800s* by Wilbur Herbert. I flicked through the pages, scanning the bright orange post-it notes I had used to highlight sections relevant to Barrington. There:

'Archie Hargraves, the young biographer who lived with the widow Rosalind Barrington before escorting her back to England, wrote in a letter home to his fiancée Clara Forsyth of a 'grave, coated in flowers that smelt of rot and ruin.' Sadly, the would be biographer's life was claimed by the Great War, before anything could be published...'

A grave. And now a body. But not Barrington. It seemed too big a coincidence to be nothing. There were rumours of a journal of notes from Archie's time in Australia, but as nothing had ever been released, it was a lead I had discounted early in my research. But what about Clara? What else had Archie told her about his time with the widow? Did he know of some other woman living on the estate?

It seemed thin.

Yet the bones were an indisputable fact. Who was she? And how could anyone cover up two disappearances so thoroughly?

No, there was something here and someone knew. Archie and Clara were gone, but their families remained... An idea began to take form. I collected up my books, shoving them into a satchel before heading to the bathroom for a quick shower, hands shaking in anticipation. I needed to get to the university and see my supervisor.

17

Darkness paused. Shades muted. Hold. Hold.
Hope.
Shimmering opalescence.

London, England 2018

Three days later I stood in the passport queue at Heathrow Airport, exhausted. It had been my first ever long haul flight, and with the nerves of travelling alone and the anticipation of my plan, as well as the discomfort of commercial flight, I had not slept in over 26 hours. My eyes felt like sand had been poured under my lids and my skin was hot like I was developing a fever. Worse, it was only 6 a.m London time, so even after I got through immigration I couldn't check into my hotel and sleep for hours yet.

Despite my feet being on British soil, my mind hadn't caught up with the quick turn of events of the last two days. Still riding the excitement from my time in Goolwa, I had visited my supervisor with my plan: to use my untouched research grant to go to England and find the relatives of Archie Hargraves and Clara Forsyth. To discover what else they might know about the life and disappearance of Edward Barrington. Mr Tuft had regarded me over glasses perched on the tip of his long nose, 'That was a privilege you won last year Ellie. One that you turned your back on.'

'I know Mr. Tuft. And that's on me. But now, after being to Goolwa and seeing where Barrington lived… I just know there's more to find, more insight to his last days, when he wrote *The Fall*. If I speak to the families, I might be able to find some answers.' *Like who those bones* belong to and whether there is any connection to Barrington's disappearance, I thought to myself.

Peter had leaned back in his chair, fingers steepled before him, and my shoulders had slumped. *Idiot Ellie, after all the stuff ups of the last six months, why should you be granted such an opportunity? Like dad always said, 'you have to earn experiences, they don't just land there for you'.* I'd been ready to take my leave when Mr Tuft had nodded. 'Ok, I'll talk to the grants department. With all the press Barrington is currently generating, after finding those mystery bones, I just might be able to swing it. '

My jaw had dropped. Quickly recovering, I thanked him profusely making for a swift exit before he could change his mind. 'But remember, Ellie,' Peter called to my retreating back, 'your thesis is on *The Fall*, and Barrington's last known days. Not the woman buried on the farm. No matter how intriguing that all might be, don't get distracted.'

I nodded and rushed out the door.

And now here I was, in England.

I made it through passport control, found my bag (lucky bright purple) and navigated to the Heathrow Express. I had planned on taking the cheaper Piccadilly line, but by now my exhausted brain was too frayed and the simple option was all I could face. The train whizzed through the outer suburbs of the UK capital, passing rows of brown brick houses with cute back yards filled with flowers, hedges and the occasional plastic slippery-dip set. After a few quick train changes, I arrived at South Kensington, my destination. I left the station and plodded out onto the street. All around me rows and rows of white townhouses, 3 or 4 storeys high, stretched off along the curving streets, glowing in the gentle sunlight. The sky above was pale blue, the morning breeze cool against my fevered skin; it felt fresh, despite the smell of street and car that came with it.

I checked in at the Best Western and stored my bags, then with hours until I could take my room, headed out to explore. Though overtired, the sights and smells had awoken my mind, filling me with a heady energy. I had to see everything!

I took off down the high street, marvelling at the increasingly hectic morning traffic, feeling in a dream of sorts as I passed the wrought iron fences of Hyde Park. At length I came to a quieter street curve, which soon opened out to a large paved circle before an enormous building. Buckingham Palace, mammoth and ornate, reclined before me, the shiny gold tips of the fence glinting in the strengthening sun. I stood in silent awe, taking in the splendour. Continuing on, I crossed through the smaller Green Park, spying several grey squirrels racing through the trees and countless pigeons pecking at the earth, not stopping until the Thames spread before me, wide and rushing.

And stole my breath.

Coursing dangerously in its tidal flow, the river looked fearfully grey and unpredictable. I stood in the centre of Westminster Bridge and filled my eyes with its expanse. A sense of infinite possibility and of doom seemed to ride the current. So much came from this dank and deadly tide; its waters renewed themselves everyday, pushing the old out into the ocean, cleansing itself. All along his banks commuters in suits walked briskly, joggers in active wear worked up a sweat, laughing tourists snapped selfies. The river itself was a hive of activity: boats, ferries, barges, a small group of kayaks twisting between them. The London Eye loomed to one side, to the other, sitting regally on the riverside, the Houses of Parliament. All this in one vista: the history of the empire and the crucible of nationalism.

I bought a coffee and a croissant from a nearby café, waded through tourists buying souvenir key rings and flags, took a seat on a park bench and just watched. Around me the city hummed and popped and shouted and beeped and rushed on.

Sometime later I realised I had dozed off, slumped to the side on the bench. Not a good look. Jerking awake I re-traced my steps back to my hotel, my earlier burst of energy well and truly burnt away. Thankfully my room was ready. Heading in, I planned a shower before taking a nap, but found the bed was simply too inviting. I flopped down on the spongy mattress, barely remembering to set my alarm before sleep claimed me.

It was lucky I set my alarm, as four hours later I was deeply unconscious as it's blare filled the small room. I rubbed my burning eyes, groaning to myself and stumbled to the shower. Beautifully warm water rained down my back as I soaked, trying to feel human again through the jet lag. Dressed in jeans and a neat red blouse I headed back out onto the streets of London.

I was meeting with an academic acquaintance of my supervisor, who now lectured the Arts at the University of London. He had agreed to meet me after work for a light dinner before he headed to a play with friends. As well as being a highly regarded professor of literature, he was a fan of Edward Barrington and for this reason had been happy to offer his guidance to me while I was in town, or so my supervisor had said.

We were meeting at the Social Eating House in Soho. I took the tube, gripping the hand rail to keep from falling as a mass of commuters piled into the train around me. Hot, stale air mixed with the dewy musk of perspiration and the acrid scent of brake dust that permeated the subterranean tunnels; it was a relief to get back out onto the street, though the personal space wasn't much better. Soon enough, I made it to the restaurant and headed inside.

The space was small and dimly lit in an inviting, comforting way. I scanned the room. On the far side sat the only man who looked of an age with my supervisor. He looked up and a bright smile split across his ageing face. As he rose I was shocked at how tall he was, all limbs and long fingers. He offered me his hand in greeting, 'Christopher Pickering,' he said.

'Ellie Cannon.'

'It's a pleasure to meet you my dear. Please, take a seat. How have you found London so far?'

'Oh, thank you. Um, well I only arrived this morning, so I'm still adjusting to the jet lag. But I enjoyed a walk to the Thames earlier and found it really quite beautiful. But very busy.'

"If a man is bored of London a man is bored of life!" he quoted. 'Haha, it is definitely a busy place. Lots of people. But that's what makes it exciting. How long are you staying?'

'Two weeks.'

'Well, you'll want to get your skates on, then. Lots to see and do in that time.'

'Very true, I've always dreamed of seeing London. But much of that might have to wait for another trip. I am really here about my thesis on Edward Barrington…'

'Still, you must at least make time for the Tower! Now, let's order. Then we can get down to business.'

'Ok,' I scooped up the menu and browsed the options. Lots of pork. I settled on baked salmon with a walnut crust and rocket salad with pear and goats cheese.

Mr. Pickering (call me Chris) ordered us a bottle of red to share. 'One from South Australia,' he laughed, 'to make you feel at home. Don't believe the hype, French wine is not all it's cracked up to be…' Pouring me a glass we fell into a comfortable conversation ranging over things to see in London, the weather (fabulously sunny, just as June should be), the challenges of lecturing, who was suited to such a job. As our finished plates were taken away, Chris poured out the last of the wine into our glasses and fixed me with his eyes. I waited, tense. I hadn't had a cigarette all day and now I felt under scrutiny. A challenging combination.

'You are a kind person, I think Ellie. Good to people and understanding.'

I wasn't sure it was a question, but I answered, 'Well, yes, I mean, I certainly try...'

'I have something for you.' He reached round to the breast pocket of his jacket, slung over the back of his chair and produced a slip of paper, handing it over to me. I opened it. A list of names and a single phone number.

'What's this?'

'Peter told me you were interested in knowing more about Barrington's life in Australia, about what happened there. I'm afraid that's not something I can help you with. There are only two families around who could be of assistance: Archie Hargraves' family at Harrowbow, who refuse all interview requests and have made it their solemn duty to block any investigation into Archie's time in Australia with Rosalind Barrington, and Clara Forsyth's relatives. The Butlers.'

'You found the Butlers?'

'Wasn't as big a challenge as you might think. I looked them up when I was around your age and traced them to Barking, in London's East. The only remaining relatives are Clara's second daughter, Audrey, and her daughter Jennifer. Jennifer is her carer. Audrey is a very old woman now. And that there, my dear, is their home number. No mobile, they are too old for such fancy things.' He chuckled to himself.

'Wh.. thank you! This is incredible! I was expecting to have to spend most of my time here tracking them down. But now I can just get straight to talking...'

'Careful now, it's just a contact. There is no guarantee they will want to discuss the past. Circumstances surrounding Clara and Archie were not, positive.'

'You mean because of the break of their engagement?'

'There was more to it than that. But unfortunately, that's all I have time for this fine evening. I don't want to miss the start of the play. Give them a call. Be honest. Say who you are and why you are here and hopefully they will be willing to talk to you.'

'Mr Pickering, Chris. Thank you, really. I promise I will be very polite.'

'Good girl. Well, night now Ellie. Enjoy your time in London. And good luck.'

And with that he left me to ponder my next move.

18

Transparent winds whisper: distances past, journeys to come.
Faceless. Nameless.

I caught the London Overground across central London to Barking. At first the streets were mostly lined with brick apartment buildings, some old, some modern but slowly these gave away to sheds and factories, tall, dirty chimneys rising to the sky. Worn looking, though well maintained terraced houses made up Mrs Butler's street, pots of bright geraniums in various colours hanging from window sills and entranceways. A bin had been overturned in a neighbours yard, empty tin cans, the residue of tomato soup still clinging to the rim, rattled in the unseasonably chill breeze that whipped down the road. Coming to number 51, I double checked the address before I pushed the gate open and felt its hinges give. Flustered, I tried to pick up the little wooden gate and find a way to re-attach it to the fence post, my satchel bag a nuisance banging against my side. Not a good look to break someone's property before you'd even met them. I fussed, getting nowhere, feeling rather conspicuous and silly, until a woman with dark roots topping her blonde mane, cried from next door.

'Forget it love! Postman'll break it tomorra anyhow... the old duck won't notice.'

'Thank you,' I waved, setting the gate to lean against the fence and adjusting my jacket before walking up the cracked path to the door.

The front garden was overgrown with weeds, a line of roses grew like bushes under the front bay window, thick and wooden from lack of pruning. Taking a deep breath, I pressed the doorbell. And waited.

The doorknob twisted; I was glad to see it didn't fall off. A woman stood in the doorway. From her face I guessed her to be in her early sixties, though the deep lines on her forehead and cigarette puckers around her mouth made it hard to judge. She stood in a defensive posture, arms crossed over her breasts, offering no greeting as she waited for me to speak.

'Um, good morning,' I began, 'I am Ellie Cannon, PhD Candidate from Sydney University. I am here to speak with...'

'I know who you are,' the woman interrupted, 'You think she gets visitors often?'

She scanned me up and down. My face felt tight, I tried to relax.

'I'm Jennifer, Audrey's daughter. She's waiting for you in the back sunroom. I will bring some tea, if you take it. Don't be long with her alright, she's not so well.'

I nodded and followed Jennifer to the back room. Though the wall paper was pealing at the edges, the inside of the house was clean and neat. Family photos lined the hallway walls, straight and well dusted.

'I clean the place for her once a week,' Jennifer said, seemingly embarrassed, 'Hard to keep up two houses.'

I smiled. 'You do a fine job,' I said genuinely, but thought the compliment sounded backhanded.

'Through there,' Jennifer gestured to a door. 'She'll be waiting for you.'

Thanking her again, I headed through into the sunroom.

Sitting in a rocking chair dressed in a pale pink knitted cardigan and matching cotton skirt, sat a small, withered woman. Her ash white hair lay in thinning wisps over her crown, her shoulders stooped towards her middle. I coughed gently to alert her that I was there. She looked around.

'Mrs. Butler? Ellie Cannon from Sydney University, thank you very much for agreeing to meet with me at such short notice.'

'Come in young lady,' she gestured to a soft looking lounge to her left, 'Please, take a seat, Jennifer will be along shortly with some nice tea. I hope she thought to ask how you like it, sweet and white, very white, that's my pleasure.'

Her smile was warm, her eyes filmy and unfocused. I settled in my assigned seat and took out my note pad and pen.

'Since you rang I've been thinking on the past, what I remember of my mother and my older sister, Gracie,' she continued. 'Perhaps there will be some details in here that will help you.' She tapped her head

with a thick curled finger. 'The name of a relative, some information...
look here, a picture of my mother...' She handed me a furrowed black
and white snap shot. 'She was quite the looker no?'

I grinned politely, taking the photo. It showed a young Clara
Forsyth, hair in ringlets, face solemn, the largeness of her eyes the main
attraction of her face.

'She was a remarkable lady, my mother, I only wish my Jennifer
could find her way in this world. But we make do...'

Jennifer entered with tea and biscuits.

'Here mum, very white as you like it. Miss Cannon, I was not sure
how you take it so I have left it up to you. Be leaving you then.'

'You aren't staying for tea?' Audrey enquired.

Jennifer leaned over and kissed the old woman's papery brow.
'Gotta finish the cleaning love. I'll only be in the next room.' She exited
quietly.

Audrey brought her tea slowly to her mouth. A quake in her hands
threatened to shake the tea onto her blouse. Hoping not to offend, I
reached over and steadied her hand, helping her to drink.

'Thank you,' she whispered, smiling warmly at me once again. 'My
mother was very young when Gracie came along,' she began, then
paused. 'No, that's not the start. She was engaged, as you know, to a
very wealthy young man, Archie Hargraves. But the war,' she shook
her head. 'Those were tough years. I wonder at the lives and dreams
destroyed because of that horror.' She looked off towards the window,
tea cup settling in her lap.

'Did your mother talk much about her former fiancé? In particular,
anything at all about his time in Australia?'

'Australia? Why, yes, she did mention it once or twice. He went off
after their engagement. Wanted to write a book, or some such. But he
never did get the chance. Mother only ever had wonderful things to
say about him. She made sure Gracie knew all about him, even if my
father was perhaps less than pleased to hear another man's praises
sung. Archie was a good man. So many good men lost...'

She drifted off to some far away memory I could not follow. I waited
patiently for a few minutes before realising the old lady had fallen
asleep.

'Mrs. Butler?' I asked softly, but was greeted only with a soft
murmur.

I took the tea cup gently from her lap and placed it on the table.
Turning I found Jennifer standing watch in the door way.

'She's not well Miss Cannon. Let me see you out.'

She led me down the hall. Pausing at the front door, she turned to me, 'He was scum, I'll have you know. Whatever she told you, it were a fancy and a lie.'

'I am sorry...' I began, surprised at the venom in her tone.

'Archie whatever his damn name was! Left Gran Clara. Disgraced her name.'

'I believe they'd been engaged, no?'

'Yeah… that's all that matters, hey? Intention,' she rolled her eyes, 'Look, you got time for a coffee?'

I stared at this woman, the sudden invite taking me by surprise.

'Well, um, sure.'

'Come on, I know a nice place. Follow me.'

Jennifer and I walked to a small, brightly lit community café that rested near the Rippleside Cemetery. As I settled down on a flimsy wooden chair, Jennifer went to the counter and soon returned with two black coffees and tea biscuits. I took a sip, harsh and strong. Jennifer dumped her large handbag on the table and sat down heavily.

'Mum likes to focus on the good in people,' she began. I nodded to show I was listening. 'She doesn't like to admit this story is full of arseholes, like Archie Hargraves.' She was watching her spoon circle her cup, eyes down. 'Are you ready to hear the truth? Not the dressed up hero nonsense of my mother, but the truth?'

'Yes,' I nodded, 'I am.'

Clara

19

The breezes pass. Across the world. Alone.

Gloucestershire, England 1910

Clara leapt across a muddy creek, feet landing lightly on the wet stones, laughing. Around her broad oaks stood tall, shrouded in the light mist of mid-morning, pale sunlight glinting through the yellowing leaves. 'Wait!' she called to Archie, out ahead of her and pulling away. She was just out of being a child, the change had come so suddenly she hardly yet knew it. But as she chased her childhood friend across the field, something in her body felt different. The young friends, grown together in the lounge rooms of their parents grand homes, knew only the time spent in each other's company. Clara's father, Harold Forsyth, and Archie's father, Lord Arthur Hargraves, had been at boarding school together in the North; a natural friendship, borne of matching social status and the homesickness of all children away from their mothers.

Archie slowed his pace and allowed Clara's frantic running to catch him. She lunged forward and wrapped her arms about him by way of claiming her victory. It was an old gesture, from before. Today, as they stood pressed against each other, both of them felt a shift. Clara dropped her arms but did not move away. Archie stared into her face. No words were needed. Regardless, neither would have known what to say. The sky above them was filled with grey clouds, sweeping quickly in the valley winds, a turmoil of shadows playing over the ground.

Clara felt her heart beat quicken, heat coiling long her limbs as she stared into Archie's deep brown eyes. *Was this it?* she thought, *Will I be the first of my friends to be kissed by a boy?* Archie breathed in deeply and Clara braced herself, swallowing a lump that had formed in her throat, leaning slightly towards him. A flicker of confusion flashed across Archie's face and he took a step back. Clara breathed in sharply, the heat of before evaporating, embarrassment staining her cheeks. Unsure what to do to break the tension between them she defaulted to the little girl she'd so recently been. Throwing her head back she laughed, full and loud, breaking the moment before running up ahead of him. Archie grinned to himself as he watched his friend racing into the distance, relief lightening his heart. Nothing had changed.

Later that afternoon, the two families gathered in the Forsyth's dinning hall. Sitting across from Archie at the long table, lit by many candles, Clara stole quick glances at her friend. At almost 18, Archie's shoulders had broadened since last summer, his jaw strengthened into masculinity. Sat beside his younger brothers Graham and Benjamin, his maturing was even more obvious than when she had chased him through the trees. Watching his elegant movements in the candle light her mind drifted to thoughts of what she might like him to do to her with those long fingered hands... Archie looked up, flicking a flop of black hair from his eyes and, catching her mooning over him, smiled. A hot flush threatened to give her away, so she looked down to her meal demurely and focused on delicately cutting her chicken. A little furrow formed in the centre of Archie's brow.

His discomfort was quickly redirected however, as Mr Forsyth began an announcement to the table. 'So, let us delay it no longer. As you know, we asked you here today to tell you our great news. We are relocating to London. We have found just the place, right in the centre. Much better finishing schools, we are thinking Cygnet House, I can be assured of Clara's education...'

'London?' Archie interrupted, a new sensation, like a subtle burn, pulsed along his spine. He flicked his gaze to Clara. Body pulled in upon herself, she had lowed her head, her eyes darting furtively up to his and away. All the merriment that had danced in her face that afternoon had vanished.

'Don't worry, my darling,' Clara's mother, Ada, smiled gently. A regal woman, Clara had most certainly inherited her looks, if not yet her baring. 'You will always be welcome to visit. And, when you start at Cambridge in the new year, we will actually be closer for you to visit.'

'And you will still come back for the summers surely?' Archie's mother, Lady Violet, prompted, 'to check on the estate?'

'We have sold Beauwater. Found just the right fellow too. He'll get much more out of these acres than I ever have,' Harold announced boldly, then busied himself pouring another round of wine, not waiting for the serving boy to return.

Silence fell across the table.

It stretched, becoming a physical presence pressing down on them all. Clara looked up at Archie, her eyes pleading. Archie took a breath, 'Well, I think this is very exciting news,' he began. 'London is such an exciting city. I'll be sure to visit during my study breaks.'

'Precisely,' Ada said, turning a forced but thankful smile towards him. 'See dear, it won't be so far from your friends.' Clara glanced up at her mother. Ada raised an eyebrow at her daughter and sat up straighter. Realising her poor posture, Clara straightened and, smile plastered on her lips, looked directly to Archie. 'And I have always wished for a penpal,' she said. 'I shall write to you. You can tell me of all your university adventures and I can tell you of my times in London.'

'It's settled then,' proclaimed Arthur, 'London is not so far away. And we always enjoy some city life, don't we Violet? Here's a toast: to old friends and new places.'

'Old friends and new places,' the group chimed together. The servants entered to clear away the empty plates and make room for dessert and the friends fell back into conversation. But for Clara the warmth of the candle light and comfort of the company were gone.

That night as Clara prepared for bed, a soft knock sounded on her door. Sitting at her mirror, she quickly wiped away the tears that had been wetting her cheeks since Archie and his family departed. Turning to her door, Clara nodded politely as her mother entered. Ada looked down at her daughter, all blonde hair and blue eyes, red-rims giving away the emotions she had been indulging. So young, just a child really. She suppressed a sigh and strengthened her resolve. Taking a seat on the edge of Clara's bed she patted the mattress beside her, gesturing for her daughter to come to bed. Dutifully, Clara rose and climbed under her covers. Ada tucked her daughter in and took hold of her hands.

'I know that London scares you, that you do not wish to go. Nor do I, my daughter. But you do know why we must go? Why we must sell

Beauwater?'

'Yes, mother. Because there is no more money.'

'No more money,' Ada shook her head sadly and heaved a heavy sigh. 'Oh my child, this is not the way I pictured you blossoming into your womanhood.' She paused, her thoughts drifting back to her own presentation: balls and gatherings, suitors and parties. Not for Clara. But all was not lost.

'You are a beautiful girl, Clara. And our name is strong. You will marry well and soon, and all this will be behind us.'

'Marry?' Clara sat bolt upright in bed, eyes wide in the soft light.

Ada gave a soft laugh, 'Don't be coy, I saw the looks you were giving Master Archie this evening. And might I say, your father and I fully approve. His family and ours are firm friends, and despite our *changed* circumstances, I am sure Lord Hargraves would overlook anything for the happiness of his son.'

'But mother, Archie and I are just friends. We've never... well... done anything...' Clara shrank in on herself, eyes studying the bed cover.

'Well, I should hope not!' Ada admonished playfully. 'If that were so Archie is not the young man I believe him to be. But well, I know he is a good boy. Truth be told, I'm not sure he has even figured it out himself yet.'

'Figured it out?'

'That he is in love with you, my dear. You two have been inseparable since you were small. Now he is a man and you nearly a woman. He will ask you for your hand, Clara, it is inevitable. And we must ensure it happens.'

'Archie is in love with me?' Clara breathed, staring up at her mother.

'Isn't it obvious dear?'

'But when we move to London, I will hardly see him...' A wail of despair threatened to escape her lips.

'A little separation never hurts. It reminds a man of what he wants. Do not worry my darling. You will write to Archie and he will visit and we will be courteous and welcoming, a 'home away from home' while he studies. And once he has finished, he will realise what has been right there before him all this time. You.'

Ada reached out and tucked a golden curl behind Clara's ear and cupped her daughter's chin. 'You are a beauty my child. You will marry Archie Hargraves and live the life I've always dreamed for you. I promise you that. Now, it is time for sleep. We have much to do in preparation for our departure to London and I suspect there will be more visits from the Hargraves, so you must get your rest to look radiant, like always. Goodnight my darling.'

'Goodnight mother.'

Clara slipped down under her covers, pulling them up around her shoulders and settling her head against the goose feather pillow. Ada took her candle, blowing out the others in Clara's room. 'Sweet dreams my daughter,' she whispered as she pulled the door closed behind her.

In the dark Clara lay curled in a ball, hands pressed to her chest, holding in the beating of her heart. *Archie loves me!* She thought with glee. Rolling onto her back she spread her arms wide and let out a small giggle of delight. She clasped her hand over her mouth and waited in silence, hoping her mother didn't hear her being so childish. No, the time for such behaviour was past. Now she was a lady. A beautiful lady, her mother had said, a lady who would one day marry the astonishingly handsome Archie Hargraves. She curled onto her side again, grinning to herself and, carried by girlish fantasies of stolen kisses and secret love notes, drifted off to sleep.

Down the hall her mother slipped into her own bedroom, pausing at the door. He would come to her tonight, after their visitors. Even if the thought of his touch repulsed her, she would oblige. It was her role after all. A pity he had not kept his part of the bargain struck when they married. Harold's mind, once so sharp, was slipping, burying them under mountains of debt so high she did not know if they could regain their standing, even after selling the family estate. Generations in the Forsyth name and now, someone else's. The shame sat heavily on her chest, deepening the smile lines that straddled her mouth.

She took a breath to steady herself. She would see her daughter avoid this fate of poverty to which her husband's debts had diminished them. Even if she had to manipulate the son of her oldest friends to do it.

Nothing would stand in her way.

20

Beneath the currents of the sky I remain, passed by.

London, England 1913

'Archie!' Clara exclaimed, eyes wide with joy and surprise. It was mid-summer and the heat was stifling. Attempting to find some respite from their stuffy, overheated townhouse, Clara had convinced her mother to take an afternoon walk. Leaving behind their brown brick abode, they'd followed the shimmering wall of white terraced houses that bordered Regent's Park and entered the gardens. Vivid green leaves covered the trees, flowers in bright bloom bursting from bushes and shrubs, the park was glorious at this time of year, though the grass was perhaps a tad dry. A gentle breeze was blowing through the grounds, bringing with it much welcomed relief from the oppressive heat. She'd known that Archie would be on semester break from university, but had not had word from him as to when to expect a visit.

And yet, there he stood.

Archie. Naturally tall, he was hunched forward, a smile playing on lips pressed almost against his companion's ear. Telling some silly joke no doubt.

Overjoyed at the unexpected encounter, Clara unlinked her arm from Ada's and hurried towards him. A powerful urge to throw her arms about his neck gripped her, but thankfully she remembered herself in time.

It had been three years since her family had moved to the London townhouse and Archie had begun his studies at Cambridge. He had been a most attentive and punctual friend, writing to her regularly to regale her with his stories of new acquaintances, travel and his favourite authors. Each semester break he would pay her and her parents a visit, dining with them and sharing their company. Slowly but surely, despite the distance between them, Clara felt their connection grow and solidify. All those years ago, as her mother cooed to her of Archie's budding love, Clara had felt doubts. But the intervening years were proving Ada right.

Coming to Archie's side, she beamed up into his face. Expecting to see her own joy mirrored back in his smile, his hesitance surprised her. He nodded to her saying stiffly, 'Miss Clara, Mrs Forsyth. What a pleasant surprise.' His uncomfortable stance and tight voice gave away the lie.

He stepped to the side, opening a space between himself and his friend.

Clara forged ahead, refusing to be put off by the unexpected reservation in his greeting. 'I did not know to expect you in London so soon. Was the summer poetry class cancelled? No matter, I'm so pleased to see you. When did you arrive? Where are you staying?'

'Clara, dear.' Ada said softly, coming up beside her daughter, 'be calm my child, you haven't given Archie a chance to answer your flurry of questions.'

Clara felt her cheeks redden. At seventeen years old she was desperate to prove her maturity and class, but struggled to reign in a natural enthusiasm that seemed bound to her blood. 'Sorry mother, Archie. I am just very happy to see you. And meet your friend.' She nodded respectfully to the tall blonde youth who had been sharing conversation with Archie just moments before. The man smiled uncertainly, eyes flicking from her, to Ada and back to Archie. *A shy one*, she decided.

'Why, yes, do forgive me,' Archie stuttered, 'This is my friend from Cambridge, William Wright. We take Classics together.' Clara beamed at William. He wasn't one she had heard of. Archie often spoke of Phillip and Paul, and she had even met dear Harry. Their mother's were friends…

'Pleased to meet you,' Ada said, an edge in her tone caught Clara's attention. Her mother had fixed William with a cold stare. *What was wrong?* Tension buzzed between her mother and Archie. Clara tried to move the conversation along. 'So you and Mr Wright travelled here together then? Sometime on holiday? What a wonderful idea. I should like to travel with friends someday.'

'We haven't been here long,' Archie said hastily, 'Only just arrived really. I was planning to write to you shortly.'

'But of course you were,' Ada cut in smoothly. 'We have no doubt. Well, this has been a wonderful surprise but I fear we must be getting on. Come Clara, dear.'

Clara glanced up at her mother in consternation. There was no rush. They could take a walk together... but when Ada gave a direction... 'Well,' she fussed with her skirt, trying to compose herself, in turmoil from her mother's cold behaviour, 'it was lovely to see you Archie. And to meet you Mr Wright.'

'Lovely to meet you also Miss Clara.'

'And we will be seeing you soon...'

'Of course dear,' Ada called, already turning away. 'I will have an invite sent to your hotel today, Mr Hargraves. Where was it you said you were staying?'

Archie looked sharply at Ada, arms stiffly by his side, 'Brown's Hotel, in Mayfair.'

'Good day for now then.' Ada said and, linking her arm to Clara's, led her daughter slowly away down the sunny green lined path.

Clara's forehead felt tight, her cheeks flushed, and not from the sun. When they were a good distance away and out of ear shot, she hissed, 'What was that mother? Why were you so dismissive?'

Ada strolled on in silence, not changing her gentle pace. Clara felt the tension charging through her body, urging her to pick up speed and get... somewhere. After a few moments Ada spoke softly, facing forward as if talking to herself, 'Sometimes a man needs to be shown that you aren't just there when it suits him. But that he must also make the effort.'

Clara glanced up at her mother, confused. But Ada did not look down at her daughter, only straight ahead, nodding politely to the other pairs of ladies walking arm in arm down the garden path. In their white lace gowns, dainty umbrellas or jauntily worn summer hats shielding them from the sunlight, Clara was reminded of how elegant city ladies were, of what she longed to be. Remembering herself, she straightened her back and returned her focus to their stroll and the etiquette required from a grown woman. In her mind she ran through her mother's words and actions, hoping desperately that with enough thought, she might come to understand. Yet again her mother had demonstrated the importance of poise. Archie always looked at her with such admiration. Clara wanted to be on the other end of that gaze.

Arriving home, Clara retreated to the library, picking up a little volume of poetry Archie had gifted to her last year. Out of the blue he had visited, bearing the small book. 'I have found my path to greatness Clara,' he had exclaimed. 'The mystery of Edward James Barrington. He was a poet. I bought you a copy of his first works. I think, if you try, you will like them.'

'Greatness? Why Archie, you are already 'great'!' she had protested. Archie had gifted her a strained smile and pressed the small volume of poems into her hand.

'It's like he wrote the words for me,' he said. 'Don't you ever feel like no one understands you? Like you are hidden by shadow?'

Clara certainly did not.

She had heard the rumblings of the women calling themselves 'Suffragettes'. They'd even had a large rally in Hyde Park earlier that month. Clara remembered her mother's dismissive tone when Harold had mentioned the disruption they were causing the city. 'It's never a good thing to stir up trouble,' she'd declared, eyes daring Clara to disagree. But honestly, Clara had no understanding of what they were complaining about. Did Archie mean something like that, but for men? Unsure how to respond she only nodded, confusion furrowing her delicate brow.

'Ah,' Archie had sighed deeply, 'he travelled to Australia. All that way away. And shaped himself a whole new life. Can you imagine? Your own life, of your choosing.'

'I'm not sure I should like that at all,' Clara replied.

Archie had smiled indulgently at her, as though she were still a child. Some emotion she could not place sat within his eyes. 'Try the poems,' he'd said and left.

That Christmas, he had asked her what she thought of the works. Ashamed, Clara had tried to bend the truth, saying she had not had the time, what with comportment classes and charity work at the church. Archie had grinned at her, his eyes sparkling at catching her in the lie. Her chest had tightened, a sense of indignation rising up to blurt defensive excuses at him. Thankfully, he had spoken first.

'It's alright Clara, I didn't really expect you to enjoy them. I know poetry is not to your liking. But I do know you enjoy a good story. And that is what will make Barrington the perfect subject for my intended book.'

'You want to write a book?'

'Yes,' Archie had said, exasperation creeping into his tone. 'Why does that surprise everyone?'

Feeling rebuked, Clara had gone quiet. Archie came to site beside her on the couch. Then, lips inches from her ear, he whispered the story: a scandalous divorce, an older woman, a famous poet and a journey to the other side of the world, for love. And then, the disappearance of the poet himself. A mystery never solved. Clara was enraptured, hanging on Archie's every word.

'And that's not even the worst of it,' he had whispered, his breath tickling her neck, taking full advantage of their moment alone and sitting almost pressed against her. Her breathing came faster.

'They say the widow has lost her mind, all alone in the bush. She turned to witchcraft. Growing herbs and consorting with the natives.'

Clara had looked at him sharply, her breath stuck in her throat. 'Are you trying to trick me? I am not a child!'

'And this is no fairytale. No Clara, I confess, I think those rumours are unlikely to be true. But, can you imagine if we knew? '

He'd leaned back on the couch and sighed, eyes to the ceiling. A soft winter sunbeam tracked across his face, lightening one side of his raven black hair and turning his left eye translucent. 'If I could go there, to Australia and meet the widow... Oh, Clara, can you imagine the book I could write? I would be my own man, not just the son of my father. I could make a name, for myself.'

Such desires confused Clara. Archie's father was a wealthy Lord, a title Archie would inherit. What more could he want? From his position flopped back on the couch, Archie's head had swung casually to the side, taking her in. Then he sat up straight, pulling his jacket down and righting himself. 'Well, thank you for at least trying to read the poems, Clara. It means a lot to me.'

'It was my pleasure Archie. And I really do love the book. It's so sweet.'

He'd leaned forward and pecked her on the forehead gently. 'So are you,' he smiled and rose to leave the room.

Now, sitting alone in the library, the little book was no less sweet, and no less boring. She put it down and went to see if the cook, Maeve, would let her help with the pastries.

21

Deserted.
Colours bleed.

A knock came at the door. 'Ouch,' Clara cried, pulling the cheeky needle from her finger and sucking away the blood before it could stain her embroidery. It was late for a visitor, and with her parents out at a dinner with friends, Clara would have to receive them. Checking that she had stemmed the flow of blood, she tucked her embroidery aside and waited, enjoying the cool breeze that blew through the open window.

Mr Jones, the butler, entered. 'Master Hargraves to see you Miss. I wasn't sure if you would be available?' His tone made it very clear that he believed, with her home alone, she should not be available. She sat up at attention. 'Archie? Well, send him in,' she said. Jones paused, caught between his duty and his morals. After a moment of hesitation he turned stiffly and walked for the door. Clara leapt to her feet brushing down her skirts and patting her hair into place. She really did wish he had called ahead to warn her.

Shortly, Archie strode into the room.

'You may leave us,' Clara said to Jones and the butler nodded, politely shutting the door behind him. Leaving them alone.

She looked to Archie. He seemed to take up more space than usual, standing solidly, feet planted. He fixed her with eyes feverish and intense. Such focus on his face, as if he were staring her down. Her heart started pumping and she took a deep breath, fixing her shoulders, head high. She was about to speak, when Archie lurched forward, taking her hands. His were cold, but firm, larger than she'd realised, engulfing her own. He seemed to sway on his feet and as he breathed she was sure she could smell the acid tang of whiskey on his breath. 'Archie...' she began warily. Had he been drinking? What was he thinking coming here in such a state? She was suddenly very glad for her parents' absence, for a very different reason. 'Would you like a seat?' she offered, struggling to navigate her way through this unexpected social situation. She moved to guide him to the couch but he seized her by the upper arms, pulling her round to face him. She froze at the unexpected contact, the aggression in the action. 'Archie...'

'Marry me.'

Words of protest died on her tongue, replaced by wordless shock. She realised her mouth was hanging open and quickly clamped it shut. 'Pardon me?' she said, voice little more than a whisper.

In response Archie fell unsteadily down on one knee before her. His hands fussed at his jacket pockets a moment, before a frown crossed his face. 'I will need to get you a ring. I meant to...' he trailed off. Clara remained frozen in stunned silence.

'Clara,' he reached up, gently taking her hands once more, the tension on his face fading away, 'I'm sorry to have burst in this way, but... Clara, will you do me the honour of becoming my wife?'

A joy, more intense than anything Clara had ever known, flooded her body. She felt her knees go weak and before she knew what she was doing she too was kneeling on the carpeted floor, arms wrapped about Archie's neck. 'Yes, yes of course I will marry you!' she exclaimed. They locked eyes. It was not the proposal she had imagined, whimsically daydreaming her way through comportment school, but now that it was here she realised grand gestures and shiny rings didn't matter. Archie loved her. Her mother was right. She was going to be his wife. She smiled shyly at him, anticipating what would come next to seal the new relationship between them. But Archie stood, a flash of concern floating across his face as he helped her to her feet. He burped loudly into his hand and then looked at her in embarrassment. She giggled, too overcome with the moment to be annoyed at his indignity. And really, what did it matter if he'd needed a drink for courage?

Looking suddenly overwhelmed, Archie stepped back from her. 'Of course, I will need to ask your father's permission before this can be official.'

She closed the space newly opened between them, 'He will say yes, there is nothing to fear. And mother will be delighted! She always hoped we would marry.'

Archie's face fell, a shadow passing over his eyes. Clara's chest tightened, she'd said the wrong thing. Again. 'But that's not why I said yes,' she said quickly, 'I want to marry you Archie Hargraves. I love you. Since we were children and always. I love you.'

'I know,' he whispered gently, raising a hand to cup her cheek, 'and I love you too.'

Happiness so complete she believed she would burst from it coursed through her at his simple, but perfectly beautiful words. He pulled his hand away, leaving her cheek cooler without his touch. 'I must go. It wouldn't do for your parents to find me here alone with you. Goodnight Clara. I will visit again, very soon.'

Disappointment filled her heart, surely now they were engaged they could remain alone a little longer at least? But she knew Archie was right, there was a way these things were done.

'Until tomorrow, fiancé,' she said.

Archie gave her a quick smile, air snorting out of his nose and turned to go.

That night Clara did not sleep, her thoughts and dreams filled with one name: Lady Clara Hargraves.

Archie didn't call the next day, or the next. Waiting, Clara felt herself filling up with the unexpressed joy. Bubbling like a pot of water about to boil over. Finally, one sultry afternoon, her father strode into the lounge and announced he had given his consent to their engagement.

'You spoke with Archie?' Clara asked, flustered.

'Yes, this morning, while you and mother were at church. He asked to be remembered to you, and that I beg your forgiveness on his behalf. He has left for Harrowbow. To tell his parents the happy news and begin the planning.'

Crestfallen Clara looked down at the embroidery in her lap.

'What is this?' Ada said, standing and walking to her husband, 'Archie asked permission to wed our daughter, but has not formally proposed?'

'Not at all, he asked her first!' Her father grinned indulgently over at her, 'I could not say no to what my daughter's heart wants.'

Clara felt the hot stare of her mother burning into her from across the room and kept her eyes averted. But when Ada spoke, it was only joy she heard in her mother's voice. 'Well, this is the most wonderful news. Clara! How did you keep this quiet? There is so much to do, so much to plan. We must start a list.'

'And I'll get some brandy,' her father said.

Ada came beside her, paper and pencil in hand.

'I'm sorry mother,' Clara said, eyes still downcast.

'Whatever for my dear?'

'I'm sorry that I didn't tell you sooner, I just...' she couldn't find the right words to smooth this over, to make her mother understand.

'Darling,' Ada said firmly, her tone commanding that Clara look up. She did. Where she expected to see anger and resentment shone only pure happiness. 'You are to be Lady Clara Hargraves. From now on you get to decide what and to whom you wish to share any personal detail. Now come, we must think. Tell me of the wedding you've always imagined. We must make sure we don't miss anything.' Clara felt a smile break out across her face as she and her mother leapt into the task, her father sipping brandy by the window.

A few weeks later an invite to the wedding of William Wright and Christine Albury came in the mail. Clara remembered the bride-to-be from her years in Gloucestershire. Tall and elegant, Christine was a few years Clara's senior, so they had not socialised much. Regardless, Clara was not surprised that the statuesque beauty had caught Archie's friend's attention. The flutter of excitement she felt at receiving the invite, the first to an event she would attend as Archie's betrothed, threatened to entirely undo her composure. When she heard that the train from Cheltenham would whisk her fiancé back into London the very next day, she positively exploded with joy.

Clara's parents greeted Archie warmly, then made equally implausible reasons to leave the two intended alone together. Clara felt a familiar shyness mixed with warmth infuse her body as she watched Archie pace before the fireplace.

'Clara, there is something we must discuss,' he began,

'Yes, I agree. In light of William and Christine's wedding invite, we should be sure to choose a date suitably spaced from theirs. We will have many mutual guests after all.'

Archie turned to her, shock on his face. 'You received the invitation already?' he said, tone oddly flat.

'Yes, it arrived yesterday. Just before you.' She offered him a grin, hoping to coax him into calmness. But he would not settle and took up pacing the room once again.

'I suppose that *is* what we must discuss…' he said, as if to himself.

'And of course we must ensure your brothers can make it up from Eton. To be present.' Clara folded her hands gently in her lap and waited patiently. She was deeply committed to her comportment practice, now more than ever.

'Clara,' Archie said, perching himself on the couch beside her. So intense, Clara stifled a giggle. *How is it men are so incapable of hiding their emotions?* She waited. 'You remember the poet I spoke to you about, the one who moved to Australia?'

Clara frowned, this was not where she had expected the conversation to be going. 'Of course you don't,' he said to himself, misunderstanding the reason for her frown. 'Barrington,' he continued, 'the poet who went missing, leaving his wife alone in the wilderness.'

'Of course I remember,' Clara interrupted, desperate to show him that she had been listening. 'The widow everyone says is into witchcraft.'

Archie smiled, 'Yes, that's the one. Clara, I have come across an incredible opportunity. Rosalind Barrington has invited me to Hathrone Farm in Australia, to learn more about her husband, for my book.'

The words were in sentences, but Clara could not find the meaning of their phrases. She frowned again.

'I leave in three weeks.'

Time stopped. 'Leave?' she stuttered, 'Where are you going?'

'To Australia!' Archie said. More words, and still Clara could not find her way through them. Archie rose to his feet, impassioned. 'Don't you see Clara? The magnitude of the opportunity before me? Before us? I cannot put this off. Do you know how many years people have been trying to gain an invite to Hathrone Farm? This will make my name, our name Clara. The book I can write after such an adventure. I will be famous. You will be famous!'

He sat again, taking her hands in his, 'This is the highest honour. I cannot refuse.'

Blinking rapidly to prevent the threatening tears from cascading down her face, Clara choked out, 'How long will you be gone?'

'At least 9 months, perhaps 12. And then, as soon as I return, we will be married.'

'12 months… you will miss William's wedding.' As if that were the most prominent issue.

Archie cupped her face, turning her gaze up to him. 'Clara, I do not make this decision lightly. This is truly a remarkable opportunity. It will bring us a future beyond anything we ever imagined.'

I only ever dreamed of you, Clara thought, but bit her tongue. It was clear, his mind was made up. His ticket booked before he'd even spoken to her of it. There was nothing she could do but smile and accept.

'We can write to each other?' she asked, dreading the response.

'I will write weekly, daily. The letters will be delayed, but they will come to you. Oh and I almost forgot.'

He reached into his jacket pocket and pulled out a small black box. 'I hope I guessed your size correctly.'

Clara's breath stopped. She took the box, knowing exactly what was inside; but this wasn't how it was meant to be. A sudden heaviness overcame her body. She opened the box with a clack. Inside nestled an enormous emerald stone on a golden band. 'It's beautiful,' she said dutifully, though in truth she hardly cared.

'Allow me,' Archie fussed, pulling the ring from the box and sliding it carefully onto her finger. 'A perfect fit,' he said, clearly pleased with himself. She forced a smile to her tired lips. Archie took her face in both his hands. 'I know this is not the engagement period you were expecting. And I know it is hard to understand now. But Clara, I promise you, this short time apart - this is nothing in the grand scheme of what our marriage will be. It will be hard, and I will miss you, everyday. But the rewards will make it worth every moment.'

'You will miss me?' Her voice cracked on the words, the tears finally winning their silent battle and coursing down her cheeks. Archie leaned forward and brushed his lips against hers, softly, like flakes of snow across her mouth. She tasted the salt of her tears but could not stop them. 'Everyday,' he whispered against her lips. 'Everyday.'

22

Trapped beneath the mirror surface, danger lurks.
Hidden. Unseen. Waiting.

London, England 1914

Clara stood at Euston train station, one hand clenched around the letter from Archie, the other steadying herself against the nearest pole. The letter had arrived 'express' on a mail boat that had left just days before Archie's vessel, bringing the news she had been longing to hear for over twelve months now, Archie was coming home. Obviously the decision to leave had been made with haste; tensions in Europe had reached a crescendo. Against the murmurings of conflict people were consolidating, pulling close. And he'd been right to come home. Only last week the announcement had come over the radio: England was at war.

Clara forced that thought aside, all that mattered was that Archie was coming back to her, finally.

His letter had also brought the news that he was bringing the widow Rosalind Barrington to stay, as part of finishing his research. Clara could not understand how there could be more left to do after almost a year in the field, but her joy at his return made that detail almost insignificant. Widow or not, her fiancé was returning.

She had raced to tell her mother the news and the two women had set about preparing the house for visitors, the heaviness of a year in limbo sluicing from Clara's shoulders. As Archie and Clara were not yet married it would be necessary for him to find separate accommodation, as always. Luckily for the widow, Clara's family home was large for a city address and there were several guest rooms on the second floor. Clara had busied herself prettying the house with flowers and buying Archie's favourite English treats, sure he had had no access to such delights in that far off land. Her parents shared Clara's joy. Especially her mother, who always warmly welcomed Archie into their home, like a son.

Their time apart had been hard on Clara. Long months without the distraction of parties and friends, she had whiled away her time reading and waiting for his infrequent letters to arrive. Even her father Harold had noticed how his once vibrant and joyous daughter had begun to shrink from the world. *Understandable*, he had decided, *given the times*. But now, watching Clara practically jumping out of her skin with excitement, he could not help but find a smile upon his lips. So long lost in his book keeping and finances, and the strange malaise he found shrouding his mind from time to time, taking a moment to enjoy his beautiful daughter's company was a joy he realised he forgot to indulge.

Clara stood by the pole, eyes fixed on the track, impatiently checking the large overhead clock every few seconds. Harold could feel her impatience. It was his eyes, not Clara's, that noted the prevalence of young men in uniform departing for the Front. War with Germany. He shook the thought of his daughter's salty cheeks from his mind. *Today is a happy day*, he reminded himself. *It will be over by Christmas anyway.*

Finally the train shuffled into view, preceded by a plume of thick coal smoke. Clara wriggled, a barely suppressed squeal of excitement escaping her lips as she rose onto her toes to see over the waiting crowd.

'Don't they know,' she hissed, 'I have been waiting longer than anyone here to see our guests!'

Harold smiled at her youth, a frown of concern simultaneously creasing his brow. Bringing her into the world had been difficult, he and Ada lost many children to childbirth and pregnancy. But then Clara had survived. How Harold had loved her, right from the first moment he saw her. Standing now beside his child, her energy so infectious, a sadness pulled at his heart. He was soon to lose her to marriage. Harold resolved to spend more time with his beloved daughter, before she wed. The thought however, turned grey, its edges curling and like a mote of dust floated away.

The train sounded its arrival, pulling into the station, its horn bringing Harold back to the moment. Passengers began to disembark. Clara's eyes flew across the carriages, scanning every person as they stepped from the train. Surrounding her were people laughing and hugging, shaking hands. *What if I no longer recognise him,* she worried, *it has been a whole year.* She thought of her own appearance, knowing her girlish figure had blossomed well in his absence, nervous as to how he would respond, but also excited. Men looked at her differently now. Always a pretty girl, her large blue eyes the main feature of a small impish face, Clara had been late blooming, coming into the fullness of her womanhood only in this past year. Dressed now in a white fluid material from shoulder to hem, her tight bolero jacket warming her and emphasising her shape, Clara patted her curled honey locks and fixed her sight again on the track. Jittery with anticipation.

Her father tapped her on the shoulder and indicated a young man stepping from the train. Clara looked over, familiarity flooding her eyes, irrepressible joy taking over her body. She would have run like a child to him, thrown herself into his arms, who cared what people thought, except that he turned away. She watched as he helped a lady dressed head to toe in black, clearly older but still with good baring, step from the train. In that moment of contact a flame of jealousy ignited in her heart. They appeared too close, too familiar. Clara felt a stab of hatred shoot from her body at the woman who had spent the past year with her fiancé. That feeling passed, however, the moment Archie looked up and saw her. He squinted his eyes, as if deciding if it were really her. She waved and pulled herself up tall allowing her body to sit at its most flattering angle. Arm linked around her fathers, they walked with an air of forced calm to Archie and the widow Rosalind.

'Mr Forsyth,' Archie nodded, shaking his future father in-law's hand heartily.

'I trust your journey was comfortable?' Harold asked stiffly.

'Why yes, the train from Port of London is always a pleasure.'

Clara waited impatiently, her whole being screaming for Archie's focused attention. Then it came. His eyes took her in with one sweeping glance. Pausing a moment at her feet, a wry smile came to his lips. A slight shake of the head. Clara felt herself frown, but quickly smoothed her forehead. This was a time for confidence and happiness, she reminded herself firmly. Their gazes locked and the two stood in each others eyes, Clara filled with the excitement of promise, Archie coy and unsure.

Archie broke the spell, introducing them both to 'Mrs. Rosalind Barrington.' The lady stood stooped next to Archie. Up close she looked dignified, but withered, her eyes downcast behind a delicate lace veil. Clara wondered at her remaining in full mourning dress 25 years after the death of her husband; some took more firmly to tradition, she supposed. Harold offered Mrs Barrington his arm as escort, freeing Archie to take Clara. He stepped forward, arm cocked. Clara slid her hand into its crook, their touch like lightening shooting up her arm, and together they walked the few hundred metres to her home.

It took the rest of the day for Clara to contrive a moment alone with Archie. And it wasn't even a moment she could take credit for.

First, he had to greet Clara's tearful, joyous mother. Then he wanted to personally help Rosalind to settle in, carrying her bags and ensuring she knew the layout of Clara's family home. Archie's care for Rosalind was dedicated to the point of almost being rude in not allowing Clara's mother, Ada, to do the job of welcoming their guest herself. Ever the gracious hostess however, Ada saw enthusiasm in Archie and was happy to give him the responsibility of settling the widow. He would, after all, shortly be a part of the family. Next, Archie had to write to his university and inform them he had arrived safely in England.

'It is most important that Professor Jefferyson receives a personal letter. He is the Head of Literature after all,' he said.

Clara felt it was a task that could wait a day. Petulance convincing her that had he really wanted time with her he could wait before announcing his return, allowing them some uninterrupted time. As evening approached and Clara was called to prepare for dinner, her irritation at what she perceived as Archie's disinterest had festered to such a point that she considered claiming illness and staying in bed. *That would teach him,* she thought, crossing her arms angrily across her newly ample chest as she pondered her evening makeup in the twilight. It was as she sat there, indulging in childish sulking, that a soft knock came at her door.

She sat up straight, wiping some stray tears of frustration from her slightly flushed face. Expecting the visitor to be her mother wondering why she was not yet down for dinner, Clara called entrance. Still clad only in her under garments she quickly sprayed herself with rosewater and started applying the blush she had been agonising over. Eyes fixed to the mirror, she did not realise just who had entered until she felt two hands on her shoulders. Looking up into the mirror, Archie's eyes smiled to her. She spun around, frantic with shock.

'But...' she sounded, glancing to the door she was relieved to see he had closed.

'It's alright,' he smiled. 'Your mother sent me up for you, said no doubt you were upset with me and would only come down if I knocked on your door.'

He smiled softly again, 'I see from your attire she was quite accurate?' An arched eyebrow carried light mockery, from their childhood. But she was no longer a child. Now, she would have none of it.

'Are you surprised?' she almost snapped, fighting back the temptation to abandon herself to his stare. His eyes roaming across her nude coloured silks were filling her body with a fresh excitement of a different kind.

She shook her head, determined to stand her ground. 'It has been a year and then you ignore me. It isn't fair.'

She turned her face away, tears burning her eyes once more, hating the childishness of her vexation. These thoughts racing through her mind, she barely felt Archie's hand as it took her chin and moved her face to his.

'I am sorry,' he sighed, 'Clara there is just so much I have to do. So much to consider. But soon, I promise, this will all be over. Please, Clara, please understand. I'm doing this for you, for all of us,' his eyes searched her face for forgiveness.

Clara's resolve melted. Archie saw it at once and swiftly kissed her before she could regroup. Losing herself on his lips, as she always had when he took this liberty, Clara felt her anger evaporate. As Archie pulled away elation filled her breast. He tweaked her nose gently and nodded his head.

'I will tell your mother you will be down shortly.'

With that he let her go and strode out the door. He did not look back.

Within two days Archie was leaving again, heading for Cambridge to meet with his professors and discuss his research and book outline. The widow accompanied him, and was then escorted to Harrowbow, Archie's family estate, where his family welcomed her as a long term guest. Envy coursed through Clara's veins, but she reigned it in. She would be welcome there even more so, and soon, as Archie's wife.

Through her father's boastful ramblings to his friends over dinner, not from Archie himself, Clara learned that Archie had almost completed his work. Clara tried to be excited for Archie, always sure to match her father's smile as he spoke of her intended. But the knowledge of Rosalind in his home, while she languished here alone, stuck in her side like a thorn. The mysterious black clad figure represented Clara's lost time, the last twelve months of waiting. And Clara was still waiting.

'Why is she so important? She is so uncommonly silent,' Clara whined to her mother. 'She's not good company at all.'

'She is a lost woman Clara, that is all, a lost woman. We should do our best to respect her privacy and be understanding.'

And so Clara worked to push her doubts aside, knowing them to be the folly of a bored mind; Rosalind was a subject for research, something borrowed, she would go back. And yet she could not fight the misgiving within her stomach, the sense that the widow somehow mattered more to Archie than she did. Laying awake at night, Clara burned with the realisation that she was beginning to see Rosalind as a rival.

23

Thick rivulets course down.

In Archie's absence Clara fell into a deep depression, worse even than when he was in Australia. To have him home, yet not with her was intolerable. He wrote, but infrequently. He professed his excitement over their coming nuptials, but set no date.

Outside the narrow focus of Clara's discontent, the nation pulsed with tension. The war was not going well for England, its long reach breaching the safety of the channel and bursting into Clara's lounge room in the form of Mrs Elderdown, wailing for Ada. Ada responded quickly, taking her the bewildered friend into the back sunroom and ordering Clara to give them privacy. But Clara did not comply. Edging quietly to the doorway she listened in on their conversation.

'It's Harry, he signed up,' Mrs. Elderdown sobbed, 'He's been called to the Front. Oh, Ada, they are running recruitment campaigns across the city. How could he do this?'

'Now, Emma,' Ada soothed, 'you know how. It is his duty. It is every man's duty.'

'That is easy to say when you don't have a son!'

Clara retreated to her room and pondered the conversation. Mrs Elderdown's words were in stark contrast with her father's teary pride every time he heard of a new solider leaving to fight. It seemed this, 'silly German business' as her father had once dismissed it, was becoming rather more important. When she asked her father about it he assured her all would be well, and then turned away, his eyes looking far off, focused on something she couldn't see. The future suddenly felt very uncertain. She needed Archie; she needed reassurance. But her childhood friend, her fiancé, was back in Gloucestershire.

'So that is where we shall go,' Ada declared one chilly afternoon, as the last of the leaves fell from the trees, the winds carrying a bitterness that heralded snow.

'But mother,' Clara said quietly, 'we've not been invited.'

'Not invited? Not invited indeed!' Ada exclaimed. 'You, my dear, are Archie's fiancée, and I might add a very patient one at that. And with the war, the danger, it is only fitting that he would want you in the safety of his country estate. Right Harold?' Ada looked over at her husband, sitting reading by the fire in the early dark of November nights.

'Hmm?' Harold started out of his reading and looked up at his wife. Seeing the flush of her cheeks he sat up straighter, 'What was that you asked my dear?'

'Clara would be safer with Archie, in Gloucestershire. With all this war business. Wouldn't you agree?' She fixed her husband with eyes of ice, daring him to contradict her.

'Oh, yes, very much so, yes. Indeed Ada, indeed.'

'So that's settled then,' Ada took a seat on the lounge closest the fire, taking a moment to arrange her skirts before, 'You will write to Lord Hargraves in the morning explaining the reason for our visit. And Clara and I can start our preparations. We can be there in under a week.'

'Be there?' Harold looked at his wife in confusion.

'In Gloucestershire, dear,' Ada said firmly. 'Staying with the Hargraves. Until this ghastly business on the continent is over. Or at least until Clara is wed.'

'You are going to Harrowbow?'

'Yes dear, you are going to write to Arthur yourself for us. First thing in the morning. It's the only way for Clara and myself to be safe. Don't worry my darling. I will remind you.'

'Oh yes, yes of course.'

Clara watched her father return to his reading. His greying hair falling into his eyes. Eyes once so bright with intellect, now swallowed by the wrinkles of years. She had noticed a change in him lately. His mind, usually so sharp and always ready with a quip, would lose focus momentarily, leaving him confused. Subtle, but there. Her heart ached to leave him here in the townhouse alone…

'Now dearest,' Ada said, smiling warmly to her daughter. 'We won't have much time to prepare. Which dress maker would you prefer, Henrietta or Claudine?'

'Dress maker?'

'But of course my darling. You will need new winter outfits for our visit to Harrowbow. After all, we will be visiting your fiancé.'

Concern for her father's fracturing mind vanished as her mother spoke. Images of lace and ribbons of cream and pink flooding through her mind. Perhaps her mother would even agree to her trying one of the new tailored overcoats that pinched at the waist.

'I've always rather preferred Claudine.' Clara ventured.

'Then that is where we will start.'

The next week was a flurry of appointments, measurements and fittings, as Ada arranged a new winter wardrobe for Clara. How she managed to convince Claudine to take the contract at such short notice Clara had no idea. The reality of a depleted clientele and subsequent discounts due to the war never crossed her mind.

She hardly had a moment to think her days a whirlwind fashion choices: *which shade of rose do I prefer, does Archie like me in blue?* Before she knew it, she was on the train to Cheltenham. Sat by the window, she waved fervently to her father. She could see his smile through the rough glass of the carriage, warm and happy, as he tipped his hat to their departing train. Clara could barely sit still. Finally, she was going to be with Archie.

Gloucestershire, England 1914

Arriving at Harrowbow was like something out of a dream. Clara had spent hours at the estate in her childhood, but her years in the London townhouse had eroded her memory of the grand sweeping gardens, and the height of the ceilings. The family butler, Mr Stevens, welcomed her and Ada, showing them to their twin rooms and informing them that the family had invited them for drinks after they had refreshed from their journey.

Clara had been in a flurry to change and race down to their invite, but Ada had taken her firmly in hand. 'Now daughter, I know you are excited to be here. But remember, you are not yet a Lady of this house. You are merely a fiancée.'

'Mother,' Clara had said, astonished. 'I am to be Archie's wife. What are you saying?'

'I am saying that you are not *yet* his wife. And you should act accordingly. Remember your manners, your comportment. Be a Lady.'

And so Clara had been forced to allow her mother to primp and preen her for near an hour longer than her own enthusiasm warranted.

But her mother had been right. Coming down the stairs and stepping into the dining hall of Harrowbow, Clara was overcome by the immensity of the space. Two brilliantly glowing chandeliers graced the ceiling. A deep velvet rug cupped the mahogany dining table, matching chairs lining its sides. Space for a small party. Archie and his father stood by the fireplace, wines in hand, chatting casually as she entered.

Dressed in her finest silk gown, waist wrapped in a crimson sash, Clara made her way across the room to them, silently thanking her mother for insisting that they re-curl her hair. Archie watched her every step, the firelight casting hoods over his eyes, making them seem to sink into his skull. The effect was chilling. By the time she made it to his side, Clara felt goose flesh rising over her arms. And then Archie smiled. Leaning in to kiss her cheek, breathing deeply as he did so. The warmth of years playing chase across the grass flowed out between them and Clara knew, all would be well.

The days and nights blended together calmly over their initial weeks, though Archie was too busy to give his fiancée much of his time. Occasionally, Clara glimpsed him walking the grounds the widow on his arm, heads tilted close, the mist of their breath mingling in the frozen air. He never found time to escort her on such walks. She pushed her resentment aside, determined not to dwell on negative things. She was here in Archie's family home. It was enough. Ada and Clara made their own entertainment, and spent many hours in the company of her soon to be mother-in-law Lady Violet. As the colder winds brought fog, rain and eventually snow, Clara took joy in watching her mother and Violet re-connect, Ada coming alive in a way Clara had not seen in years. *Not since the sale of Beauview*, she realised. Even if Archie was diverted, it was wonderful to see her mother so happy. A pleasant distraction from the ever present tension of the war in Europe.

As an extension to the muted New Year celebrations of Harrowbow, Lord Hargraves decided to throw an impromptu gathering to celebrate his son's coming nuptials.

'This is our moment, my dearest daughter. Tonight we return to society, triumphant!' Ada announced.

Clara returned her mother's smile in the mirror and watched as her hair was twisted into a heaping pile of curls and rounds upon her head; it was as though her mother thought the height of her hair could somehow overcome the fall from society they had endured. Descending the stairs, her new blue silk skirts swishing gently about her, neck adorned with shimmering pearls, she felt lifted up, and for the first time, that she belonged here. Head held high, she entered the reception room, a calm confidence settling over her.

Until she saw the women.

Gathered together by the fireplace in a tight circle stood three ladies. She knew them all from before: Mabel Harrot, Pauline Deseter and William Wright's beautiful wife Christina. The cold memory of the last time she was in company with these women chilled her blood and threatened to take her knees from under her. William and Christine's wedding. Such a glamorous and beautiful affair. But Clara had been sidelined. Invited only because of Archie, but attending alone. It had been the first time she really understood the feeling of being 'outside' society that her mother so railed against.

But, unlike that day, this evening Archie was here with her for all to see. She squared her shoulders and strode over, only to overhear: '...I feel so terribly for her. She has been so patient. But even now, look at how he dotes on the widow,' Pauline was saying.

'You know what I heard?' Mabel said, picking up the tale, 'That he is not just doting on her, but her lover! You know she was one for the younger men... She was seen with him, in town, without her veil on.'

'Oh Mabel, you do exaggerate!'

'Not at all. Something is holding him back from marrying the girl.'

Christina's eyes flicked up and, spotting Clara, flashed wide for a moment.

'Clara,' she exclaimed walking around her companions and coming to take her hands in greeting. Clara's fingers felt like ice against Christina's warm skin. 'Well look at you. Beautiful,' Christina crooned. The others turned, showing not a single sign of concern they may have been overheard. Perhaps they simply didn't care. The floor seemed to shift beneath Clara, a hole opening up to devour her. She plastered a smile upon her lips and falling back on social etiquette said, 'It is good to see you Christina. You and William are well, I trust?' She scanned the room, looking for Archie, wishing him to come to her side and banish their horrible words. Christina seemed to read her eyes.

'Very well, thank you. William is out in the yard with your fiancé

134

now. Talking of man things no doubt. A long time since they have seen one another. But don't worry, Archie was sure to settle Mrs Barrington in well before they escaped. '

Clara didn't miss the subtle barb. 'Yes, of course.'

'Well, darling Clara. All grown up,' Mabel cooed, joining their conversation. 'How it must feel to be back here after, well, all that business with your father and the debt collector. I imagine the rooms feel positively enormous after your time in London. My father insists on large rooms even when in the city. I myself think a cozy little bed sounds a delight, but I will never convince him.'

Realising she was gaping at the incredibly rude comment, Clara snapped her mouth shut, heat rising on her cheeks. Her mind whirled, her breathing coming in tight bursts. She felt she might faint, ruining any dignity she had left.

A hand gripped her elbow.

Relief flooded through her as she turned to face her fiancé. But it was not Archie she found at her side. The widow smiled at her gently from behind her veil, her hazel eyes bright in the firelight. Linking her arm with Clara, she guided her away from the women without a word. Once across the room, she indicated a chair and Clara sat down, fighting desperately to regain her composure. Leaning forward, the widow whispered, 'I was so glad to see you arrive my dear. At my age, one doesn't have the stomach for those who prefer gossip to real life. You look an absolute delight.'

'Why, thank you,' Clara stumbled. It was the first time the widow had addressed her directly.

'Archie will be very pleased to see you looking so well. But, while he is indisposed, let us see what we can do to disrupt those nasty rumours shall we? What woman is friendly with her fiancés lover after all? What a silly little piece of gossip that is. Don't you agree?' Mrs Barrington fixed her with warm watery eyes and Clara felt the sincerity of her words. Her tension dissolved. Smiling, Clara said, 'May I offer you some champagne?'

'I'd be delighted.'

24

Suction pulls, dragging down, down, down.
I fight, I flail. I sink.
Cased in the cold wet dark.

A frantic knocking sounded on the front door. 'Well I never,' Arthur exclaimed coming to his feet. 'At this time of night.' The family was gathered in the lounge after supper, all pursuing their individual reading or embroidery, warmed by the fire and each other's presence. Now they waited, tense.

Stevens entered, bowing politely, 'Apologies, sir. A gentleman to see Master Hargraves. A friend from university. William Wright. I must warn you, sir. He is in quite a state…'

'Will is here?' Archie exclaimed. 'Well bring him in man!' Not allowing Stevens the time to obey, Archie pushed past the butler into the hall, lurching towards the door. Arthur followed. Left alone in the room with the women, Clara paused, one second, two, then made a choice. Moving fast she walked to the door and then stepped purposely across the landing. 'Clara!' She ignored her mother's urgent hiss and, padding lightly on her slippered feet, stalked to the front door. Standing in the shadows, she watched as the scene unfolded.

Will stood at the door, leaning heavily against the thick frame, a dusting of snow through his golden locks. Archie crossed the distance between them in two mighty steps, catching Will in his arms before the man could collapse.

'He's dead,' Will moaned into Archie's chest, his knees giving beneath him. 'Harry's dead.'

'What are you talking about?' Archie asked, bracing himself to take the weight of his friend.

'Word came, from the Front. He has fallen, Archie. In France... It's taken the best of us, Archie, the best of us.' His words dissolved into tears. Archie clutched him firmly, as if his embrace could take the words, this terrible truth and change it.

Arthur stepped forward, 'I think the young man needs somewhere to be safe.' He nodded gently to his son and they each took an arm and guided Will down the passage and to another wing of the house.

Confused and afraid, Clara returned to the women. ' Well, what happened?' Violet asked, voice urgent.

'Henry Elderdown is dead,' Clara repeated, 'In France.'

The room fell silent, each woman alone in their own horror at the news, the far reaching fingers of the terrible conflict abroad and their own memories of the boy Henry had been.

'It is late,' Ada declared, 'I think it's time we went to bed. Clara?' Ada held her hand out to her daughter.

Unable to find words, Clara took her mother's hand and allowed herself to be guided to her room.

In her sleep she heard Archie's soft voice, as it always spoke to her, in her dreams. His warmth sliding into the bed beside her, holding her close. Rolling over her hands felt something solid but soft.

'Archie?' she realised in surprise, eyes flying open.

'I'm sorry. I, I needed to see you.'

Excitement coursed through her. She felt his hands upon her body as a husband's had right to be, the way she had longed for them to touch her. A heightened mix of fear and anticipation turned her breathing ragged. She felt his lips caress her neck, his fingers on her thigh, higher, higher. It was alright, she knew, because they were together...

It was not until Archie moved between her legs, spreading them carefully with his hips, adjusting his weight on his arms, that Clara realised what they were about to do. Piercing pain ripped through her centre and she gripped hard onto Archie's muscular arms. She squeezed her eyes shut as he moved inside her, each thrust bringing more pain. She threw her head back, wanting to scream. Then her breath was knocked from her lungs as Archie slumped down on her body, his full weight on her chest and stomach. Clara watched Archie lying above her. Her nightdress was pushed up around her throat, pulled tight by her body's upward motion during their act of passion. It tightened as he moved. Part of her willed him to take his weight from her, the other wanted to prolong the closeness. The horrors of the war raging so close to their sanctuary had hammered a death nell into their lives. Right now, she needed more than the friend Archie had been. She needed her husband. She clung to his body, holding him tight, working to stay just a little longer in this moment between realities. Finally, moments before Clara would have been forced to try and push his weight aside, Archie rose to his elbows and looked deeply into her eyes.

'You are alright?' he asked, concern flashing across his face.

Clara could see in his unsure expression that this was new for him also. She could not answer him, too overwhelmed by what they had just done and the emotions it had unleashed within her. Archie reached a hand to her brow and wiped a stray lock of hair from her face.

'I, I'm sorry. I just. I needed...' his words dissolved into racking sobs. Clara twined her hands around his torso, pulling him back down.

'It's alright. It's ok,' she crooned gently into his ear, hand stroking his hair.

'Harry. Harry is...' he sobbed.

'I know. I know, my love. It's ok. I have you.'

'You don't know!' Archie exclaimed, pulling himself from her embrace. She felt something warm rush from her and quickly moved onto her side to stop it from finding the bed sheets. Archie was re-buttoning his trousers, straightening his shirt.

'What are you doing?' she asked.

'Returning to my room,' Archie said. 'This was a mistake. I'm sorry. I shouldn't be here.'

Shock resonated through Clara. She stood, going to Archie and taking his hands. 'Mistake? Archie, I am to be your wife. This... this was no mistake!'

Archie looked at her. His red rimmed eyes flicking back and forth, frantic. She tried what she hoped was a calm and gentle smile. To reassure.

'I'm so sorry, ' he said, voice choking.

'Archie,' she gripped his forearm, holding him back from the door. 'Wait, please talk to me.'

He rushed at her.

Savagely taking her into his arms, Archie mashed his lips to hers in a passionate and painful kiss. When he released her the force of his rejection was so strong she nearly fell. Confused, she stumbled landing on the edge of the sweat damp bed.

Archie moved back from her, almost staggering, anguish on his face.

'I've been lying to you. And I can't tell you the truth. I can't tell anyone the truth.'

'What truth? Archie, you can tell me anything. Anything.'

Head swinging side to side, eyes wild, Archie cried, 'I'm a fraud. I haven't been working on my biography. I haven't written a thing. I can't write it, I can't reveal... I have to protect Rosalind. Don't you see? *Whatever the cost*. The cost is too high. I can't do it, Clara.'

Confused, Clara rallied, 'It's alright my love. You don't have to write the biography. It doesn't matter. And Rosalind, Rosalind is safe and well here now, you don't have to worry about...'

'I cannot marry you.'

Clara stopped, mouth agape, 'Archie...'

'I am sorry Clara. But I cannot do what is right by you. I cannot protect you both.'

'Protect me? Archie, what are you talking about?'

'I am almost glad for the war,' Archie's voice was horse. 'It will give us some distance...' he muttered, face turned away.

'W-war?' Clara's mind could not process everything that was happening, the sudden shift.

'It's my duty Clara, my duty to England. To Harry. Will signed up today, he ships at week's end.' His voice went low, a fierce light in his eyes. Clara sucked in a startled breath. Afraid of him, for the first time.

'I will sign up. And I will be with him. Always....' He paused, staring at his hands as they clenched and unclenched before him. 'I am sorry Clara. I cannot marry you. I know you probably don't understand this now... but, in time...'

Impassioned Clara shot to her feet, anger in her words, 'Your duty? Your duty? This is nothing to do with duty. This, this is something to do with me. With us,' the horrid words of Mabel Harrot flashing through her mind. 'Even after... this. Even after tonight. You just think of yourself. You take what you want, and leave me behind. You never think about me. You always leave.'

Archie's face flushed with shame, then clouded into darkness, 'Is that what you think of me?' he whispered.

His lips quivered, on the verge of speaking further. Something held him back. Clara held his eyes, watched the anger disperse, replaced with a distanced sorrow she did not recognise.

Without a word he turned to leave. Clara felt the cold of his words, the emptiness of his leaving reaching up to her from the icy floorboards.

'To war...' she piped, almost choking on the words.

The sound of her neighbour's fevered tears, the black words on white of the newspaper reports, the cold of the winter outside these walls, filled Clara's mind as she gripped her belly subconsciously.

Archie paused facing the corridor, his shoulders tight.

'I have no choice,' he whispered

He moved as if to continue into the corridor but something stopped him and he turned. Looking down at Clara she saw the tears begin to form in his eyes. Seeing her chance, she moved swiftly to him, pulling him into her arms. His strength left him and together they crumpled to the cold floor. Tears of regret, guilt, and fear streaming from both their eyes.

The months that followed were like a suffocating dream for both Clara and Archie.

Archie's training lasted a mere two weeks before his battalion was called to the Front. Initially kept at a distance from the fighting due to his father's name, August found him at Ypres. Battle after battle he survived. Exploding shells burying him beneath the earth, the taste of mud and the salty blood of others on his lips. This was a war that would not easily be won. He wrote home to Clara regularly, though few made it through the battle lines.

Clara waited, the desperate hope that he would come home and set everything right coloured her every moment. But as the months passed, a new problem grew for Clara. Their one night of confused passion had sparked a life, more precious to her than anything in the world.

Disgusted, and afraid for her reputation, her parents gave Clara an ultimatum: a removal or leave and never return. Never believing his daughter would defy him, Harold watched, chest aching with regret, as Clara packed her bags. He longed to take back his words but pride held his tongue. Ada, crying silently beside him, did nothing to intervene.

Alone, Clara sought refuge at her local church and prayed for Archie's return. Father Peters, though saddened by her sin, was horrified by her parents suggestion. 'That is a far graver cross to bear, my dear.'

He directed her to the support of Ivy House, newly renamed as Mothers' Hospital, a hospital for pregnant women out of wedlock, run by the Salvation Army. Clara made her way to Hackney. The women were kind and understanding. They helped Clara find a room and board, and work sewing and washing for the local society women. When her time came, they ensured the healthy delivery of a baby girl, Grace Annabelle Forsyth.

Three months after the birth of their daughter a telegram arrived at Clara's door. Archie had fallen.

Ellie

25

Without I cannot be. Without I will remain.
Nothing. Empty. Floating.

London, England 2018

I stood alone in the cemetery, the winds of the morning had died down to a gentle breeze, the early chill giving way to a warm June day. Trees lined the walkways, their green leafy branches reaching up to the low slung English sky. Around me, many mourners were gathering to pay their respects in the mid-afternoon sun. Occasionally one would nod to me, or even pat my shoulder as they passed, such was the collective nature of inferred grief. I kept my head down, staring at Clara's grave. A cavern of secrets. One small plot in a row of hundreds. A presence came up on my side. I knew it was Jennifer without turning, the smell of stale cigarettes hung in the air around her; I really needed to stop smoking. Jennifer bent down, placing a bundle of carnations on the grave, yellow, bright.

'Was her favourite colour,' she explained. 'Said it brought the sunshine every day, even in this shit hole.'

I smiled at her crude expression, eyes still lowered respectfully.

Jennifer placed a gentle hand on my arm, a genuine gesture of care and for the first time I saw the kindness behind the bitter mask. How could a trip to discover the life of a poet become the story of this woman and her family? She linked our arms, her warmth spreading into my chilled body. I did not trust my voice to speak, only stood, allowing myself to take comfort from human contact.

'The women at Mothers' Hospital were wonderful to Gran Clara. After Grace was born, she volunteered there. With the war on, there was no shortage of pregnant women left alone. They expanded and opened their doors to all women, not just the unwed. That's how she met Tom Wilkes.

'He brought in his sister-in-law in 1919, his brother hadn't returned from the war. Was a returned solider himself. He carried a lot of wounds, mental and physical. But so did Gran, so I guess they had shared grief.

'They married in 1920. Tom worked as a labourer, there was a fair bit of construction work going after the war. Well below her station, as it was before, I guess. But he loved her, Ellie. Took on Grace as his own, never said a thing against Gran for having a child unmarried. He was a good man.'

She sighed, releasing my arm, pulling a packet from her pocket and lighting a cigarette. She offered me one, but I rallied my resolve and shook my head.

Breathing out a stream of smoke, she continued, 'After they married, Gran struggled to get pregnant again. Ironic, hey? Their boy, Clive took three years to come along. Then another five years later, my mum, Audrey. There were some happy years there, I think.'

Jen, sighed, long and deep. I waited.

'The depression hit them hard. Tom took anything he could get, but couldn't earn enough to feed them, so Gran had to find work. She washed and ironed for people, tough, unforgiving work. But she just got on with it, no complaints. Mum used to help, carrying the baskets of clothes, folding the clean ones.

'Was mum who found Tom hanging. Suicide. Couldn't pay the bills, the rent. But maybe it was more the memories from the war, I don't know. Mum said he used to have nightmares, flash backs. She was only 10 years old.'

A felt a shudder run through my body. The thought of such a small child seeing such horror.

'Couple years after that war broke out again. Clive signed up to fight, by choice...why, I don't know. Shame perhaps, dead dad and all. He died at nineteen, somewhere on the Western Front. Snow always made Gran cry after that. Made her think of his grave all that way away, wherever he ended up...'

Tears for the woman resting before me trickled down my cheeks.

'That's when Gran started talking about Archie again, I mean fully.

She kind of regressed back to being 18. Not all at once, but steadily. She used to sit and talk with him. Drinking tea, sitting in the garden. By the time I came along, I think she completely forgot she was Mrs Wilkes, like Tom never happened. She went missing a few times. Found her in random places, by rivers, always talking to Archie. I don't know how mum coped.'

I was full of pity, and did not know how to hide it. Jennifer didn't seem the type to take sympathy well.

'Did Grace ever make a claim to the Harrowbow Estate? Prove her bloodline through technology...' I asked.

'And what would she do that for then?'

'For money, comfort? To claim who she was?'

'No, she didn't. And I'm not surprised. They turned her mother out.'

'Turned her out?'

'Archie left Gran Clara his journals from Australia, in a crackpot Will written from the Front. Signed 'Brigadier-General Archie Hargraves'. What bull. '

'Archie left a Will?'

Jennifer nodded. My heart skipped a beat. 'You mean, there are journals from Australia? From Archie's time with Rosalind Barrington on the farm?'

'I've no reason to doubt it. Can you believe the arrogance? Heir to a fortune and he left her, what? Some useless notes he never even bothered to turn into a book! After Archie died Gran went to Harrowbow, pregnant with his child. And they refused her. Lady Violet Hargraves wouldn't even see her. Why?'

I stared at Jennifer blankly but my mind was racing. Journals from the Barrington Farm did exist. But the Hargraves denied Archie's wishes. Why indeed? What secrets waited on those pages?

'From what I hear those estates aren't doing so hot these days,' Jennifer continued. 'Proof there was nothing worthy in those journals. If there was money to be made the Hargraves would have sold them for sure by now.'

'And Rosalind Barrington? Did your grandmother ever say anything about her, or anything about Archie's time in Australia?'

'She was just the widow. Kind enough to Gran, but they weren't close. I'm sorry, I don't know anything else.'

I nodded, distracted. Stones crunched on the path behind us. A broad woman came to stand beside Jennifer.

'Ellie, this is Bel. My ride,' Jennifer said simply. 'I am sorry I can't help you with your research. This family is too full of its own pain to dig up someone else's. You need a lift somewhere?'

'No, but thank you very much for your time. I really appreciate it.'

Bel wrapped an arm about Jennifer's shoulders and I watched them walk away together down the cemetery path, Jennifer's hands fumbling to light another cigarette.

'Woah, that's one hell of a story, can't help but really feel for Clara... I mean, I know it's the poet you are interested in. But there is more to all this. Right?'

I breathed deeply into the phone, releasing some of the tension that had been filling my chest since meeting with Jennifer yesterday. Waiting the 12 hours for an acceptable time to call Taj had been torture.

'I think something terrible happened at the farm on the Finniss, and Archie found out, or was involved somehow... Something bad enough to stop him publishing. And then, caught between that secret and love for Clara he couldn't find a way through.'

'But ultimately he chose Clara. When he died at the Front, she was meant to get the journals - and use them.'

'How different things could have been. But what was it between him and the widow? And what's in those journals? What could be so important that he wanted to hide it, but also knew it would make Clara money?'

'They did find a body at the farm...'

I blew out another breath. How did Taj always seem to hit on exactly the same things I was thinking? The body. There had to be a connection.

'Something big happened at that property,' he continued.

'I think so too. That's why I had to ring you. Thanks for listening Taj.'

'Anytime. So what's the next move?'

I blinked, brain frozen momentarily. 'Next move?'

'Yeah, what's the plan to get your hands on those journals?'

'Oh, that would be great. But it's not going to happen. The Hargraves are notoriously quiet. They have never answered any questions about the journals.'

'Because it's something worth hiding. You should go see them.'

I burst out laughing. 'Go see them? Taj, these are landed gentry. I can't just walk up to the front door...'

'Why not? The postman does. Ellie, seriously, they're just people. Go see them. I bet you can find the address on Google Maps.'

'I already looked it up,' I chewed my lip nervously, 'It's only a couple of hours on the train from where I'm staying. But, Taj... I can't just rock up! They will have gates.'

'So press the buzzer. All big gates have buzzers. Look, Ellie, you aren't a reporter. You are a student, studying. Just tell them who you are and why you are there. What have you got to lose?'

I thought about it, nothing actually. The story was intriguing. A dead body without a name, a missing poet without a burial place, hidden journals, the resignation of *The Fall*, it was all connected somehow, I was sure.

'Something happened at that farm,' I said.

'So go find out what.'

26

All to give, nothing to take.
To wait, to hope, to feel, relief to fall.

Gloucestershire, England 2018

I pulled on a white shirt and jeans, I was going for the casual student look. Heading out from my hotel, I hired a bike on my way to the station and took the train out towards Cheltenham. The ride began taxingly. Crammed into the window seat, next to a woman with long greasy curls piled atop her head, mobile attached to her ear, I was pressed against the glass, and stuck listening to half a conversation. Apparently last night had been quite the romantic adventure for my fellow traveller. I strained my eyes out the window, searching for a long reaching view, but the industry of London gated my gaze. Just as I felt I would have to excuse myself and feign a toilet excursion for some space, the buildings stopped, almost as one, giving way to a glorious view. Before me stretched green pastures and small stone houses, the shimmer of sunlight cast all in a golden glow.

I felt my body let go, physically relaxing into the view, so peaceful after the bustle of the inner city. Even my companion took stock, hanging up her call and settling back into her seat to rest. She was soon snoring softly. I kept my head turned to the countryside slipping past: green hedge rows, pocket sized towns in valleys, gentle brooks arched by stone bridges, birds on the wing.

Exiting at a beautiful old station of dark brick and cream signs, I mounted my bike. My journey took me through several small villages, houses built flush against the road. A few people walked along the narrow streets, but mostly it was just me and the little cottages of Cotswold stone, gardens of bright flowers in pink, purple, yellow and crimson. Between the towns the roads wound up, down and around, sometimes lined by fences of meticulously stacked grey stone, sometimes open to the fields of green farmland beyond. The sun peeked gently through a canopy of impossibly green leaves, casting a dappled light along the road before me. Birds sang and peace settled into my bones. I almost forgot the nervous tension that had been roiling in my gut since I woke this morning. Almost.

At length I came to a sweeping stone fence, higher than the others. It wrapped around a bend in the road and curved down a gentle hill. Coming round the bend the elevation gave a perfect view of the valley, and the manor house at its centre, Harrowbow. The lavish building stood three storeys high, constructed of the same cream stone as the village houses, square, lined with tall windows, strong and immovable, timeless. It ducked behind the trees that bordered the estate as I taxied down the road, looking for a gate, driveway, and buzzer…

As I neared the bottom of the gently rolling hill, a gap in the fence appeared and I saw a long drive leading into the property. No gate. Sucking in a deep breath for bravery, I veered onto the drive and cycled up to the front of the manor. It was even more impressive from ground level, rising up above me, a mix of regal splendour and country charm. A large circular driveway encased a small fountain, though no water was currently spilling from its taps. I stopped by the fountain, dismounted and walked slowly towards the front stair. But for the chirping birds flitting to and fro in the trees, the place was silent and still. Though the gardens were immaculately tended, I wondered if perhaps it wasn't even occupied anymore? Leaning my bike against the stair pillar, I strode boldly up to the heavy oak door and before my nerve deserted me, lifted the brass knocker to bang loudly, three times. And waited. A gentle breeze blew past. I knocked again, four times. The hammering of my heart began to slow, a strange disappointment taking its place in my stomach. I realised that though I had dreaded coming here, I really did want to meet the Hargraves and at least try and find some answers.

Shoulders slumped, I'd turned to walk down the stairs, a wasted day, when I heard the heavy click of a large door latch. I looked back to find the door pulled open, a diminutive man in pale trousers and a blue shirt standing in the entrance way. Quick eyes took me in before, head cocked to the side in an expression of open curiosity, he smiled. 'Well hello there. I wasn't expecting any visitors today. Are you lost?'

Momentarily speechless, I stood dumb. Then rallied, 'Um, no, not lost. I was looking for Lord Hargraves. Is he in residence?'

'He is. But there are no appointments in his schedule today. Who may I ask, are you?'

'Right, um, I'm Ellie Cannon,' I approached the man with my hand held out to shake. He took it in plump, soft fingers, giving me a light squeeze. 'I'm a PhD candidate from the University of Sydney. I am studying the last known poem of Edward Barrington, you might have heard of it, it's called *The Fall*? I have been looking into his last few years of life, in Australia, and my research has lead me here. I was hoping to speak with Lord Hargraves about the research journals of Mr Archie Hargraves, to try and fill in some blanks. I won't take much of his time…'

The man held up a hand and I realised I had been rambling. I took a deep breath, clenching my hands into fists to try and still the shaking that had suddenly taken them over.

'Sydney University? You have come a long way indeed. Well, I'm not sure there is much I can offer you, but as it happens, I have a free few hours. So please, Miss Cannon, come in. I would be happy to answer your questions, if I can.' He stepped back from the door and gestured me inside.

'You are Lord Hargraves?' I asked as I walked past him into the dimly lit hall.

'I am, pleased to meet you Miss Cannon. Come this way to the reception room. Take a seat wherever you like.'

I entered a small but elegantly furnished room to the side of the entrance. Chairs and couches clad in matching red and gold lined the space, facing a large window, curtains open to the natural light of the day. I took a seat closest the door. Lord Hargraves took one on the other side of the room, crossing a leg and hunching slightly over his knee. He must have been in his late forties, younger than I had thought the current Lord would be.

'My christian name is David,' he began, 'if using our birth names is suitable to you, Ellie?'

'Yes, of course. Thank you for being welcoming. I apologise for just turning up. But I didn't think you would agree to a meeting…'

'Unless you were already here?' His lips quirked into a grin, 'No, probably not. I'm not much for 'interviews' these days. But, you are here now. What can I do for you?'

'My research has brought to my attention the journals Archie Hargraves kept during his time in Australia. I believe your great-grandmother took possession of them after he died at Ypres? I am hoping for some information on the journals. Or perhaps, even to see them, if I may?'

'Ah, the famous journals of Archie Hargraves. Oh how the gossips have wanted access to those over the years.'

'Oh no, not to gossip, not at all! I am trying to fill in the last few years of Edward Barrington's life. Archie Hargraves was the only person his widow, Rosalind Barrington, spoke to. I am not looking for scandal. Just some facts.'

David raised his eyebrows, a knowing smirk on his lips. 'So this has no connection to the mysterious female body found on Barrington's Australian Farm some months ago? Or the rumours of Archie and Rosalind's illicit affair? They always said she had an eye for the younger men.'

I felt the heat of my blush rise up on my cheeks and ducked my head in embarrassment. 'Lord Hargraves...'

'Ellie, let me stop you there. I am not offended. Quite the opposite really. No one has shown any interest in the history of my family and our famous connections for years. Decades even. Once we were a wealthy, prosperous name, mixing in all the grand circles. My great-great-grand father even dined with the King! But times have changed for the Hargraves name, for many of our echelon. The economy has diversified, the population expanded and adapted. Owning land is no longer the greatest indicator of status, or of wealth. We find ourselves heir to great estates, grand houses and lands, and pitiful bank accounts with which to run them. Some of us have been lucky, securing the interest of the entertainment industry, using the manors as the setting for great movie romances or series on TV and garnering a new public interest through that fame. Tourism has been a lifeline for many of my friends. How I have longed for such interest to find it's way to Harrowbow.'

'There was that interest, after the war, when people learned Mrs Barrington had returned from Australia.'

'Indeed there was. But my great-grandmother chose not to lower our name to the creeping gossip mongers of the press. We still had a reputation to lose then.'

'And now?'

David smiled, gentle but grim. 'I find myself struggling to make ends meet. With the cost of upkeep on the manor and the estate, I have had to let all my house staff go. And the gardener runs on a skeleton team. If I had a way to improve the standing, to create interest in Harrowbow, I would take it.'

'So the journals...'

'Yes, the journals. They do, in fact, exist. However... well, I hate to disappoint you Ellie, especially when you have come this far, but from memory there really wasn't anything particularly interesting in them. In fact, by not releasing them all those years ago, my great-grand mother probably created more trouble for herself, and for Rosalind, than there would have been if she had.'

'Then why did your great-grandmother keep them from Clara Forsyth, Archie's fiancée?'

'Ex-fiancée,' David said, then sighed. 'Power, I suppose. And the girl claimed to be carrying an heir. A scandalous lie. Why would Violet give her anything? She had two more young sons of her own to care for. Ellie, you must remember, times were different then. We had to protect the sanctity of our family.'

'Clara's relatives don't agree with that assessment.'

A hardness entered his tone, 'Well naturally. Look what they think they stand to gain.' David gestured to the manor around us. 'Too long ago now anyway. What's done is done.'

I swallowed, sensing I was on dangerous ground. Time for a new tack, 'So, no scandal?'

'Not by today's standards, no. Though I believe she was protecting Archie's good name.'

'Because of the broken engagement?'

'Something like that,' he said evasively.

'But she took in Mrs Barrington,' I pressed.

'Yes, she did.' his face softened. 'Archie cared for her, so did Violet. The widow had her own money, the remainder of her inheritance from her husband's passing and then the sales of his new poems after the war. Violet encouraged her to release the poems in a timely fashion. After the war people were desperate for distraction, to forget the recent horrors and indulge in the hyper hope of the future. They were ready to lap up the mysteries and scandals of the past. Violet always had an eye for creating interest.'

'But Rosalind still remained here. Didn't move into her own home?'The widow had no one after Archie died. A few relatives, a niece and nephew I believe, up in the North. But they never visited. So she remained here and after a good many years of peaceful solitude, died here. Left all her money to the Arts. She and Violet were firm friends.'

'And to your knowledge, did Rosalind ever speak to Violet about a friend in Australia? Or anything unfortunate occurring?'

'No, she did not.'

I'd known that answer was coming. Resigned, I sighed, 'It's nice to know Rosalind found some peace, at the end.'

'It is. Whatever you may have heard about Violet, she valued loyalty and friendship. She was a complex woman, true. But family always came first.'

'You seem to hold her memory close.'

'She is the heart and soul of Harrowbow. Her management after the Great War and through the depression is the only reason the estate has lasted this long. She was a shrewd and intelligent woman.' His eyes blazed with passion, his fingers gripping the chair arms.

'Great-grandfather Arthur fell into a deep depression after the loss of his first son. One from which he never recovered. So many young men from the area died, Henry Elderdown, William Wright. It was a terrible time. Violet held this family and this estate together.'

I nodded, gathering my thoughts. 'Thank you for your candour, David. I wonder if I may ask to see the journals. I understand there is nothing explosive in them. But maybe in Archie's words on Australia there will be something that is relevant to my research or at least gives me a bit more context for my thesis.'

'I would be happy to let you read the journals, Ellie. But first I would have to find them. No one has asked after them, or read them, for years. This place has been downsized multiple times since I was born, belongings boxed up and stored or sold. Sitting here right now, I honestly don't know where to look to find them.'

'Could I ask you to just try?'

'Of course. I will see what I can find. Perhaps in the attic. How much longer are you in the UK?'

'I leave next Tuesday. I'll be in London until then.'

'So I have 5 days. I will see what I can do. If you leave me your hotel address I can have them posted up to you, if I have any luck. But I can't make any promises. This house is a warren of history. Well, if there is nothing else I can help you with, I will show you out.'

We rose and headed for the door.

'Say, before you go, would you like to see the widow's grave? She is buried here on the estate.'

'Yes, thank you.'

'Not at all.'

We walked down the front steps and David lead me across the estate, through a line of trees to a quiet open space. In the centre sat a series of tombstones, encircled by an old wrought iron fence. To the side, slightly separated from the others sat a lone grave.

I stood in silence, looking at the unassuming stone. 'Rosalind Barrington, beloved wife of Edward Barrington. Loved in life and after. 'Into the end I walk, with open eyes. Ready and willing. To the arms of mine own."

'It was the widow's own inscription. I always find it sad for some reason.'

'Yes,' I whispered, re-reading the words. Memorising them. 'She was ready to be back with Barrington, it seems.'

'To find such a great love,' he said wistfully. 'Well, Ellie, thank you for your visit. But I really must get on. If I find anything I will let you know. Enjoy the rest of your time here in England.'

'Thank you David, for being open and willing to talk with me. It means a lot.'

'Well, I am sorry I could not be more help, but there we are. Take care Ellie. All the best with your thesis. Cheerio!'

We shook hands and I made my way back to my bike. Cycling back to the train station the peaceful joy of the morning did not return. In its place a heaviness sat squat and dull in my chest; Rosalind's last words echoing through my mind. Her resting place another barrier to the truth.

27

To fall
To fall
To sink beneath.

Derbyshire, England 2018

Before me, surrounded on all sides by sweeping grass and manicured gardens of roses and lilies, stood the large grey mansion of Hathrone. Not as imposing as Harrowbow, or the famous Highclere, but still stately and refined. I'd caught the train to Manchester that morning. Then, squeezed into a tour coach with my fellow travellers, rocked past the tall brown stone buildings and wide open streets and squares of Manchester and into the lush green countryside of Derbyshire.

Alighting the bus, I crunched along a gravel path to the doorway, past the ticket check and into the former home of Edward James Barrington. The main entrance was large and high ceilinged, lined with dark wooden panels and gilded tables holding shining silver candelabras. A faded red carpet muffled my footsteps on the old oak floor, the painted eyes of kings and queens, lords and ladies, watching from large gold framed portraits. The window shutters were closed to the morning sun, casting all in shadow. Pausing at the far end of the hall I imagined the small Edward standing, solemn and silent, in this hollow and impersonal place. 'No wonder Barrington felt so alone,' I whispered.

'Your first visit to Hathrone?' I looked over and saw the kindly face of an older man dressed in shirt emblazoned with a National Trust

155

logo. His name badge said 'Albert'.

I smiled,'Yes, it is. It's a very large space.'

'The main hall most certainly is... Miss?'

'Ellie,' I offered.

'Nice to meet you Ellie. Yes, it is a large entrance, most houses of the time were designed this way to make an impression on distinguished guests and the like. We have tried to keep it as authentic as possible. But there are multiple family stories to try and tell at Hathrone. May I ask if you have a particular interest in the estate? Or are you more a fan of the grand houses in general?'

'I am actually studying a poem by Mr Edward Barrington. So I guess that is my main interest in this house.'

His eyes lit up at that. 'Well then, you have seen the Hathrone of his youth: dark, impersonal. But, if you will permit me to guide you, would you like to see the Hathrone of his married life?'

I cocked my head in curiosity, 'Yes, yes please.'

Albert turned and led me up a staircase to the second storey of the house. Here there was a tighter hallway, lined on both sides with smaller rooms. I glanced in one as we passed and saw what appeared to be a study, floor to ceiling book cases filled with old leather bound volumes, an imposing oak desk at the centre. *Formidable,* I thought and continued on.

Two doors down, Albert stopped and gestured me to enter. Pensive, I stepped through the doorway, and into a room bathed in light. The walls were covered in cream wall paper with small yellow and pink flowers climbing up in a repeating pattern. The furniture was sparse but finely crafted, a large cream rug by the open fireplace. Windows thrown open to the sky revealed a pretty view across a small lake to the side of the house. The space felt, welcoming.

'This was Mrs Rosalind Barrington's day room,' Albert began, 'when she and Mr Barrington married there were many changes made to the living rooms of Hathrone. From her diaries, we surmise she wanted to create a home. A family home.'

Albert let the weight of his words hang in the silence.

'They never did have a family,' I said.

'Not for want of trying, it seems,' Albert drew my attention to a connecting door. It led to a room in pastel pinks and blues, a white, lace lined cot nestled against the wall. 'The nursery. Beautiful, don't you think?'

'Yes,' and despite the sadness embodied by the unused cot, I felt myself smile. There had been happiness here. Joy and hope.

'We believe even Mr Barrington found a love of Hathrone while living here with his wife. But, as you know, that time came to a tragic end. Still, I find it soothing to know it wasn't all gloomy.'

'Thank you for showing me. I agree, this is nice to see.'

'Of course, the house underwent further changes after Mr Barrington sold it to Mr Alistair Harbinger in Australia. He was a good man though, kept on the staff, maintained the house. It stayed in his family until the 70s, when it was passed to the National Trust for maintenance and upkeep. It's looking somewhat older now, but we do our best to preserve our heritage.'

I nodded. 'Is the apple orchard still here?'

'Yes, indeed. Just go out the front, turn right and follow the curve of the house. You will see it.'

'Thank you very much for your time, Albert.'

'My pleasure, Ellie.'

I strolled the grounds, savouring the warm sunshine that lit the canopy of oaks, exposing the veins of the leaves, until I found the orchard, shining green in the summer light, the place that Edward and Rosalind first acknowledged their love. Standing beneath the apple trees I realised that Hathrone really did feel like it could be a home.

I left with a confused heart. The sense of Rosalind's influence in the upstairs rooms of Hathrone, gentle, fragile but hopeful, remained within me. I knew so much about her husband, but so little of her; the woman who stole his heart, who made Hathrone a home; the woman Archie strove to protect. But from what?

The tour arrived back in Manchester early, so with time to kill before my train, I took a stroll to the town hall. Standing before the grand stone building, the money of the Industrial Revolution brimming from the architecture, I imagined being Rosalind that fateful day she attended a poetry recital that would alter the course of her whole life. Betrayed by her husband, she did not cower at home, but ventured out, skirts swishing, head held high; even here she seemed a figure of hope, striking out against her circumstances, fighting to have a life worth living. Before today she had been no more than a means to an end. A clue to Barrington. But who was she really? What secrets did she hold in death?

As the sun lowered in the sky, Manchester underwent a transformation before my eyes. So stoic and refined this morning, now there was an undeniable energy on the streets. Young women were gathering in their heels and sparkling skirts, makeup bold, ready for the dim light of clubs and bars, young men strutted in open shirts and ankle length trousers. I felt the pull of the city, a pulsing undercurrent inviting me in, and turned away. Manchester was a city of history, it's streets lined with stories of success and failure, love and loss. But it was also a city of the present; people shaping their lives, creating stories to add to the brickwork, sweat and smog.

As the train rocked me back to my London hotel, I pondered that reality. I lived in a world of the past, yet all around me moments were being created: new hopes, fears and dreams. *Life isn't static, things are always in motion*, I realised. The thought felt good.

London, England 2018

Instead of filling my last day in London with a tour on the hop on hop off bus (the queue was ridiculous), I took my notes from meeting with Clara's family and headed to Green Park. Deciding to act like I was English, I hired a sun lounge for the afternoon. Arranging myself into the green striped lounge was more hassle than I expected, but eventually I found a comfortable balance. Above me white clouds wandered lazily across a pale blue sky, the warmth of the sun on my skin tingling gently. I took out my notes and highlighter and soon lost myself in the story of Clara and Archie. It really did seem a tragedy. Archie had left for Australia excited and inspired, but it all fell apart. Why? It truly seemed he was aiming to shield Rosalind from something on their return to England. And, despite his best intentions, that protection had caused Clara to suffer mightily. At least Rosalind had been able to live out her life in peace; David's estate was beautiful and nicely tucked away from prying eyes.

It was strange to think how young Archie had been when he died. Of course I knew, academically, that so many young men died in the war, but to hear the story of one, and of the woman he left behind, both younger than me… it hit home.

As the shadows lengthened I gathered up my notes and slung my bag over my shoulder, heading for my hotel. A premonition of disappointment sat heavy on my chest. David had seemed so open and willing to talk during our meeting, yet I had not heard anything from him since I returned to London. Had he been unable to find the journals? Had he even tried? Or was there something in those pages worth hiding?

With a start of surprise I realised how thoroughly I had re-engaged with my thesis. This new mystery had reignited my passion for *The Fall* and given me a way back into my research. Armed with this realisation, I resolved not to care if David came through or not. I would move forward regardless and finish my work. Somewhere inside though, I still hoped.

On my final morning in London, chewing my way through marmalade toast and stewed fruit, I gave up that hope. I would be leaving for Heathrow within the hour, and David still hadn't made contact.

A sudden snort of laughter broke out from my nose. I shook my head at myself in rueful silence. *Listen to yourself,* I thought. *There is no big secret or conspiracy. There is just a family who for once did the honourable thing and protected an old widow's privacy.* The most extraordinary element was that they had had the famed widow in their home. If there was nothing of note in Archie's diaries, then it made sence to keep it quiet. That way intrigue and interest was created, without having to back it up. Trundling up the stairs to collect my bags, I realised the folly of my excitement and conspiracy theories. People like the Hargraves were master manipulators, David had said so himself of his ancestor Violet. He was no different and I had fallen for it, just like everyone else back in the 20s. Sullen, I acknowledged I would have to go back to traditional research to analyse *The Fall*, in books.

So it was no act of surprise that rendered me speechless when, as I was checking out of my hotel, David himself walked through the hotel doors and smiling broadly, handed me a stack of melamine folders full to bursting.

'Ellie, my dear, I'm so glad I caught you. The traffic was ridiculous this morning! Here, these are for you. I had the journals photocopied, the pages are numbered, each section in its own folder. There are 3. Lots of pages I am afraid. Archie was quite the note taker.'

I took the stack of folders from him, cradling them in my arms. 'David, thank you.' I managed, still lost for words at his unexpected arrival.

David shrugged, 'I said I would look for them. Took me longer than I expected to find them, then I had to find a photocopier… couldn't part with the originals. But there you are. I hope there will be something that helps you. Time for Archie's words to be free to the world, I say. If nothing else it's a cracking description of how he viewed Australia.'

'I look very forward to reading them. And I promise I will treat the information respectfully.'

David waved me off. 'It was decades ago. Everyone from then is dead. Use what you wish. I hope it gives you something more to add to your thesis.'

He walked me to my cab, holding the hotel door open in a bustling display of chivalry. 'Safe flight Ellie. I've left my number and email in the first folder. I'd love to hear what you make of the journals. When you have time of course.'

'I will certainly let you know. Thanks again. See you later.'

Sitting in the cab I thumbed through the first few pages. Line after line of beautiful, floral prose in an elegant and artistic hand. Archie clearly loved words and description. Despite my earlier negative thoughts on the journals' prospects, a little bubble of excitement, sparked when I first saw David lope unassumingly into the hotel foyer, started to grow in my belly and I couldn't wait to get onto the plane and in the air. An uninterrupted 26 hours of flight and transit time to read and think awaited me.

Archie

28

No scarlet haze to blur my eyes.
No emerald green and fawn.

Australia 1913

Archie's dark eyes scanned the little breakfast room of the Coffee Palace Guest House, taking in the country style furnishings and thin curtains. They looked almost homemade. Glancing out the window he paused, savouring the cool colour of the sun that filtered through the sandstone buildings of the main street.

After a month at sea, alone in a turmoil of seasickness and driving determination, he'd arrived in Port Victor the previous evening and taken a room for the night. A walk along the coast of the town had stretched his legs and refreshed his mind after the weeks of travel. The scent of seaweed assaulted his nose as he stood on the sand, gazing out at the two islands that framed Port Victor's coastline, Granite Island to the left, the Bluff to the right, rising solid against the misty horizon. Archie breathed in the crisp salty air and sighed. He had arrived, was standing on the land he had dreamed of visiting. Australia. It was a beautiful country, in its way, though Archie doubted it could ever rival England in his heart. He should have felt triumphant. Yet standing alone in silence, waves breaking gently on the shore before him, all he really felt was restless.

Now, as he tried to focus on his newspaper, passing the time as he awaited breakfast, he still could not shake the sense of impatience in his chest.

'She's mad you know.' Archie turned from his newspaper to take in a small pixie face, framed with golden curls. 'Mad from sadness,' he leaned in closer, lifting a small hand, the final traces of childhood almost gone from the curve of his wrist. 'She even drinks herbs, and mixes potions.'

The boy stared at him intently, not a hint of mischief on his little face, eyes wide with his appeal to be believed.

'Samuel, away with you. Stop pestering the guests,' a short woman with matching curls, though shot through with grey, bustled into the dinning room, tray of food in hand. The scent of blackened bacon and warm scones filled the room as she placed the tray before him.

'Thank you for the warning,' Archie whispered to Samuel. The boy nodded earnestly and scampered off. Archie fought to suppress his smile as he turned to his hostess.

'I am sorry, sir,' Mrs Smith said, 'It's my fault, I fear. He always likes to know who is staying at the guest house. And, well, you are an unusual guest.'

'It's no problem Mrs Smith, I assure you. I was once a boy, prone to such fancies.'

'Well, I'm not sure it's all fancy I am afraid. But that's enough from me, you enjoy your breakfast.'

Archie nodded his thanks and took a sip of tea, warm and soothing, just what he needed after his long journey. Shaking his head at the superstitions of the locals, *not all fancy indeed*, he scooped up a mouthful of scrambled eggs and chewed slowly.

To be fair to Samuel and Mrs Smith, he too had enjoyed the rumours of Edward Barrington's wife, using them to tease Clara. 'Witchcraft,' was the word he had used when recounting the stories of strange rituals the widow was rumoured to indulge in. And then there was the maid, Mary, and her herbal garden.

'They say she corrupted the devoted wife, led her into an unsavoury life...two women, alone in the bush, conjuring spells to bring the husband back...'

'Ooo!' Clara had squealed, 'Stop it! You will unsettle me.'

She had turned away, but moved closer in the same action. So keen to play the grown up, so much the little girl. If he had found amusement in the gossip while living on the other side of the world, why wouldn't the locals? Behind rumour some truth often lurked.

Soon after Mrs Smith cleared away the breakfast dishes, a horse and carriage arrived, sent from Hathrone Farm. Its driver, introducing

163

himself as 'Just Percy,' was a middle-aged man with the look of a farmer about his powerful shoulders that, despite the lines on his face, still betrayed youthfulness. Archie, dressed in his finest black suit, extended a hand in greeting. After a pause, Percy accepted. He helped Archie with his things: one small pack of clothes, and two boxes of books and papers, heavy but not intrusive. Percy opened the carriage door, but Archie waved it away climbing up to sit on the driver's stoop next to the man so he could enjoy the view. The man nodded and, with a mix of excitement and trepidation churning through his core, Archie began the final leg of his journey.

Rocking on the carriage seat, Archie thought of the first time he'd read a Barrington poem. First year literature at Cambridge, Professor Jefferyson. The words had seemed to reach into his mind, pull his own thoughts from within him and lay them on the page. Archie saw his own loneliness within those stanzas. He felt *seen* for the first time. Not as the man who would inherit his father's wealth and title, but as the human trapped within.

Now he was almost there, at the home of the famed widow Rosalind Barrington. On the cusp of starting the work that had driven him to the other side of the world, to write a biography of the late poet. To make a name for himself. And Clara, *no this isn't about Clara*, he pushed the thought down firmly.

The wind blew past his face, reddening Archie's cheeks, the smell of dust and salt-heavy air filling his nostrils as he gazed out at the grey, churning seas. Percy turned inland. Great clouds were forming above Archie's head, his view now blocked by close-knit trees, white ghosts in the grey light, pressing in from all sides. Archie rolled his shoulders and stretched his lower back, a small tingle had formed at the base of his spine, as though someone were watching him. He glanced back at the thick bushland. The trees loomed out towards the cart, only darkness between their trucks. He shook his head at his over active imagination. Travel exhaustion, certainly nothing more.

At length the driver slowed the carriage, turning into the long drive of Hathrone Farm.

The entrance gate was worn, the lettering of Hathrone faded and broken. Weeds had won the battle for the dirt drive, with only a faint line where horses might occasionally run visible through the green. Percy pulled the carriage to a stop. Archie dismounted and walked around taking in his surrounds. The homestead, large and clearly once stylish, faced the river below. Its roof appeared to slope to the left, as did the wooden verandah. White paint pealed from the walls and railings and an old table lay on its side by the front door. A mess of bushland, barely restrained by the poorly maintained stone fences that lined the yard, reached towards the house. Archie stood for a moment. He'd never seen such unwieldy trees and bushes, the opposite of the cultivated gardens of home. Hathrone Farm was not at all what he had expected.

The driver dropped Archie's belongings beside him and gestured Archie to come. *How rude,* Archie thought. Collecting up his belongings he followed Percy across the run down farm. Smelling the dust and decay, Archie felt the throb of rumour pulse in his temples. There was something unnatural about this place.

Coming into the dimly lit hall of the homestead, Percy announced, 'Make yourself at home, I'll let the widow know you have arrived. First on the left.' Archie nodded his thanks as Percy lumbered on down the hall.

Archie frowned as he opened the door, worried over what he might find inside. Then released a long breath of relief. Though small, the room appeared tidy and neat. There was a wooden floor, not polished but soft, a cot made up with green blankets, a side table with a candle and a plain glass shade to project the light, electricity had yet to find its way this far from town, and against the far wall a desk and chair. He walked over to the ensemble and found an unexpected smile on his lips, for resting on the desk was a small vase of roses, pink and white. He picked up a pink one so tight in bud it must have been cut that morning, and pressed it to his nose. Clara loved the smell of roses, constantly spraying herself with rosewater perfume. His gut clenched tight at the flood of memories that assaulted his senses, shame heavy on his chest. He felt his eyes grow hot and took a series of deep breaths, fighting to resist the darkness that pulled at his mind. Just then he heard a shuffle at the door. Wiping his eyes quickly and dropping the rose on the desk he turned, pulling himself up tall, expecting to see Mrs Barrington at his door.

Instead, there stood the driver, cap off, pensive.

'The widow said she's not up to seeing you today. You are to make yourself at home, as I told you, and are free to get familiar with the property,' his voice catching over 'property' with a sense of unease. 'She says she'll leave some dinner on the stove, you're welcome to it when evening comes. Hopefully she'll be ready for you tomorrow.'

Archie pushed his disappointment aside. *So be it,* he thought, *I must be understanding. She has been alone here some years, I should not expect too much.* He followed Percy out to the carriage.

'I'll make a special trip back tomorrow,' Percy was saying as he mounted the carriage. 'I usually only come once a week to help with the upkeep, the widow likes her solitude. Was surprised she invited you,' he added off handedly. 'Now, you take stock of what's here, down the path from the house is the out-house, watch for spiders. Beyond that is a herb garden, I try to keep them happy but the soil here is unforgiving. Other side of the house is the widow's roses, how she keeps 'em so fresh I do not know. Best not to interfere with them, been her salvation these years I think. '

Archie wondered over the emotion in his voice as he spoke of the flowers. He must have known the family for some time.

'I'll take a stroll, have a look around,' Archie said, more for something to say, to keep Percy there another moment before he would be alone.

'You'd be free to, but don't touch anything. She knows. Like I said, take stock, and if there is anything you'll be needing before next week let me know tomorrow and I will bring it out for you. My farm is off over the next hill if there is trouble.'

Above his head the sunlight dimmed. The clouds that had been threatening rain were gathering strength. Archie turned and looked out across the farm and sighed. It was an altogether depressing place: farm in ruin, homestead in disrepair. It pained him that the memory of such a great man was resting here; it did not suit his glory. He wandered aimlessly towards the river bubbling below until a flash of brilliant colour caught his eye. On the far side of the homestead sat the roses Percy had mentioned, unexpectedly beautiful and fresh against the wild backdrop of native flora. Strolling to them he paused to smell the pink bush, a sense of emptiness settling in his heart.

Then he saw it.

Just over from the bushes lay a mound covered completely in roses. The top layer was fresh, obviously cut within the last week, but underneath the petals were more and more wilted as the layers lowered, becoming ripe with decay, the bottom layer made only of their stems, the petals having joined the earth beneath. As Archie came closer the smell of floral foliage, old and fresh, mixed with the water-saturated air, creating a heavy, pungent scent, thick in his throat. Involuntarily, he took a step backwards, the wall of scent a physical presence holding him away

He stood there for some time, taking in the scene. It was one drenched in pain. *She's made a grave*, he realised, a *place to mourn her missing husband*. A simple pile of flowers to mark the loss of Edward Barrington. A place to grieve, but empty of a body at rest. The site sat heavy on his chest. The top layer of roses shone in the withering light, reflecting love and remembrance. But their beauty was marred by the decay beneath them, its smell rising above their sweet one to fill the air with rot. A sense of foreboding entered his heart. Archie hurried away, his stomach rebelling against the uncomfortable sight and scent of death.

In the homestead a pair of curtains flickered.

29

White cloud mist rain light.

Outside was coloured the dark blue of impending nightfall. Against the silence of the countryside, so complete it ached, Archie pulled his writing kit from his bags and began his journal entry for the day. It helped, he found, with the homesickness. As the ink slid across the page Archie's heart tightened in doubt and longing. He didn't really know what he had expected here on a property in Australia. But it wasn't this. Around him the old homestead creaked in the cold winter night and Archie huddled down lower under his blankets. *At least the room is well sealed,* he thought. It might not be an English winter, but there was a true chill to the night air. Mind wandering, he thought of the widow, no doubt asleep only a few doors down. Old, alone and vulnerable. She had not even met him, and yet here he rested, under her roof.

Outside the rain began to fall, softly at first but soon developing into a powerful downpour, the percussion of its droplets connecting with the tin roof above his head beat an unfamiliar lullaby. The scent of wet dust and river mud floated on the breeze.

Why am I here?

The thought gripped him firmly, the memory spilling from the gaping emptiness in his chest and transforming his little room from the dark shades of candle light to the warm tones of an English summer afternoon...

London, England 1913

Smooth, sleek skin beneath his hand, his head resting comfortably on a feather-down pillow. The gentle rise and fall of his companion's chest his only timer. Archie shifted his elbow and hooked a hand under his head, allowing him to gaze down on his friend.

'What?' Will said, 'Surely you aren't ready again so soon?'

Archie blushed furiously, lowering his eyes. How did Will always read him so easily? Will rolled over and the two men lay face to face, only their breath between them. The moment was everything and nothing at once. Swimming in Will's eyes, Archie's heart felt safe and content. They always took two rooms when they stayed together, careful to use them both to keep gossips at bay. This afternoon it was Will's bed they shared, sated and alone.

Will reached out and tucked a stray lock of Archie's hair behind his ear. Archie caught his hand, bringing its palm to his lips.

Will sighed, 'I think you should do it,' he said simply. Archie paused, his lips still pressed against Will's skin.

'Do what?'

'Marry Clara,'

'Oh Will!' Archie complained, dropping his hand. 'Not this. Not now.'

'I don't think this can wait,' Will said and turning his back to Archie pulled himself out of bed and started to don his clothes. Archie rested his head on his arm, content to lay in silence watching his lover dress. The toned lines of Will's body, lightly browned from a summer of rowing and hunting, shifted elegantly in the afternoon sun. 'Stop doing that,' Archie whispered, 'Come back here.'

Will paused, hands on his trousers, and seeing Archie's eyes gave him a knowing smirk. 'Why do you think I am dressing?' he chided, 'I know you won't listen to me otherwise. Mrs. Forsyth is right. Clara would make a wonderful wife.'

'Will!' Archie exclaimed, 'I have no desire to marry. I have everything I want right here.'

'Not forever,' Will said, then looked down, averting his eyes in a search for socks.

Archie sat up. 'What do you mean by that?'

Will sighed and perched himself on the bed edge, sock in hand. 'They saw us Archie, together.'

'We were being subtle.'

'Always, but you saw her eyes. You said it yourself, Mrs Forsyth emphasised how 'discreet' Clara would be as your wife.' Will stopped, staring at Archie.

Archie shifted. Suddenly feeling very naked he pulled the sheet up to cover his dignity. He knew Will was right. They had run into Clara and Ada just that morning. Where Clara was simply delighted to see him, Ada's shrewd eyes left no doubt as to her intended machinations. And then she had come here, to the hotel, to speak with him.

'Clara would make you a solid wife. A *discreet* wife. Think it over Mr. Hargraves.'

It had been a threat, really. A promise to keep her own counsel if Archie made her daughter a bride.

'It's ridiculous,' he said, flopping back against the pillows. 'Clara is just a child.'

'She is not,' Will said. 'Young yes, but she is a woman, and ready to be wed. Look, I know this is difficult. But really she is a great option. She is a friend, she cares for you. Clara would make a wonderful wife.'

'But I don't love her, Will. Not like that. She is like a little sister to me.' Archie said, catching Will's eyes and holding his gaze. The moment stretched, oceans of words spoken between them across the quiet space of the hotel room.

Will turned away first. 'I'm engaged,' he said.

'Pardon?'

'I am engaged. Her name is Christina Albury. We met at a dance last winter. She's a lovely girl and...'

'You are engaged? Why...why didn't you say anything? We have been here together a week!'

'Because of this!' William exclaimed, gesturing between them. 'Because I wanted, this, like it was, like it can't be again. One last time.'

'Will,' Archie started, rising from the bed to go to him.

'No, Archie. Please, just wait.'

Archie paused. Will ran a hand through his hair, and took a deep breath. 'Archie, you know how I feel. But this, us... this can't continue. It is my duty to wed and have a family, as it is yours. And Christina...'

'Don't do this Will. Not yet.' His words came fast, running together as he sought the right phrase to change the course Will had set in motion. 'We are going to travel together, see Australia. Just you and me. And I'll write my book. Father will pay our passage, we could leave anytime.'

'Your father's money can't fix this Archie! And what would running to Australia change? I'm still me and you are you.' True anguish twisted his beautiful face.

'But we are young, there is time.'

'Time for what?'

Tears sprang into Will's eyes, threatening to spill down his face. 'Stolen moments, secret letters. Months apart, alone. And then a few fevered nights in a London hotel. Archie, I can't do this anymore. I want...' He breathed out harshly. 'It doesn't matter what I want, it can't be. *This* can't be. And the sooner we accept that and move on the better.'

Archie stood in stunned silence, watching as Will dashed a few escaped tears from his cheeks and collected his jacket and suitcase. 'This is goodbye, Archie. I am engaged, and I won't betray Christina any further. I will do my duty and live the best life I can. You should too.'

He strode for the door. Archie reached out a hand to touch him as he passed, to prevent him from leaving, but stopped. His hand flopped to his side, his mouth opening and closing. Too many words and none at all. He watched Will's broad back walk away and out of his life.

He'd got drunk then. Really drunk. And, in the hollow of rejection, asked Clara to marry him. Once he sobered up and realised the enormity of what he had done, he ran home to his father. Walking the grounds of Harrowbow, the hole in his chest a void of unfathomable depth, suddenly, the biography he always swore he would write became more than a dream. It became an escape. He begged his father for the funds to travel to Australia.

'I just need one big adventure before I settle father, something just for me.' As always, Arthur had been more than accommodating, indulging his son's request with hardly a murmur of caution. Archie sent a flurry of telegrams across the equator. And now, two months later here he was. On the other side of the world in a small, cold room, the guest of a woman who would not speak to him.

But no less alone than he had been from the day Will had walked out their hotel door.

30

White. No darkness either, to conceal.
All revealed.

Archie sat bolt up right in his bed. The wind outside blew stronger but that wasn't what had called him from his slumber. Ears straining, Archie listened. The wind whipped boldly around the house, whistling and screaming through the eaves. But there, beneath it all, a voice. A voice crying out in pain. Archie stood and quickly but cautiously stalked outside and into the rain. He paused in the night sky, giving his eyes a moment to adjust to the moonlight, fragile and distant. The gum trees swayed in the wind of the storm around him, the pale light turning them a ghostly white. He waited. Steady raindrops fell on his head. He did not notice.

It came again.

Clearer now, stronger. A human cry, coming from the river. Archie's body reacted, driven by the instinct of protection. Bolting down the hillside he tripped and nearly fell, his legs catching on the overgrown tangle of grass and weeds. When his bare feet squelched in the soggy mud of the river's edge, he paused, ears tuned. But the sound did not come. He waited, needing to hear it for direction. Still nothing. Archie concentrated on slowing his rasping breathing, sucking in great gulps of air and holding them to still his nerves.

The rain continued to fall, soaking through his night shirt. He ran a hand through his sodden hair and pealed his ears once more.

'Hello?' he called to the river, his voice echoing across the water's surface.

Only the wind replied.

Archie waited a few moments more before he was sure. Cursing his nerves, he turned back to his room, annoyed that he had ruined his bedclothes for no good purpose. Above his head lightening cracked in the sky, illuminating the homestead in an eerie white, accentuating the gnarled shadows cast by the gum trees surrounding him. Archie hurried back to his room, disliking the isolation of this place, the wild bushland that surrounded him, the foreign scents and sounds. Reminders of how far he was from home.

Rounding his door, Archie stopped dead, hand flying to cover his mouth. It was all he could do to halt the scream that rose in his throat. A figure dressed in black hovered in his room. Archie stared, frozen, as the figure lit the candle on his bedside table. The flame took, its amber glow revealing Rosalind Barrington.

She was dressed head to toe in black silk trimmed with lace, a sheer scarf covering her shoulders, widow's veil across her face. Her hair, dark despite her age, was pulled into a loose bun, exposing the slender arch of her neck, firm of skin and pale in the soft light. Rivulets of water coursed down her bodice, pooling silently at her feet.

For a moment Archie saw her as Barrington must have: small and frail, pale and elegant, the candle light smoothing aged skin. He stood in the doorway, transfixed.

Rosalind looked up into his face, her eyes blurred by the veil and candle light. She watched him, as if expecting something. Still dripping from the rain, Archie moved into his room, the wooden floor rough against his bare feet. He swallowed, unsure of how to proceed through this unexpected introduction.

She spoke first, 'I heard lightening. It's a different beast in this country. I thought I should check on you.'

Her voice was soft, a mere whisper against the storm outside. She held his gaze a moment more then turned away. The outside world continued to rage but in this room, time had stopped.

'I found your room empty. I looked for you, outside. But it's such a dark night.'

Not yet calm from the exertion of running, feeling exposed dressed only in bed-wares, Archie stammered, 'W-w-hy thank you Madam. I do apologise for disappearing like that. I thought I heard… I thought… well. '

Rosalind smiled softly and gathered her skirts around her. 'It is rather loud in the silence,' she said.

Moving slowly she walked past him and out into the hall, limbs fluid, no sign of ageing joints. Without looking back she floated down the long hall and into her room, out of Archie's view. Archie watched after her for a few moments before closing his door and returning to a bed in which sleep refused to calm the beating of his heart, nor order the turmoil in his mind.

The next morning Archie rose early. Unsettled by the night's events he couldn't sleep. He didn't know what to make of his imagination and the unexpected meeting with the widow. Coming outside, he noticed the verandah table that had been turned over on his arrival had been righted. On it sat a fresh loaf of bread. Pensively, he moved forward, unsure if his presence would be welcome. Rosalind came through the door holding a silver tray covered in fried eggs and mushrooms. Her veil caught the gentle breeze. She placed the tray on the table and gestured him over. Archie complied, still trying to shake the night cries from his mind. Taking up his seat beside her, he followed her lead and took some eggs and bread, trying to relax into his chair.

Rosalind lifted her veil and turned her face to the sun. In the soft morning light he observed his companion. While the sense of youth remained, it was clear in the day light that she was older, all be it well kempt. Her eyes, famed for their bright green, were more a dull hazel, sunken into prominent cheekbones. As he watched her sun her face more signs of age betrayed themselves: the lines of her forehead, the slight stoop to her shoulders, the hang of skin on her chin. Pale fleshed to the point of pallid against the harsh black of her mourning dress. Even in her youth, she would have been an unusual looking woman. Yet, despite all that, there was an aura that shone from her. He found himself oddly drawn to her. An enigma. Archie shifted in his seat. The sound brought her eyes to his, gaze locked quizzically.

Archie coughed nervously, finding his voice, 'Thank you for the breakfast, and the other meals, and for my room. You have been most kind.'

She nodded gently, settled her veil back over her face and rose to pour tea, long gloved fingers curling about the ceramic pot.

'I-I hope you did not miss too much sleep last night... on my account?' Archie flinched at the memory of being in his bed clothes.

She arranged herself in her seat and looked to Archie.

'It is a pleasure to have you here,' she whispered, voice raspy and tired.

Archie smiled and drank his tea, unsure of what to say next.

'Percy showed you around?' she continued. 'Good. Well the place is yours. Feel free to roam and write. Our,' her voice seemed to catch over the word. She paused, cleared her throat and continued, 'His things are in the back room, you may look though them but don't take anything. I am not sure they will be much help to you. But satisfy yourself.'

With that she stood to leave. Archie hurriedly rose to show her proper respect. The lines around her eyes creased as in a smile of approval and she left him to his breakfast.

Archie sat back down, his appetite weak from his fitful sleep. Leaning back into his chair he scanned the horizon. Around him the trees dripped from the soaking rain and birds sang in post-storm joy. Sunlight caught droplets of dew laying thick over the grasses and shrubs, creating little sparks of light across the yard. The farm looked fresh and clean, open, unlike the shadowed horrors his mind had conjured the night before. The river bobbed smoothly and Archie could hear the reeds rustle in the breeze. Across its banks was an expanse of bushland, vast and free. He rose, subconsciously lured by the calls of the night and strolled down to the waterside. On its bank he stopped, watching the water eddy and flow, waiting for stillness to fill his body. The brown murky water whispered gently, its surface littered with reed beds through which tiny insects played and hunted. Archie observed how the reeds seemed to force the river into tracks, guiding its flow in winding paths around their clusters. *One could get lost out there*, he thought, a shiver running down his spine. As if on cue the wind flashed up briefly from the muddy ponds, rustling the reeds against each other. It felt like a warning. Archie's stomach flipped. The enclosed, secreted river, hidden by the dry overgrowth, echoed with the cries of the night. Such a strange place. Archie turned for the homestead, his hand rubbing the small of his back.

This tension was soon forgotten as Archie headed for Barrington's study. Following Rosalind's instructions he walked the dark hallway, floor rough and splintering, paintwork peeling and faded, heart beating in nervous anticipation. The study door creaked as he opened it revealing a room cast in a wash of pale sunlight, drapes pulled back to allow a view of the rose garden and grave. The walls were painted in a yellowing white, the floor scrubbed to a bright polish. A large oak desk with an emerald green inlay sat beside an elaborate stone fireplace, chairs of a deep brown leather lined the walls, dusted and clean. Floor to ceiling, brown wooden shelves, filled to bursting with books. Archie ran a hand over the smooth, cool leather covers. It was like stepping back in time.

He closed his eyes, breathing in the scent of the room, a mixture of the freshening outside air and of the knowledge in book dust. Barrington's presence still lingered in the walls. The man who travelled to the far side of the world to claim his own life. Archie felt his excitement return in a flood of passion and conviction. There were answers here, he knew it, he would find them. And he would write his book, and claim his future and his name.

Something for himself.

31

White. And alone, beneath the currents I wait.

Archie buttoned up his finest suit, dark woollen, tailored just right. He straightened his hair and paused to check his reflection. Suitable, he looked the gentleman he was. Thus armoured he departed for his meeting in Goolwa.

Months of working through Barrington's study had heeded some interesting insights to the man, like his love of Christmas carols and distain for church, but his diaries had regressed over his time in Australia. Slowly, he wrote less and less, the long descriptions of emotions morphing into lists of supplies and plans for the farm. For his book to be anything special Archie needed more. He needed Rosalind. But as the days lengthened into summer she continued to keep to herself. A mystery behind a veil.

She'd left him no choice but to take matters into his own hands.

Frustrated at his lack of progress, Archie decided to try a new tack. Writing to the local paper he placed an advertisement asking to speak to anyone with knowledge about the Barrington family.

Now, a week later, Archie found himself at a small public house on the main street of Goolwa. The Corio's golden stone walls, trimmed with green painted woodwork shone in the bright sunshine. Across from him sat Ernest Fuller stirring sugar into a cup of coffee.

'Thank you for meeting with me,' Archie said, offering the shy older man a smile. Ernest nodded his balding head and blew across the cup. Furtive eyes glanced up at Archie, squinted as if considering and then returned to the cup.

'Not sure you're going to like what I have to say,' he began. 'Never sat right with me, the whole story.'

Archie waited, pencil pursed as Ernest took a sip of hot brown liquid. Archie's own teapot sat untouched beside him. After a moment he prompted, 'You were the deputy officer on the case, when Barrington disappeared? You interviewed Rosalind Barrington and visited the homestead? Were on the search party, too I believe.'

Ernest nodded solemnly. 'Never did make sense how he could disappear like that. None of his belongings were taken, so he didn't run away. No sign of a scuffle.

'And he'd recently purchased the property. Mr Harbinger, the man he bought Hathrone from, said he was giddy with joy over the purchase, like a 'child with a bag of sweets'. And his doctor friend, George, gave a statement attesting to Rosalind's improved health. Everything seemed to be, well, just right really. Strange timing.'

'But he was having financial problems, back in England.' Archie said.

'We thought that was a lead,' Ernest nodded, 'but no. Sold his Estate there to buy the one here. Made a tidy profit, so that was a solved issue too.'

'An accident then. On the river?'

'We searched that river, all along her banks, in the shallows. It was coming into autumn, but the rains hadn't really started, so the rivers weren't running strong yet. Rivers can be unpredictable, though. His boat was moored at the homestead, he wasn't out fishing or rowing. You can't slip in that river and drown by accident...'

'Are you suggesting suicide?' Archie felt his heart beat quicken at the shameful possibility.

Ernest shrugged without commitment. 'Mary, the housekeeper, was away that weekend, visiting friends in town. And their two aborigine boys were back at the mission. It was the perfect time for something to happen. But... '

'But?'

'We never found a body, on land or in the river. Dead bodies always float... eventually.'

Archie coughed subtly to clear his throat. Feeling nauseous at the thought of a dead Barrington, bloated and rotting drifting on the river currents.

'It was Rosalind's story never sat right with me,' Ernest continued.

'But she was cleared, 'Archie replied.

178

'Officially, yes.'

Archie looked up sharply from his notes. *What is this?* he thought. Ernest paused, scanning Archie's face, he seemed to come to a decision.

'Mr Barrington was missing for five days before anyone made a report,' he began. 'Percy came with supplies and found Rosalind locked in her room, refusing to come out. Saying Edward had abandoned her. Sounded tragic. He had disappeared, leaving her alone with no way to get help. Her too frail to ride a horse into the town.'

'That's awful. Five days alone and isolated. So vulnerable, out there by herself.'

'I thought so too, we all did. Under such strain we understood why she refused to come out and speak to us. But then the aborigine, Balun, came to make a statement. Said he'd been down at the house three days before Percy. Said he went to work the land, feed the sheep, but the place seemed deserted. So he knocked on the house door. Rosalind didn't answer, so he let himself inside.'

'The native went in the house, uninvited?'

Ernest gave Archie a long stare, 'The Barrington's allowed their aborigines some strange freedoms. Anyway, he said he spoke to Rosalind, asked where Mr Barrington was and she told him he was just out fishing for the day and to come back next week. Paid him for his time, even though there was no work done.'

'But if that's right, Barrington had already been missing for two days. She could have got Balun to raise the alarm.'

Ernest shrugged again, 'As it was it took the little fella over a week to come forward with that information. By then, Mary had coaxed Rosalind from her room to give a statement. She was so quiet, I'll never forget that. Voice no more than a whisper. Wouldn't look us in the eyes. Wearing black lace, like she already knew he was dead.'

'She must have been in shock. She could well have mixed up the timeline.'

'Or the black fella did, not the most reliable sort. But that's not the end of it.'

He paused, draining his coffee in one large slurp. Archie glanced at his tea, cold now, no steam rising from the spout.

'Before Mary got Rosalind to talk, George Harbot tried. Took him most of a day. Finally she let him in to speak with her in person. They argued. Loud. We all tried to be respectful and keep our distance, but we could hear the tone of the exchange. When he came out he slammed the bedroom door and strode from the house. I was by the front steps. He paused by me and said, 'Ask your questions, I hope you get more truth than I have.' Then stormed away to his horse. He never visited her again, didn't even go to the funeral.'

Archie felt his brow furrow. 'But that's terrible! He was their closest friend in Australia. How could he abandon her?'

Ernest held his hands up in the universal gesture of defeat. 'Officially, we ruled accidental death. But something happened on that farm. Rosalind's testimony was so cold, so detached. And young Percy, he couldn't talk without sweat pouring down his face. That lad, so anxious, face white like he'd seen a ghost.'

'You suspect foul play? That Rosalind was involved?'

'I don't know what I think boy, but there was more to this than the report suggests. Someone on that farm wasn't telling the truth. And a man is dead because of it.'

Archie stared at Ernest for a moment, allowing his words to sink in.

'It sounds like a fool's theory, I know. My Sergeant wouldn't listen to me when I tried to bring it up with him. Said to use my eyes. A sick, fragile woman, a farm boy and a black. What was the motive? None of them stood to gain anything. Told me to let it go. But I couldn't. It festered and soon I found being a policeman just wasn't for me. So I left the job, went to work on the new train line that was just being set up. Forged a good life. But, it's always haunted me... what happened to Mr Barrington.'

They had parted ways soon after, Archie agitated from the meeting. Sitting awkwardly beside Percy on the carriage stoop, Archie fought for calm while his mind whirled furiously trying to piece together everything he knew. Was he sitting beside a murderer? Or had there been a farming accident, and Balun thought he would be blamed? And Rosalind. Small, mysterious Rosalind. She'd invited him here, yet actively avoided him. Why? It just didn't add up. The thoughts twirled and twirled, twisting his mind and his guts in knots.

Combined with the oppressive heat of the noon sun, by the time they made it back to the farm Archie was in such a state he was struggling to breathe, his limbs heavy and numb. He strode from the cart without even thanking Percy, grabbed his towel and headed straight for the river.

Stroking smoothly through the cool water another possibility tormented his mind. Suicide. Had the man he revered taken his own life? Archie knew Edward wasn't particularly religious. But to commit

180

such a shameful act? To leave his wife alone in the Australian bush? What could possibly have pushed him to such despair? Archie had come here for answers, to find himself. But all he had was dust and mystery.

Rosalind sat at the table on the verandah watching as Archie stroked across the river. A cool breeze had brought her outside to enjoy the last wisps of spring before the heat would set in firmly and without restraint.

He will leave soon, she thought to herself as he changed direction, heading back for the bank. Rosalind stood and retreated inside, a heaviness in her heart. Taking up position behind the front window curtain she watched as the young man walked up from the river, body glistening in the sun, beads of water dripping from his nose and running down his chest.

32

The waters travel forward. The winds pass over.
And on and on and on.

Weeks passed. Summer arrived in full force. But nothing changed for Archie. He'd long since finished with Barrington's journals and hadn't seen Rosalind since New Years Eve - a shared glass of sherry and an early night. Despite hours alone in contemplation he could not make the facts of Ernest's investigation align with his own knowledge of Barrington and the people he had met on this farm. One eve, wet with sweat and mind still in turmoil, Archie dragged a blanket out into the night and lay on the dried grasses that surrounded the homestead, under the stars. Impossibly dark, the moon no more than a sliver, the air hot and still not even a breath of wind whispered up from the water. Archie tossed on his blanket hearing the dry undergrowth crackle beneath him. The song of insects buzzed through the dark.

That's when he heard it.

Reaching from the water's edge the low 'oh' from his first nights at Hathrone called to him. Archie sat bolt upright, ears pricked, mind filled briefly with images of murder and death. It had been months since the cry had first shocked him. He'd put it down to travel fatigue and the storm of a foreign land. But in tonight's stillness it could not be so easily dismissed. Frozen, he sat listening. It came again, louder this time and more intense. The sound resolved itself in his ears. It was the cry of a desperate woman.

Archie leapt to his feet, determined this time to find the source of the noise. He jogged swiftly to the water's edge. The cry sounded again, now closer, a wail of sorrow piercing the darkness. Archie followed his ears along the riverbank, feet crunching through the dried and wilted reeds, weak from the heat.

On he ran under the pale moon until a dark figure came into view. He slowed his pace, stopping just out of sight, watching. Hunched over the water's edge the figure moved slowly, rocking itself back and forth on its knees. Repeatedly its hands dipped into the water, cupping the brown liquid and pouring it back out again, like an offering. Archie watched the hands, large and firm as they pooled the river and gifted it back. The cries had stopped, as had the buzz of insects in the deepening night. Archie watched the figure as it rose from its knees, framed by weak silver moonlight, height and breadth imposing. There it stood solid against the darkness, erect and powerful. A horror. A black vision of death. Unnatural.

The figure turned, whites of two eyes catching the moon and gleaming in the dark. Archie shuffled back, not wanting to be seen. The figure turned away. As it moved from the riverside Archie saw it hunch down, shrinking into the darkness. Archie sank down to his knees and realised he was shaking, his breath coming in short shallow bursts. What had he just seen? Consumed by fear he could not move.

Hours later, as the first rays of sunlight began to warm the already overheated earth, Archie made his way towards the homestead. His first instinct was to go for help, to make a run for Percy's farm just over the hill. He had to tell him - what? That the fancies of a blonde haired boy had gripped his mind? A ghost of the stories of murdering natives was alive by the river? As he passed the grave by the rose garden his knees gave out beneath him and he slumped in the dust. He did not hear the breeze rattle the dry gums overhead, or the warbling call of a magpie in the distance. In the bright sunlight of morning the truth of last night's vision was stark. Overworked, stressed and sleep deprived, Archie had driven himself to a breakdown. His mind, fevered by his own torment had created a figure cloaked in midnight, his own fears made physical. This dark, forbidding land, with its vast space and walls of trees had cracked his weakened soul.

Palms pressed to his eyes, the tears came, rolling down his cheeks, wetting his neck and chest. He could no longer deny the truth. Will had broken his heart. Archie had let himself believe the foolish notion they could have a life together. A hopeless dream. And, in response to Will's honesty, Archie had betrayed his oldest friend, Clara. How could he have been so selfish to play with her heart so? Running from reality he had abandoned her to pursue a fantasy 10,000 miles away. What had he been thinking? That the past of a dead man could free his own future? No, the cage was in his own heart, it would be with him always. There was nothing he could do, no path left to him. It was time to return to England.

A soft footfall broke into his reverie.

Archie looked up. In the rose garden Rosalind was cutting a fresh bunch of pink flowers. He watched as she sliced the sharp knife through their stems, her practiced hands avoiding the dangerous thorns.

Slowly, as if unaware of his presence, she moved to the grave. There, bowing her head, Archie could hear the whisper of her voice but could not make out the words. She placed the flowers gently on the mound, adding more to the decaying pile of years.

As if in a trance, she moved back from the grave. After a few minutes standing in silence she came and sat herself in the dirt beside him. Surprised, Archie wiped his eyes and waited.

It seemed that ages passed, sat together in the dust of South Australia. The magpie overhead warbled again and its mate replied from further a field. Rosalind and Archie looked up as one to watch the bird's flight, up and way from them, to its mate in a distant tree.

Rosalind, eyes again glued to her husband's grave, removed her veil. Folding it carefully she set it in her lap and spoke, 'I always had a gift for flowers. Everyone would say so. But getting these to grow here was quite another story. The first few years they died, only the big one, in the front, the pink rose, alone she survived our first summer. I cried when they died; shed tears for each bush that passed. After a time they began to toughen but I have had years to strengthen them. I was not always so good in these climates.'

She looked directly into Archie's red rimmed eyes, 'This land can break you. Can confuse your mind.'

Shocked, Archie sucked in a sharp breath. How did she know what had befallen his own imagination? They gazed at each other in silence, a delicate balance hovering between them. Rosalind smoothed the veil in her lap and looked back to the grave.

'Our second autumn here, after George, our physician, had pronounced me well, I found myself to be with child. We were so happy despite the warning George had given us. We felt my body must be ready. I – Edward – was not as sure but the joy made this country shine even brighter. It gave me hope.'

She gripped her stomach with both hands, thrusting her fingers into its age softened muscles.

'It was a sign,' she continued, 'though I did not heed it, I was not listening. This place, it warns you, but you have to listen.'

Rosalind bowed her head, tears leaking silently down her cheeks as Archie relaxed his shoulders and prepared to listen.

33

I wait. Stagnant. Transparent. Unmoving.

Hathrone Australia 1888

Rosalind lay on their marriage bed, skin slick with sweat. Her body burned, her mind screamed as the next contraction bore down upon her. Within the hour Allambee returned with the doctor. Edward met them at the door and led them to his wife. Face blanched with fear Edward entered the room, George by his side, but he already knew they were too late. On the bed between Rosalind's ghost white legs stretched a sea of vivid red. Rosalind's face brightened momentarily as she saw George, believing he would make it right, he always made it right. But the shadow that drifted over his face spoke the truth her heart already knew. She looked down between her legs and saw the wet feeling was more than just perspiration.

'No' she breathed, head swinging side to side, 'No, no, no. Edward, don't let it be. Don't let it be!'

Edward rushed to her side; taking her hand in his, he pressed it to his lips. George opened his doctor's case. Stethoscope in hand he efficiently assessed her condition, listening to her too small belly, heart beat and lungs. Sadly, he shook his head.

'No,' she cried pushing herself up from her laying position. She grabbed Edward's arms and shook him, hard. He let her, his sorrow too great to resist hers.

George leaned down and whispered to Edward, 'She is still to birth it, you must leave.'

Edward shot a look of pure disgust at his friend, 'I will do no such thing. Do what you must, I will remain.'

And so he knelt on the floor beside his wife as she laboured the night away to birth an already dead child.

The boy arrived with the pale hues of the morning sky, his tiny body shaded blue by death. George handed the infant to Mary who, guided by Edward's rushed gesture, took it from the room. Rosalind lay motionless on the bed, unseeing eyes fixed on the white ceiling above.

'She must be cleaned,' George said softly to Edward. 'And she must rest. I will send a nurse to check you both. I am sorry for your loss.'

He squeezed Edward's shoulder. 'It was just too soon for him to enter the world, and live,' and left the room. Rosalind rolled onto her side, turning herself away from Edward.

'My love,' he whispered, 'I must clean you, please, my love.'

But no amount of gentle persuasion could make her move. She stared blankly at the wall in numbed exhaustion. He left her and walked into the dark of early morning alone.

Mary sat on the verandah stair, cradling something small, swaddled in white. *My son.* Hot tears burned his eyes as Edward took the tiny bundle from her, so small it fit within his palms. He unwrapped the cloth. Mary had cleaned away the red blood of birth revealing a tiny, but perfectly formed baby. Eyes closed, neatly detailed fingers curled, like a carving made flesh. He looked to be sleeping peacefully in his father's hands. Six months of love and hope never to be realised.

Edward cradled the child to his chest, as if holding him close could fill the gaping void that had opened there and walked to the water's edge. The air was thick with the promise of rain, ready to break the suffocating heat. Sweat plastered Edward's shirt to his back. But all he felt was the cold lump against his chest. The baby boy, gone from this life.

At the river he knelt and gently, so gently gave the boy to the currents to drift away, calm and free, forever.

As he watched the dark waters swirling, Edward knew: Rosalind was not whole, she never would be. His decision to sell Hathrone and buy this farm in Australia had been the right one. If her body was not strong enough to carry a child, their child, how could it carry her own health in that cold infused country? He'd heard the rasp of her breathing return during the labour. No, he was right that they should stay here. And George had been right too, he now realised. She was not ready to bear a child; the pregnancy had been a mistake. And it was one he would never risk again. Confident in what he had to do,

Edward ordered Balun to set up the spare room with a bed for himself. Not trusting his lust he would keep from her feminine body by night, clothed in daylight she would be easier to resist.

The sky broke that night, the heavens lashing the homestead in angry retribution. The smell of wet dust flooded the air, displacing the acrid stench of blood, rivulets of water coursing down the riverbank joining the currents that rushed away, cleansing Edward's loss. Focusing him on the love that remained: his sole purpose.

Weeks passed. Edward cleaned and fed Rosalind daily. She remained silent, eyes wide, dark, empty. He threw himself into the work of the farm, planning crops and sheep breeding, working the soil hard and fast, pushing himself to exhaustion. Thinking about everything but the perfect miniature baby he'd given to the river.

Eventually, the haze of loss lifted enough for Rosalind to rise from bed and venture out onto the verandah. There her Edward sat, reading a novel she was sure she had seen him read before. He was more beautiful than she remembered.

'My love,' he welcomed her, concern flashing over his face. She smiled weakly and moved to sit on his knee, her skin almost translucent in the morning light. He held her tight against him, his fear of losing her still raw from the miscarriage. *All that blood!* Driven by his grief and his desperation to ensure her safety, he told her of the sale of Hathrone and the purchase of this farm, all those months before.

'Hathrone Farm I have decided to call it. It is ours my love! I so wanted to tell you sooner,' his eyes searching her face, 'But I feared the excitement might be too much with the... well... But it is for the best. I must protect you. This country gave you back to me; I will not let England take you from me. I will not let anyone take you from me.'

He buried his head in her chest suppressing the sob that rose to his throat. Rosalind placed her arms around his head, running her fingers through his hair. Face blank, staring ahead.

'The child?' her voice quavered.

'It is gone. To the river... put it from your mind. It is done, it is passed.'

That night as she readied herself for bed Rosalind's mind thought of nothing but the baby that had grown in her womb these past months. Hand on her still soft belly, muscles loose from holding the tiny life, tears formed in her eyes. She'd never even had the chance to hold him. Moving to her room heaviness enveloped her. She needed Edward with her, close and warm, the reassurance of skin on skin. Though she may not yet take him into herself, she could hold him, close and real through the disembodiment of night.

He came to her door before heading to bed, 'I am quite better now my love,' she smiled, 'Please, come back to our room, come back tonight.'

She leaned in and kissed Edward's lips, gently at first and then with more and more passion. But he pulled away. Gently he pushed her back, holding her shoulders an arm's width from his body.

'You must rest my love.' he said, 'Sweet dreams,' then turned and walked to his newly set up room.

Rosalind stood, stunned, in the doorway. Understanding filling her body, 'He blames me,' she whispered.

Slowly Rosalind's physical health returned. And with it Edward's peace of mind. Though he no longer needed the long days of farm toil to find the peace of sleep, Edward kept up his pace, driven to make the most of his land, even filling his idle hours talking to his wife about his plans. Rosalind always smiled and nodded, though she rarely looked up from the river's currents below. Driven by his own need to move forward, Edward did not see the darkness swirling in her eyes as she tended her roses, silently bringing England to this place.

Believing her husband had turned from her, she cried for every dead flower.

****

'...I was so wrong. But I loved h-' Rosalind bent her head down onto Archie's shoulder and sobbed gently. 'My boy, my baby. Gifted to the river...'

Archie placed an arm around her shoulder, as he would have his mother, if ever she had let him see her cry.

'He'd be about your age now, had things been different. I think that might be why I invited you here.'

She looked at Archie, gauging. He kept his face passive.

'It was a bad time. Balun and Allambee burned dried reeds for days. A smoke ceremony for the baby's spirit. They were horrified that we didn't bury him. Refused to work the land until our son's soul could be at peace. '

'Why,' Archie prompted, 'why not bury the child?'

Rosalind looked at him in surprise, 'He had to be free,' she said, as if it were the most obvious thing in the world. 'And so did we. Free to move on, to heal.'

She sighed, 'Edward had to work the farm alone. He couldn't leave the crops, he had no choice. But it left me alone with it all. So alone…' She lapsed into silence.

The noon sun beat down overhead, bright and unrelenting. Gently Archie coaxed the widow from the dirt and guided her inside to her bedroom before collapsing on his own cot just down the hall. Under the weight of emotional exhaustion, sleep claimed him.

34

I cannot move.

Rosalind sat waiting for him at the verandah table, breakfast laid out for two. Her veil nowhere to be seen. Hesitant he took a seat. He felt closer to her after the confession of yesterday, but was unsure of how she might feel after sharing so much of her personal world. He watched her pale face as she poured them tea, her hands moving with practical efficiency; they reminded him of Will. Archie felt his chest go tight and shoved the traitorous thought aside. To cover his unease he reached for the tea and sat back. 'Thank you,' he breathed. Rosalind's eyes flew open in surprise. Not sure what offence he had committed, he rose immediately.

'I am sorry,' he said.

'Well, it's understandable, you're still tired,' Rosalind said, calmly taking her seat again, settling her skirts about her ankles, 'But I don't know how you are planning to keep a record of my answers if you don't have a notebook and pencil. You have a biography to write. And as the sole owner of this story, I expect you to represent it accurately.'

She smiled encouragingly. Realisation dawned and, grin breaking across his face, Archie strode swiftly back to his room to collect his writing tools. *Unbelievable*, he thought, *it has happened! She trusts me.*

Hesitantly at first and then with more and more confidence, Rosalind began to tell Archie about her life and the man she loved, Edward Barrington: their time in Derbyshire, the journey to Australia, his love of the land and of her.

'And the day he went missing?' Archie ventured one afternoon as they watched the dark birds flying across an orange dusk, returning

191

home to roost after a day of feeding on the river.

Rosalind sighed heavily. 'He was just gone. I searched and searched and searched. I prayed. I cried out. But, gone.' Her answer felt uncharacteristically short; stunted compared to her elaborate descriptions of the other events of her life.

'Do you think,' Archie paused, unsure if he should continue. But Rosalind looked at him with such openness, he could not stop the words. 'Do you think he *chose* to leave?'

Her eyes flashed fire, her face tightening in a fury as pure as it was brief, before her calm façade returned. 'No,' she whispered. Where anger had bloomed just moments before, now Archie heard only exhaustion, resignation. Shaking her head slowly, 'Edward could never have left. Never by choice.'

And Archie felt it was truth.

'After Edward disappeared Balun and Allambee left me. Said this place was cursed, that I was cursed… I guess they were right. I never saw them again. But Percy, he remained loyal.'

Archie felt the warmth of anger colour his cheeks. *How could they abandon her, alone? Just like George. How cruel people could be, how selfish.* Against this betrayal Rosalind seemed even smaller to his eyes, vulnerable, deserted.

Weeks went by, talking of the past, of the present, strolling the grounds of the farm, rowing on the river. Rosalind had a particular love of the waterway; it had been a joy the couple had savoured together.

'Edward loved this boat, loved being on the water, alone, drifting, free…,' she explained one lazy afternoon as Archie pulled on the oars. "It was where we first shared our belief that we were to have a child. Water has a special power.'

The gentle sunshine tickled their faces, the water bubbling politely around them.

As she spoke Barrington came alive. And so did she. Her eyes brightened, her gaunt features smoothed. Now veil-free the sun warmed her skin and colour began to appear on her cheeks. Archie could see the pretty woman she must have been glimpsing out from her weathered face. It made him smile.

The terrors of the night did not return, slowly fading from Archie's memory.

Overtime he began to share his own stories of his childhood at Harrowbow and time in Cambridge. And through each tale resonated the companionship of the person he adored most in the world, Clara.

'She is my oldest friend. I barely remember a time that she wasn't in my life.'

'Then why the hesitation?'

'I love her. But not as a husband should a wife. When I hear you talk of Edward...'

'You should never compare, my child. Every love is it's own affair. You do what is right for those you love. Whatever the cost.'

He sat with that a while, letting her words settle into his bones; the weight of years of secrecy began to lift. He could do what was right for both Will and Clara, *whatever the cost*.

Journal full of notes, Archie could have returned home; but he did not. He felt safe with Rosalind, understood, and she with him.

Two broken souls, at opposite ends of life, finding comfort in companionship.

But the peace of those days was about to be shattered, struck by a bullet from the other side of the world, the implications rippling out across the globe. War with Germany was imminent and Archie had to return home.

Percy brought the news. The three of them sat in stunned silence as the cold winds of winter brushed over the homestead.

'The whole town is buzzing with the talk. Young men in the public houses, drinking and declaring their allegiance to England. Seems everyone thinks it's inevitable. We'll be at war. And soon.'

'Then there is no choice. This is monstrously terrible. I cannot be away from my mother, ' Archie said, beseeching Rosalind to understand.

The shadow of loneliness passed over her face. However self imposed that isolation might be, Archie felt a stab of pity for her, sharp and deep. So many years beneath the cloud of her solitude, so recently broken, she was sure to slip back into her hermit life. *What a waste*, he thought. Archie felt a sense of obligation, of protectiveness stirring within him. Leaving people was never easy, but at least those in England had known he would return. For Rosalind, this would be forever.

'Come with me,' he blurted before considering the logistics of such a move. 'Father will surely fund it,' he continued, mind racing to be ahead of his words, 'And you can stay with us. Our home is large and comfortable.' *What a coop it would be!* he thought in a momentary aside to the biography he would soon begin to write…

'Please, come home. It is what Edward would have wanted for you.'

He stopped, watching her face. Her features twisted from confusion to disgust, to fear, settling on resignation. Not what he had expected.

She shuffled uncomfortably and then fixed Archie with her eyes.

'It is late, you must rest. I do thank you for your company these past months, and for your offer of travel, but it is quite out of the question. Be sure to visit my grave and pay your respects before you leave.'

With that she stood and walked for the door.

'But Rosalind…'

'Don't call me that,' she whispered, low and venomous

Archie opened his mouth to argue, but Percy placed a hand on his shoulder, silencing him.

'Safe journey,' she said after a moment and left the two men standing awkwardly on the verandah.

A week later Archie walked out of his tiny room for the last time. In his hands he held his three cases. A heaviness had descended on him while he packed which was yet to let up. For some reason he felt sad to leave the little room, too cold in winter and too hot in summer. *Ridiculous*, he thought. He looked up at the homestead; no sign of Rosalind. Placing his things at the foot of the stairs he went to say goodbye to Barrington's grave. Respectfully doffing his hat, he saw that Rosalind had already visited that morning; new flowers lay on the heap, his hope of finding her there dashed by their fresh scent. He hadn't seen her since he asked her to return with him to England. The shield she'd kept so tightly about her when they first met had snapped back into place with force.

Archie paused a moment by the rotting mound of roses and closed his eyes, just existing in this place for the last time. He tried to focus on the experience of his time on the farm, the significance of this grave, but all he could think was that he was losing a friend. Interrupted by the sound of Percy and the carriage arriving, he walked to the front of the homestead.

Percy jumped down and took Archie's hand in his. Shaking firmly, the older man smiled saying, 'You will be missed young man. I've not seen the widow so alive in years. You did her good, visiting like this.'

Taken aback by this sudden display of affection, Archie could only nod.

'Load up, sir. I will just speak with the widow.'

Percy strode past Archie leaving him to manoeuvre his belongings onto the cart. He looked back at the homestead once more. The river murmured quietly, the reeds rustled. Peace seemed to envelop the farm in a way he had not fully appreciated until this moment. Before the confusion of leaving became too much he mounted the carriage, eyes forward.

He was consoling himself with the promise of literary success and his hope to make things right with Clara, when he felt the weight of more baggage being loaded. Surprised, he looked out his window in time to see Percy lifting a final heavy case onto the racks. Rosalind walked down the verandah stairs, pulling her long black gloves over her hands, veil firmly in place once more. He dismounted the carriage as she came closer.

She smiled at him through her veil, 'I cannot deny the truth any longer,' she said, 'Rosalind Barrington always wanted to return to England. And that's just what she is going to do.'

With that she walked to the carriage. Archie clapped, joy spreading through his body as he took her hand to help her into the carriage, composing in his head the letter he would forward to Clara once they reached Adelaide.

Archie Hargraves was coming home; the famous bride of Edward Barrington on his arm.

Ellie

35

The hope is gone, but the river flows.
Bubbles. Froths.

Sydney, Australia 2018

'This is your best chapter yet!' Peter exclaimed, adjusting his glasses and scanning the last page of my most recent chapter again before scratching his chin.

'What a discovery. A lost baby. Such a tragedy, and no one knew. You have uncovered something truly incredible here.'

'Beyond terrible for them. All the poems Rosalind brought back to England were drenched in sadness. It never really made sense, Barrington had been happy in Australia. But now we know more. I mean, I know it doesn't answer the mystery of what actually happened to Barrington, but it's something.'

'I love the interview with the rookie cop.'

'You don't think I have oversold that? The possibility of Rosalind lying? The confusing timelines?'

'You have direct quotes from a primary source. You are free to interpret them as you will. I think you have ample supporting evidence.'

'Well, I like the angle. I mean, it really raises some questions. Why was Rosalind so reluctant to speak with the police? You would think she would do everything she could to find her husband. I know Archie came to trust her, but I'm not sure. She really only told Archie one new thing, that they lost a child. She clearly avoided other questions of his. '

'The baby was a pretty powerful reveal though. The pain of a lifetime.'

'True,' I agreed, 'I thought at first the baby might have been why Archie didn't publish, but he left Australia excited to write. So it wasn't that. What was he trying to protect Rosalind from?'

'Perhaps not Rosalind, but Barrington,' Peter said. 'Suicide was considered a sin back then, and with everyone being away the weekend Barrington disappeared, it really points to suicide. Don't you think?'

'Archie didn't think so, but yes, it's a strong possibility,' I conceded, unwillingly. It fit with the despair and hopelessness of *The Fall*, but not with the Barrington I knew. Did he fight so hard to save Rosalind's life, only to leave her behind? I frowned to myself.

Peter nodded, paused, 'It's very intriguing. But don't get too distracted. You aren't a detective, you are a PhD student.'

I nodded, noncommittally. 'There are so many lies and deceits. Barrington hiding the sale of Hathrone from Rosalind, Archie proposing to Clara when he loved another...'

'Archie is a difficult source,' Peter said. 'Very disturbed within himself it seems. You have to feel for the man. Even nowadays coming out is a challenge. Simon and I only told our families when we wanted to move in together. That was the 90s, but in the 1900s...' He trailed off shaking his head.

'I think I can really tie his inner conflict to his love of Barrington's poems in general,' I said, 'It shows how people were drawn to his works because of their own emotional struggle. I think.'

'I like that, Ellie. I would speak to the family about your angle first, you want to handle Archie respectfully. They were good enough to allow you to read his private journal. What a success for you. What a source.'

'Yes,' I nodded, 'But...'

'But?' Peter looked up from my chapter and regarded me quietly.

'I don't mean to sound, well, ungrateful, but I don't think Lord Hargraves gave me all the journals.'

Peter stripped his glasses from his face, eyes boring into mine. 'What makes you say that?'

'Well, the journals, they just end so abruptly. There is no mention of the new poems. Surely Rosalind shared them with Archie first? Then there is nothing from the passage back to England, even when War was declared *while* they were sailing. A man like Archie would have had something to jot down about that... And he left Australia so ready to write. Something changed his mind, but there is no clue on the pages.'

Peter nodded slowly. 'Yes, yes, I see your point. But, well, for the purpose of your paper it's probably not important. Perhaps Lord Hargraves just gave you what was relevant to Barrington. No need to give anyway all his ancestors secrets hey?'

'True,' I said, unconvinced. I was sure there was more. Hargraves was hiding something. Archie wrote so passionately of the cries from the river. Could that really have just been in his mind? Especially now, with the body found on the property. And Rosalind, despite Archie's words I felt no closer to understanding her than I had in Manchester. She had to have known something more about her husband's disappearance. Didn't she? Was protecting her and Barrington from gossip enough to stop Archie from publishing his biography?

I didn't voice these thoughts, which told me what I feared; I was clutching at straws.

'The next step, you need to tie it all back to *The Fall*,' Peter continued. 'This is all fantastic background to Barrington's last days, when we believe he wrote the poem. You need to use it in your interpretation. Losing a baby is a big deal. Now you need to decide if the poem directly alludes to it, or if it's just a part of the darkness and sorrow surrounding Barrington at the time.'

I suppressed a sigh. I knew that. I had been racking my brains about it for weeks in fact. The lost baby was a terrible event. But as the catalyst for *The Fall*? It didn't ring true. Yes, *The Fall* was full of passionate emotion and desperation, but the end felt more like resignation. A Barrington with nothing left to fight for. With Rosalind by his side, it was hard to imagine him giving up completely.

So many new facts. Every time I went to read *The Fall* in light of them I just felt, overwhelmed. The body by the river kept leaping forward, demanding my attention. *Who were you? What do you have to do with Barrington's disappearance? Anything?*

Perhaps Caleb was right, I needed to get out of the house and socialise. I mentally committed to phoning him when I got out of my meeting.

'When do you head back to Goolwa?'

'November 29th – I want to tie it in with Deborah's birthday party.'

Peter nodded absently, 'Alright, so... let's aim to regroup again once you get back, say the first Wednesday of December? Then we can get this moving into some more analysis. Sound good?'

I nodded to the bald spot on his head as he scribbled down our next meeting in his diary. He was the only member of staff who still used a paper diary and not the online booking system. Old habits.

2 hours later I sat sipping a wine at the local bar. The wine was dry and cool, slipping down my throat. I wanted a cigarette, but was determined not to break. I hadn't had one since before England.

Scanning the room I focused on enjoying the warm lighting and casual ambience as I waited for Caleb. He was late. I tried my best not to be annoyed, but I didn't want to be out late, I still had some paragraphs to write before bed. A little hope that he might cancel popped up in my head. I pushed it away. Like I did every time I recognised that maybe I didn't really want to see him... Taking a deep breath I resolved to be flexible. Caleb had been extremely understanding of my busy schedule lately.

Just then the door swung open and Caleb entered. He stood in the doorway, one leg jigging nervously, eyes scanning the clientele, looking for me. I raised my hand in greeting and smiled. He didn't smile back, only nodded and walked briskly toward me. Something flipped over in my gut.

He pulled up a chair to sit. The physical presence of him seemed to suck the air from the room.

'Hi,' he said absently, fingers tapping lightly on the table, 'wasn't expecting to hear from you today. Or this week at all really.'

He ran a hand through his hair and hunched forward, eyes darting around the room. My brow furrowed in confusion. 'We always meet for drinks on Wednesdays...' I began.

'Not always,' he interrupted. 'You have been too busy since England.'

'I've been working on my thesis...'

Caleb turned to look at me directly for the first time. Eyes hard. Cold. 'You'd get a lot more done if you weren't drinking every night.' He flicked his chin at my wine glass. 'Couldn't even wait for me before you got started.'

The confrontation of it took my breath away. 'What...'

"Oh come on Ellie we both know what's going on here. You just disappeared on me months ago. At first I got it. That shit with your dad... and I waited. Then the body of your poet happened. And you came back to life, engaged with uni and your study, travels... but not with me.'

I went to interject and Caleb held up a hand. 'Ellie, please. Just listen.'

I sat back, automatically bringing my wine glass to my lips for a sip, cringed at my automatic response and put it back down. Caleb didn't seem to notice. He was staring off at the bar again. He sighed, turning back to me. The anger had faded from his eyes, leaving nothing more than a deep disappointment.

'I thought you were the one, you know. I really did. I figured with your dad, you'd just need time. Hell, that's normal. Everyone would. But you just didn't come back. To me. Ellie...'

He turned his body towards me and took my hands in his. Bringing them to his lips he planted a swift kiss on my knuckles then dropped them and looked into my eyes. 'I love you Ellie. But I know... I know you don't love me. I didn't want to accept it, but these last few months... I deserve better. I'm sorry. I tried to wait, but I can't anymore. I'm done with this. With us. It's best... It's best if we go our separate ways.'

I realised I was gaping and promptly shut my mouth, shaking my head to try and cover it up. Caleb's eyes didn't leave my face. Inside I was a raging cyclone of thoughts, feelings, emotions. *How could he be so selfish?* I've been in pain. I had to study. He didn't even try to understand. *It's not my fault.*

Except, there, in the centre of the vortex, sat the truth. The knowledge that I had been denying since the first few weeks of new relationship euphoria. I didn't love him. I wasn't even sure I particularly liked him. But I'd been hurt. Things with my dad. And I had needed him, for a while. But, not anymore. Not for a long time. Slowly, I nodded my head and taking a deep breath looked up and met Caleb's eyes.

I squeezed his hands. 'Thank you for giving me time. For being there for me when I needed you. And thank you for facing up to this, for both of us.'

Tears were threatening to breech his eyes. He feigned a cough, trying to cover a sob and subtly wiped his lids. My heart constricted in sympathy. I didn't love him. But I had hurt him. Deeply.

'Well then. I guess that's it.' He nodded once, then again more firmly. 'I wish you well Ellie. Whatever you do. Always.'

'I wish you well too Caleb. Thank you.'

He stood. Nodded again, then paused a moment in indecision before swooping in to kiss me briefly on the cheek one last time before turning for the door.

I watched him leave, sitting in stunned silence, breathing and processing what had just happened. Slowly my heart rate returned to normal, and with it a feeling of calm spread through me. I realised I had wanted to end things for so long, but I hadn't been strong enough. Caleb had been. For both of us. At length I reached out and drained the last of my wine before collecting my purse and heading home. I felt lighter than I had in ages. Lighter and also excited. Like bubbles were brewing in my tummy. I didn't know why, but it felt good.

36

Isolation a shadow I can't see,
Shrouded in nothingness.

Finniss River, Australia 2018

'Ellie! You're here! Come in, come in. Give me that bag. Gosh, heavy. Lucky I have you in the main guest room, it has a writing desk and all. Follow me.' Deborah was pure excitement and enthusiasm. As she lead me down the main hall of her home, formally the residence of Edward Barrington, her energy bounced off the walls. Barely two steps into the house and I already felt welcome. No, more than that, at home. Warmth spread through my body and a grin broke out on my face.

'It's wonderful to be here Deborah. Thank you so much for the offer of a room.'

'And where else would you stay? At the motel? Nonsense, this is where you stay when you come to the Fleurieu. Here, with me. Besides, my party is going to be a big one. Much easier to just stumble to your room. Now, here we are!'

She swept open the door to a room flooded with November sun. The curtains were green with a white privacy veil. The bed large and soft. And in the corner, a beautiful old wooden writing desk. Unconsciously I found myself drifting towards it, my hand running across the smooth polished top, the green leather inlay. It was beautiful.

'Was here when we bought the place. The agent said it was his, your poet's. Was in the main library room, but I had Andy move it in here, for your visit.'

'Oh, Deb! That's... I'm...'

'Speechless? Good. That was the plan. Well I will leave you to get settled in. I need to get back to planning. This party isn't going to throw itself. You have things to occupy yourself?'

'Taj is meeting me in town. We're going to the library to see if Beverly has heard anything from the locals on Facebook. Any unexpected Barrington knowledge.'

'Excellent. Give Taj my love won't you. You can see yourself out?'

'Yes, thank you. And Deborah? Really, really thank you. This is just… so nice.'

Deborah paused at the door, nose crinkled in a smile, a gleam in her eyes. 'Anytime my darling,' she said and disappeared down the hall to the kitchen, leaving me alone in the beautiful guest room. I took a moment, eyes travelling over the space and breathed in deeply. It felt so comfortable and welcoming. I hadn't felt so at home since… I pulled my thoughts up sharply. This was a positive time, one of celebration and joy. I wasn't going to think about *her* or dad, not now at any rate.

I considered unpacking my bag, but decided I'd been inside too much already today, the flight, the drive up. It was time to get outside. I drove to Goolwa, intentionally early for my meeting with Taj and Beverly, so I could take a walk down to the wharf and see the water. The air was fresh and clean. Before me the river stretched out towards its namesake curve, the wind brushing gentle ripples over its surface, two yachts bent to its breeze. Turning back Hindmarsh Island bridge dominated the view, sweeping elegantly up and over the waterway. I felt my mind drifting, imagining this space back when Barrington was alive. Being here seemed to give his poems an aura of reality that was missing when I read them at my desk in Sydney. As I wandered back towards the library my skin buzzed with anticipation, though I could not say why. Perhaps I was just excited for Deborah's big birthday bash, the main reason I was down here that weekend. Or maybe I was looking forward to seeing if Beverly's Facebook group had come up with any local information about Barrington. It would make for an interesting chapter in my thesis for sure.

Coming up beside the council building my anticipation grew. I saw Taj sitting quietly outside on the curb, knees high, arms resting on them, face turned to the sun. 'Hey,' I called strolling to his side. Taj turned, seeing me his face lit up with a grin of pure sunshine. He stood, coming towards me. My heart started pounding. *Wow, I'm really out of shape!*

'Welcome, Ellie,' he said, leaning in and brushing my cheek with a kiss. I felt my face flush, a surge of embarrassment making my cheeks feel even hotter. *What is wrong with me?*

'Great to see you,' I said, 'shall we go in?' I turned quickly to the entrance, hoping to hide my blush. Taj fell into step beside me and we walked together through the automatic sliding doors. Inside I spotted Beverly's round smiling face almost instantly. She was behind the main desk, on the phone. Seeing us, she smiled and gestured to us to take a seat and wait. We wandered over and sat at a small set of desks and chairs. I glanced over at Taj, sitting patiently, eyes gazing out the window. He seemed relaxed, completely at ease. I took a breath to settle myself, I was feeling oddly agitated. Soon enough Beverly shuffled over.

'Sorry to keep you waiting poppet. I was hoping I would have something for you, but unfortunately it fell through. Quite a few people said they had information, but it was mostly rumours of witchcraft and such. I think with the body being found it's brought out the worst in people's memories.'

I was surprised at how crestfallen I felt. I don't know what I had been expecting, it was over 100 years ago. Around me the gentle hum of the library seemed to grow loud and oppressive.

'Oh,' Beverly smiled, 'don't look so disappointed love. At least people are talking about him. Even if it is mostly gossip.'

'You mean lies,' I said flatly, feeling my hands begin to shake as a strange red filter misted over my eyes. The silence was building towards a sonic boom.

Beverly giggled, oblivious to the fire coiling along my limbs. 'I wouldn't say that love. People just like a story. Weird old woman out in the bush, it was bound to start rumours.'

'It's disrespectful. It makes Barrington and his life a cheap sideshow. Like their lives didn't even matter. Like his wife's pain didn't even matter.' I said, feeling suddenly protective of Rosalind and all she had endured.

'I don't think we should jump to that conclusion, Ellie,' Taj said, taking hold of my shaking hand. I snatched it away, his touch too cool, too comforting for the inferno boiling within me.

'Why do they do it?'

'Who? Do what?'

'People!' I shouted, faces across the library looked over at us, but I didn't see them, didn't care.

'Ellie...' Taj tried.

'Everyone, everything. It's all lies and half truths and deception and deceit. And no one cares. No. One. Cares. Not about who gets hurt, whose lives are ruined. Who is in pain. And who is missing.'

'Ellie, really, calm down,' Beverly tried. 'This is not the big deal you seem to think it is. People gossip all the time. It doesn't mean anything for your thesis. I'm very sorry to have upset you.'

'Everyone lies!' I stood up, rage surging through my body. 'Just like him, someone has lied and to hell with the consequences for the rest of us!'

'Ok, I'm going to take Ellie out now,' I heard Taj say to Beverly. 'Come on Ell.' In my peripheral vision I saw a shocked Beverly nod as an arm wrapped around my shoulders and turned me towards the door. Outside, Taj walked me through the car park to a little green space behind the council buildings. I barely noticed, my vision had narrowed to a thin dark hallway, blurry and grey.

A small lake sat in a hollow in the ground, surrounded by green grass and spindly native brush. Taj walked me to the water's edge and sat me down, taking up a spot beside me in silence. The heat of the afternoon sun still warmed the ground as we sat. In the lake a water fountain sprayed an arch of droplets over the surface, the mist catching the breeze and blowing gently over our faces.

I don't know how long we sat there, watching the water. Slowly my breathing settled and my body relaxed. Taj spoke.

'Tell me.'

That was all he said. No demand for an explanation. No anger or recrimination for my behaviour. Just a simple request. It was an offer; to listen, to share what was in my heart.

Without taking my eyes from the water fountain before us, I nodded and began.

37

My eyes are closed. Nothing to see, to feel, to taste.

Adelaide, Australia 2017

Ellie bit into the mud cake. Still warm from the oven, the dark chocolate and cream filling oozed over her tongue. Wiping the corner of her mouth with the back of her hand she grinned up at Ann. A gleam in Ann's eye anticipated Ellie's words, 'Mum, this is just delicious! You haven't made mud cake since... well, I don't remember. What's the occasion?'

'Do I need an occasion?' Ann replied as she cut herself a slice of the rich chocolate cake. 'My daughter is down from Sydney to visit. I think that is special enough.'

Ellie reached over and took her hand. 'Thanks mum. It's good to be here.' She felt the tears threaten and seeing the same sorrow reflected in Ann's eyes, quickly returned her attention to the cake.

'Well, as you know, calories don't count when it's an occasion,' Ann chirped, wiping her eyes quickly and then launching into the cake with relish.

'Dad would say calories never count if you enjoy it,' Ellie said, addressing the background sadness head on. It was her new approach when talking to her mother, to anyone. No more hiding from the truth. Dad was dead. Ellie was ready to remember him with joy. She owed him that much.

Ann looked up at Ellie in surprise, the edges of her mouth quivering with emotion. 'He always did focus on the good things in life, didn't he?'

'He did,' Ellie agreed. They both took another bite of cake, munching in silence with their own reflections. The air between them felt suddenly lighter. The possibility of happiness more tangible than it had been since the police came to say there had been an accident…

'Do you remember when he made us go camping on Yorke's Peninsular? In July? And it rained so much our tent flooded. And you insisted that we get a hotel, but he refused to come and stayed in the wet tent, all night.' Ellie said.

Ann burst into a rich full laughter. 'And all the next night as well. And then when the sun broke through he told us, 'See, you just have to have patience, then look at the reward you get.' And he stretched in the sun, wet to the bone but happy.'

'Personally, I preferred being dry.'

'Me too,' Ann laughed. They fell silent, both exploring the new spaces of remembrance that had opened up between them. Ellie felt something inside her settle. It had been a tough two years since her father had passed. Driving home from the footy with mates, no alcohol in his system, yet somehow the car had left the road and wrapped around a tree. The policeman had said how unusual it had been to find the impact on the driver's side. 'It's natural instinct to swerve to save yourself, but Ted, he turned the other way. Took the brunt of the impact. Saved his mates. That's something to be proud of.'

In the grief and sadness immediately following, through the funeral and the haunted eyes of Paulie and Mark, Paulie's arm in a sling, Mark sporting a few abrasions, that comment hadn't felt real. Like the cop was trying, but really there was no silver lining. Not even one Ted could have found. But maybe seeing Paulie playing with his new grandson, and Mark at the pub with their mates, just like old times, maybe there was a positive there. Would that have been enough for Ted to find the good in his own death?

Ellie didn't know for sure, but it resonated now, years on, more and more.

Ann collected their plates and moved into the kitchen, taking her out of view for a moment. Ellie sat in gentle contentment, nursing her memories, listening to the sounds of Ann scraping the plates clean and wrapping the remaining cake in cling film. She was pretty sure there would be a slice or two for her to cart back to Sydney tomorrow. It was good to be back here, to be home. She had been avoiding it lately. This place of her childhood where the lounge room still smelt like Ted's cigarettes. Easier to say she was too busy, that her thesis was in a 'critical stage', which was only ever half true. Now, finally, things were taking on a new shape. Not perfectly rounded yet, but smoother.

She smiled up at her mother as she bustled back into the dinning room, expecting to see the same contentment in Ann as she was feeling herself. Instead, Ann stood tensely by the dinning room table. Her hands were clutched before her as she wrung them against each other. It was also Ellie's habit to fidget when anxious. She felt her own hands come together in her lap automatically and begin to squeeze. Noticing, she forced them apart, gripping her jeans to stop her fingers from flailing.

'Ellie, there is something I need to talk to you about,' her mother started. Her eyes, bright and focused, locked with Ellie's. Ellie felt a sudden rush of cold flood through her veins. 'Okay…'

Realising she was wringing her hands, Ann scoffed at herself, wiping down her flower patterned shirt and patting her hair back in an effort to still her nerves and do something, anything with those betraying hands. Finally she sat, choosing the seat nearest Ellie. She reached out, taking Ellie's hands in hers on the table, her thumbs rubbing Ellie's fingers in a rhythm from childhood, intended to soothe. *Oh god,* Ellie thought. *What has happened?* Her mind raced away from her, darting through an endless list of terrible possibilities: grandma had had a fall, and was in hospital; Aunty Norma had lost her job; or worse - Ann was sick, terminally sick. Ellie was going to lose her mother too. It wasn't fair. Ellie felt her shoulders bunch, her core tighten, bracing for impact.

Ann gave her a weak smile. 'Ellie, I love you. You must know that. You are and always have been my first and most important priority.'

'I know that mum. And I love you too. I'm sorry that I have not visited much since dad… But I just needed time…'

'Of course darling. No, it's not that.'

Ann looked up to the ceiling, taking a deep breath.

'Ellie, I've met someone.'

The room went still.

'Actually, not 'met' someone, but 're-met' I suppose. His name is Shane. We, we were together, years ago… and well, we caught up for a drink. I didn't intend to, Ellie. But we just clicked and one thing led to another. And I have been so lonely, and…'

'Mum,' Ellie interrupted. 'Are you telling me that you have found a new boyfriend?'

'Yes, I am.'

'And you are worried about how I will react to that. Because of dad?'

'Yes.'

Relief flooded through Ellie. 'Oh, mum! I thought you were going to say… never mind. Mum, that's great. That's really great. Look, I know it must be tough, getting over dad. But mum, you're still young. You deserve to be happy, and if… Shane… makes you happy then I think that's great.'

Ann looked at her daughter, a mix of relief and fear dancing across her features.

'Really, mum. I'm happy for you.'

Ellie leaned forward intending to pull her mother into a huge squeezing hug to show her that it was all ok. It felt weird, but Ellie was an adult and she could accept, no, be happy for her mother. A hug would show that.

But Ann pulled back, head shaking gently. 'There's more Ellie.'

Ellie paused and sat back, 'Ok, I'm listening.'

Ann took her hands off the table and began ringing them in her lap once more. Ellie bunched her own into fists.

'I actually met Shane 26 years ago, the year before you were born. Your dad and I were only dating then and we hit a rough patch.'

'I know this mum. Well, I didn't know it was Shane. You told me you and dad had a small break before I came along. But you didn't look back since. I guess that would feel weird, the connection. But again,' Ellie paused for emphasis, 'if you are happy…'

'Shane is your father.'

Ellie's heart stopped. All the muscles that had been braced before constricted at once, forcing her breathing into small gasps.

'I left your father for Shane. We had a wild time together. But then I got pregnant and he left, and your father, he understood, he forgave me and he took me back, and…'

Someone had stuffed cottonwood in her ears. Her mother kept talking, but it came through fuzzy, unfocused. Ellie became aware of a pounding pain in her head and a searing burning in her lungs.

'Breathe Ellie,' Ann said, reaching out to stroke her arm. As her mother's fingers brushed her arm, the paralysis ended.

'Don't touch me!' she screamed leaping to her feet so fast that she knocked her chair over. It banged down on the tiled floor with a loud crack. Ann jumped.

'Why would you say this? I don't need a fake dad! My dad is *dead*. If you think pretending that Shane is my father is going to help me heal, then that's just fucked up.'

'Ellie, darling. No, please, please sit down. It's the truth Ellie. Ted loved me. He forgave me. And when he met you, oh Ellie, he loved you the moment he saw you. He vowed to be the best father he could be to you. And he was. He made me promise to never tell you. You were his daughter after all, in all the ways that matter. But now he is gone…'

'You decided to lie?'

'No! Ellie, please. Just… just sit down and listen.'

'No, I won't sit down and I won't listen to this shit. How dare you mum? How fucking dare you!' Ellie yelled, ripping her throat raw with the force of her anger and disgust.

She stormed from the room snatching up her bag and racing for the door.

'Wait Ellie please, don't leave like this. Please, you are in no state to drive when you are so upset.'

Ellie rounded on her mother, 'Upset? Upset? You think this is *upset*. No, this is fucking furious. You can't change the past to fit with the future you want. Ted was my father, my *dad*. No shitty fantasy of yours is going to change that. Shane is nothing! If what you say is true then what a fucking idiot you are. No! Keep the fuck away from me.'

Ellie slapped away her mother's groping hands and banged through the front screen door, slamming it shut behind her with such force that it smacked against the frame despite the soft close feature. Furiously wiping tears from her eyes, she threw open her car door, smashing it closed behind her and started the engine. Without checking the traffic of the quiet suburban street around her she lurched out onto the road and drove. She didn't know where she was going. Her luggage was still at her mum's. But she didn't care. She didn't need it. She would not go back. If Ann wanted to make up such shit then she could be alone.

'Be with Shane!' Ellie said, voice dripping with distain. 'Have a man, that's your choice, Ann. But you don't get to play happy families. You don't get him and me.'

She drove, through the city streets of Adelaide to the airport, checked into the airport hotel and booked a flight back to Sydney for the next day. Ann could collect the car herself. Fuck her!

The room had a mini bar.

Ellie, adrenalin still coursing through her body, wrenched it open.

Sitting on the short blue carpet, the white sheets of the cheap hotel stiff against her back and arms, she drank. Starting with the first bottle on the right, a Heineken, all the way through the bar and into oblivion.

****

Goolwa, Australia 2018

'That started a pretty bad time for me. Drinking, partying. I used Caleb. I didn't mean to, but I did. I think I was just running from it all.'

'When did you realise she was telling the truth?'

I looked over at Taj, it was the first question he had asked since I started. The sun was low in the sky now. The chill ocean breeze picking up in strength, bringing with it the fresh scent of the salty ocean. Taj lay beside me on the grass, head beside mine, relaxed, watching the darkening clouds as they drifted aimlessly above. I breathed in slowly. 'I think I always knew it was true. I mean, she really didn't have anything to gain by telling me.'

'Except releasing her guilt over the lie.'

That pulled me up short. 'I'd never thought about it that way.' We lay in silence, the cool grass tickling the backs of my arms and my neck. The misty spray of the fountain was being blown away from us now, luckily, or the cold would have forced us to move. And I wasn't ready yet.

'Have you spoken to your mother since?'

'A few times. The conversations don't go so well. My professor at uni knew my parents, they were childhood friends. Mum rang him. I really only answered her calls because he insisted. He knew the story. Turns out most of their friends did. Paulie, Mark, Stella, they all rang me to plead mum's case. It just made me angrier. They all lied. They all knew. It was just me who didn't. But more than that, dad lied.'

Taj waited as I gathered my thoughts. 'I was his little girl, you know? And he lied, all my life he lied. And he left me.'

'Leaving wasn't a choice.'

I sighed, 'I know.'

'When do you think you will go see her again?'

I propped myself up on an elbow, staring at Taj in exasperation. Hadn't he been listening?

'Why would I do that?'

Taj shrugged noncommittally. 'To heal. To forgive. At some point you have to get passed this. It's eating at you.'

His words were simple, but as usual hit exactly the right spot. The flare of anger subsided, replaced by hollow emptiness.

'Not yet,' I said.

I felt Taj nod beside me and we fell silent. Just us, the grass and the sky. Breathing in the silence of the evening a weight I had not even realised I was carrying, lifted. 'I miss my dad,' I whispered, tears springing to my eyes. Taj unfolded an arm, wrapped it about me and pulled me into his side, my head on his chest. And just held me. Silent, warm and solid beside me. As I cried out my grief, my loss, my loneliness. And my love. For my dad in the sky and my mum waiting to hear from me just 70 kilometres away.

38

Just time. Time. Time.

The next day I returned to the library to apologise to Beverly for my outburst. 'Not at all love. We all have our bad days,' she said with a smile and pulled me into a brief but surprisingly powerful hug, given her soft rounded belly and arms. Thanking her for her understanding I left, this time calmly.

Back at Deborah's, I set myself up at the writing desk she had so thoughtfully placed for me and began to work my way through my notes from Archie's journal. Before his disappearance, Barrington was meant to be writing for Harbinger, though as a matter of record I knew those poems never eventuated. And he was also due to release a third anthology for his publishing company in England. With so much on his plate, why would he take on the farm? And Archie, searching to find himself, drawn to Barrington's words. He'd lived here for a time, rested his head in one of these very rooms and heard a voice crying from the water. What stopped his ambition, his drive to be his own man?

Coming out of my reverie of study I realised my tummy was grumbling. I'd missed lunch, but I was sure Deborah wouldn't mind if I rustled something up for myself. Besides, I needed some time away from the words for my subconscious brain to formulate the ideas and connections my conscious brain was trying to force into order.

I made myself a hasty sandwich of cheese and Vegemite and headed down to the riverside. Wandering along the waterfront listening to the wind whistling through the reeds, I could understand Archie's fear of the outdoors. A man from the cultivation of the English countryside, in such a large and empty landscape. No wonder he thought he heard ghosts on the wind. I chuckled to myself and strolled on.

My mind was jammed full of competing thoughts: my mother, Taj, Shane, Barrington, Rosalind, Archie, Clara, they all called out to me, wanting me to focus on their lives, their pain, their secrets. My head felt stuffed full, my limbs heavy. I sat down and, removing my shoes, flexed my toes in the muddy bank and let go. No longer trying to order the voices and thoughts that vied for my undivided attention, I set my mind free, to wander as it chose.

So much had happened in the past two years, even more in the last eight months. Discovering the truth of my parentage, sinking into depression and possible alcohol dependancy, feeling trapped in the wrong relationship, facing a dead end in my thesis, no passion or leads.

And then, a body had been found here, on this estate. A woman had lost her life, many years ago, but that tragedy had been the spark that changed the direction of my own. I'd come to Goolwa, met Deborah and Taj. A warm shimmer swept through me at the very thought of his name, demanding recognition, but I pushed it away, determined to let my thoughts continue to roam freely. I'd travelled to London, talked with Clara's family and learnt of the rumours and pain of her life, met a lord and gained access to Archie's most secret journal. I'd uncovered the tragic loss of a baby, an explanation for the sorrow in *The Fall*. And yet, something wasn't right.

I was missing something. It felt like it was just there. A truth so tangible that I should be able to reach out and grasp it. A connection between it all: the disappearance of Barrington, the secrets of Archie, and the long lost woman in the earth.

Did Edward just slip and drown? He used the metaphor of the river's danger so convincingly, yet he was a newcomer to these lands. And the nameless woman, buried on the estate. Long dead, with no matching missing person that the police could find. Could it really just be coincidence? So much pain, so many secrets and deceits.

I looked out at the glassy water. Surface calm. But lurking beneath, snags, rocks and tree branches, deeper trenches, the rip of an undertow. Any number of dangers that could take you under. Had Edward fought the river's force and lost? Is that what I had been doing against the flow my life? Laying back on the cool grass I listened to the bubbling currents twist and turn and summersault and spin, until I heard Deborah calling her children and me to dinner, her high pitched voice bringing me from my musings. The patterns of my ideas broke like the surface of a pond when struck by a single rain drop, rippling away.

I sighed. 'No answers tonight then,' I whispered to the wind as I rose to join my borrowed family for dinner.

Entering the kitchen my melancholy thoughts were dismissed by the energy and excitement in the dinning room. It was the night before Deborah's big party, and everyone, even Andy, was buzzing with enthusiasm.

'Ellie, excellent! Come, come. This is the last trial of the Chicken Coq Au Vin stew I plan for one of tomorrow's offerings. Here, try some and, be honest.'

Deborah scooped a ladle of stew onto a plate and handed it to me. The salty steam warmed my cold nose and cheeks, the homely smell of chicken making my mouth water. I took a fork, pierced a large chunk of chicken thigh and chewed. Lightly spiced with cinnamon and cumin, the chicken all but melted on my tongue. It tasted like home.

'It's delicious Deb, really. That's the one. Do it just like that and everyone will be wanting seconds.'

Deborah beamed and turned to Andy. He smiled at his wife and took her hand. 'You were right darling. This party is a great idea. I am very much looking forward to it.'

Joy settled across the table, with Alison and Billy nodding, their eyes sparkling in the evening light. And we ate, and talked about the plans for tomorrow evening, who would get what and do what and when, what were we all planning to wear. And for a few wonderful hours all I thought about was this moment, here with these lovely people, and the celebration to come the next day.

39

Nothing to fight for. Nothing is left.

The evening begun with an air of anticipation and excitement. I stood in my room, assessing my reflection in the full length mirror behind the closet door. I'd chosen to wear a dress for Deborah's party, knee length black with a red swirling pattern throughout it, short sleeved to go with the balmy promise of summer on the wind. It was firm but not tight against my body. Slipping on my heals, I considered the outcome of the last hour of clothes changes, makeup work, jewellery questions and frustrated tears and realised: I looked good.

Warmth spread up through my tummy as I considered sheepishly that Taj had never seen me in a dress. I shook my head to clear the thought before the blush reddened my cheeks and kept me from going to help Deborah with the final preparations for even longer than my wardrobe catastrophe had already done. Flicking my hair back over my shoulders I straightened my back and walked from my room...

...Straight into Deborah as she careened down the hall way, flowing silver dress billowing behind her, one ear dripping with a long golden earring, her hands busy affixing the matching pair. 'Oh, Ellie!' she exclaimed, coming to a stop before me. The powerful musk of her perfume wrapped around me, exotic and heady. A huge smile on her lips, she placed her hands on my shoulders.' You look absolutely beautiful,' she said. And for the first time in a long time, the words felt true.

'And you are a vision,' I countered, 'Where did you find that dress?'

Deborah laughed in delight and honoured me with a twirl to show off the flowing silky fabric. 'Andy had it custom made. Isn't it just so me?'

'You look amazing. Are things all ready for the party? I was just coming to help.'

'Thank you darling. Yes, I believe it is mostly in hand. Taj is just finalising the table settings, perhaps you might go and give him a hand?'

'I thought he was doing the fire outside?'

'That was the plan, but he arrived in such a lovely shirt and tie I was worried he would get it dirty before you saw.' A cheeky grin flashed across her face. 'And now I see your lovely dress, I am assured of my decision. That said, I don't think the boy really knows much about table settings, so your help would definitely be appreciated.'

For once Deborah's insistent match making of Taj and I didn't annoy me. In fact, I felt strangely calm but also hasty. I smiled and kissed her cheek. 'Thank you Deborah. May you have the most wonderful birthday celebration ever.'

'Don't you worry my dear,' she crooned. 'Six cases of Verve Cliquot have that guaranteed.' She turned back up the hall, presumably heading for her room, calling to Alison and Billy, 'Hurry now children. The guests will be here any moment!'

Smile still on my face, I went to find Taj.

As Deborah had promised, I found him in the dining room, looking over knives and forks and checking wine glasses for marks.

'Hello,' I said softly. Taj jumped and looked around at me with an almost guilty expression. His eyes travelled slowly up and down my body, taking me in. I did my best not to fidget.

'Hello to you too,' his lips quirked into a nervous smile. 'You look beautiful Ellie.'

'So do you.'

'Have I done this right?' he asked, turning back to the table settings, but not before I caught sight of the slight red tinge on his cheeks and neck. Bubbles of anticipation threatened to make my voice squeak. So I played for time and strolled around the table, focusing on my breathing.

'It looks perfect, Taj. Deborah will love it. I think the addition of the wattle is a fabulous touch. A bit of nature. A bit of *here*.'

'That's what I was going for. After all, this is partly about her being a local, feeling a part of the place. I want her to feel at home here.' An anxiety I'd never seen unfolded across his face. I realised this table setting, this party, Deborah and her family, really mattered to him.

'She does Taj. And you help her feel that way.'

'Thanks Ellie. She's always been so welcoming to me. You know? Giving me the landscaping job, feeding me lunch and tea. She's good people.'

I stared at Taj, suddenly seeing so much more to this young man who had become my friend. Seeing his inner world, wanting to do well, just as filled with anxiety and worry as the rest of us. It only made my heart swell more.

Grinning, I swept around the table and hooked my arm in his. 'Come on, ' I said, 'let's get a drink.'

Shortly after the first guests arrived and the evening descended into a riot of laughter, clinking glasses, warm conversation and music. Dinner passed without a hitch, Deborah's chicken stew the clear favourite. Taj and I sat opposite each other and though I wanted to talk with him, I found myself repeatedly distracted by other guests on both sides of me. It seemed the student studying the local mystery was in high demand. As the dinner plates were whisked away I chanced a glance at Taj. He was staring at me in the half light of dusk. The earlier glimpse of vulnerability gone from his eyes, replaced with a dark, shimmering heat that set my pulse racing.

Someone turned the music up and people lurched to their feet heading for the patio dance floor, finished by the builders just this week. The nick of time. The pulsing beat began to resonate in my chest and I raised an eyebrow at Taj, an invitation and request. I saw him move to stand, never taking his eyes from mine. My heart was racing, heat flooding my body despite the cooler November evening. He came around the table, eyes low, intense and then…

'Excuse me, it's Ellie, isn't it?'

'Ah, what?' A heavy hand on my shoulder broke my focus on Taj and I looked up into the face of a man on the far edge of middle age, receding hair line, small almond coloured eyes buried in wrinkles.

I shook my head to clear the intoxication of Taj's approach and groped for my manners. 'Ah, yes, sorry, yes. I'm Ellie Cannon. And you are?' I raised my hand to shake his.

He took it in his meaty grip and pumped my hand purposefully. 'Don Lane. I work the tip site just out of town. I've been meaning to come find you. But as you're not a local I kept missing you. Bev said you would be here.'

I felt more than heard Taj arrive at my side. 'Hey Don,' he said warmly, 'I see you've met Ellie.'

'Hi Taj,' Don paused, glancing between us. 'Oh, look I'm sorry to interrupt. But I have something that I think Ellie would want to see, it's about Barrington.'

'Of course, tell her what you have.'

'Right,' Don said, taking Taj's gentle reminder to talk to me, and not about me. 'Um, well, my great grandfather actually knew Barrington,' he began. 'He migrated here on the same boat, back in 1886. Was a point of pride for my family that they were friends. Helped him get his practice off the ground when he settled here in town.'

'Your relative was George Harbot?' I asked, surprised. 'I tried to find record of any relatives to talk to, but I couldn't find any...'

'Yeah, the Harbot name died out. George didn't have any boys. We're all Lanes and Ducants now. Look, my granddad used to talk about how he met Barrington when I was a little boy, and how kind he was.'

'Well, I would love to hear everything you remember. Now I know who you are, perhaps I could book in a time to speak with you?'

'Nah, I reckon that would be a waste of your time. I really don't know much. But I have some letters.'

'Letters?' Taj and I chimed together.

'Yeah, letters my great granddad wrote to Barrington. I brought them with me if you would like to take a look?'

The heat that infused my body just moments before vanished, replaced by the familiar call of curiosity. 'Actual written documents? You have letters between George Harbot and Edward Barrington?' I said, my excitement rising. I glanced at Taj, grinning. He smiled gently down, not mirroring my own enthusiasm. *Oh right yeah...*

I turned to Don. 'Well, if you are happy to leave them here with me I would love to take a look. Perhaps we could put them in my room?'

'No worries, keep them as long as you need. They've just been collecting dust. They're out in the car. This way.'

I flashed a smile at Taj that I hoped said, sorry and we will dance soon, all at once and we followed Don out to the front porch.

The driveway, dark now that the sun had fallen behind the hills, was lined with cars. Don ambled to a blue ute and pulled open the passenger door. 'Here you go,' he gestured to the seat. I leaned in and opened the old shoe box. Inside was a pile of about ten envelopes. By the light of the car dash I picked one up. It was addressed to Barrington alright, and stamped, but unopened; labelled return to sender. I picked up the next one. It was the same. Confused, I looked around at Don. 'These are unopened,' I said.

He scratched his head. 'Yeah, grandma said Barrington and George had some falling out or something. Barrington wouldn't read his letters.'

'And you never opened them?'

'Not really one for reading much myself. But they might be useful for you. I'm happy for you to open them.'

'Well, thank you. If you are sure?'

'Yes definitely. Like I said, they are just collecting dust.'

I drew the letter up close to read the stamp detail, curiosity rising. But, something wasn't right.

'The date,' I said.

'Pardon,' said Don.

I quickly leaned back into the ute and pulled out another letter at random and checked. Then another, then another.

'Ellie?' Taj asked, 'What is it?'

'The dates,' I breathed, 'they are all later.'

'Later?' Don asked.

'Later, as in after Barrington disappeared. The dates are wrong. But George knew he was missing. He visited Rosalind when the police were searching… Why would he write to his missing friend?'

'Perhaps he was missing him?' Don offered.

'Seems cruel to the widow,' Taj countered.

'Thank you Don,' I said, 'I think I might just take these now and have a quick look. Would you like to come with and see what is written in them?'

'No thanks Ellie, I'm ready to head home. Not one for late nights these days. But Deb has my number, so when you are done with them, just give me a call.'

I nodded and thanking Don for his generosity, picked up the box of letters and headed for the house.

Taj followed me into my room, shutting the door behind us as I plopped the box on my bed. Sitting down I selected a letter at random. Resisting the urge to tear into it I edged it open carefully.

'Dated April 7th 1888,' I read aloud to Taj. 'Almost 2 weeks after Barrington went missing.'

I scanned the letter, eyes growing wider and wider with every word.

Taj leaned against the writing desk in silence. Patiently waiting.

I looked up at him, something in my face must have startled him, because he stood up and came across the room to sit beside me. 'What is it?' he asked.

My thoughts were churning, tumbling over each other, connecting the dots between all I knew and… I gasped, my hand coming to cover my mouth.

'Tell me,' he whispered.

'Taj,' I gulped, 'I know what happened to Edward James Barrington.'

The phone rang out again. 'Damn it!' I exclaimed. 'Where is he?'

'It's Saturday night Ellie, he's probably out for dinner, or at a party. Like we were…'

'But this can't wait! Taj, surely you can see how monumental this is. We, we know what happened to Barrington! People have been searching for this truth for over 100 years. And the body…we know who the body is. I should call the police.'

'Ellie, wait,' Taj gripped my frantic, failing hand and plucked the phone from my grip. 'Your first instinct was to ring your professor. To talk about proper verification. And I think that's the right move.'

'We have the letters.'

'Yes, but no cross reference to prove authenticity.'

'When did you become an academic, ' I snapped, taking back my phone, but my heart wasn't in the rebuke.

'I've had a good teacher,' Taj levelled his warm brown eyes on mine and held my gaze. I felt the corners of my mouth quirk up involuntarily and blushed.

As muffled beats of Michael Jackson's *Beat It* floated down the hall from Deborah's rocking party, I sighed and flopped on my bed, hunching over my knees. Spread on the floor at my feet the pages and pages of George's letters stared at me. What they contained…

'I'll try Professor Tuft again,' I said, already clicking through the call back screen on my mobile.

'You already left him, what, 5 messages? He will call you back Ellie. Until then, let's think, together. How can we verify the information in these letters? '

I groaned, a headache from over excitement beginning to inch across my forehead. 'I don't know. It was so long ago. The postage stamps look legit, in keeping with the time, and the writing style is definitely old fashioned.'

'But you need another vector, right? Like a triangle of facts, solid.'

'Matching facts, from multiple sources. But I just don't know.'

Taj started pacing across the side of my room, careful not to disturb the yellowing pages at his feet. 'So, what do we have?' He started counting down on his fingers: 'A missing poet whose body was never found. To whom a series of unread letters were sent.'

'Check,' I mumbled.

'An unaccounted for female body.'

'Identified in the letters.' I said.

'Well, the timing and description matches, but it's not enough to prove...'

'Oh!' I leapt up so fast I smacked my knee against the closet door, still open from my frenzied outfit search earlier that evening. The pain blooming in my knee cap barely registered though, 'I know who to ring! And it's morning there... Lord Hargraves.'

'Wouldn't it be very early morning in the UK?' Taj asked.

'Yes, but for this, I don't care if I wake him from a drunken stupor, ' I replied, already scrolling through my contacts to make the call. It rung. Bleep, bleep.

Finally I heard the click of connection, a pause before: 'Ellie,' Lord Hargraves exclaimed. 'Why this is a surprise.'

'Is it?' I asked.

'Well yes. It is rather early over here just now. And rather late where you are, if I have my time difference correct.'

'Did you know?'

'Did I know what?'

'Archie's journals. You left some pages out, didn't you? Did you think I wouldn't notice?'

A heavy sigh down the line. 'I suppose no, not really. It was rather obvious wasn't it?'

'And the missing pages. Do they... do they identify the body by the river? The woman buried here on the Finniss?'

'They do.'

'Lord Hargraves...'

'David, please.'

'David,' I paused, throat tight. 'You tried to hide it, why?'

Rustling down the line as David paused. 'A sense of duty? Such dark secrets, so much pain. Perhaps it was worth letting the past rest.'

'But then the body was found.'

'Then the body was found,' David agreed.

'Thank you David, for telling me the truth, now.'

David huffed a laugh. 'It seems you had worked it out yourself

regardless of my attempts at subterfuge. But, as you know the truth…
would you like to hear it? The pages of the journal that I kept apart?'

I collapsed to the carpeted floor and leaned against the cool metal
bed frame, legs curled against my chest. 'Yes, please.'

And I listened, Taj beside me, phone cupped between us as David
read the missing pages of Archie Hargraves' journal in a steady,
solemn tone. Tears slid down my cheeks, wetting the hand that
clutched my mobile as we learnt how the unnamed body of a woman
came to lie by the River Finniss, unclaimed for 130 years.

40

I wait.
For the inevitable.
Drifting.

Indian Ocean, International Waters 1914

'Listen to me,' the widow pleaded. Archie smiled gently at the widow, believing he understood her distress, surely brought on by the break with home after so many years in isolation. He moved to her side and placed his arms around her shaking shoulders. So old, so fragile, the confusion of age written over her wrinkled face, panic etching the lines deeper, the fake light more harsh then the candles from Hathrone.

'Loss will do this, and you now must feel you are losing him all over again. It is alright. You have made the right choice. England will welcome you warmly and honestly. You will find peace again.'

'Peace,' the word cracked from her throat. 'I have not known peace for 25 years. Rosalind wants to go home, that's why I am going home...but...'

The widow pulled away from Archie and stood before him. Hands shaking, she jolted her head violently from side to side.

'Listen to me,' she repeated, tears now streaming down her agitated face. 'It is a lie, she is dead, she is dead...I killed her...my life, my love...my reason.'

With an aggrieved cry raking from her throat the old woman fell to the floor, body convulsing in terror.

'Dead! Dead! Fix it, I cannot fix it,' she cried repeatedly, smacking her head with her gnarled old hand. 'I tried to tell you! I wanted you to see the truth, why can't you see it?'

Archie fell to his knees, his own calm broken now by the violence she was inflicting upon herself. *What have I done?* he questioned. *This is too much, she cannot cope with the change. I have been so selfish!*

'Stop, stop, please Rosalind. Stop.' He took her hands in his and held them from her face.

'I am *not* Rosalind,' the widow screamed into his face, her panic reaching fever pitch in the still of the ocean night, 'You have to listen to me!'

With that she opened her lungs wide and began screaming horror at some truth beyond explanation. Her eyes were bulbous, staring at a terror Archie could not see. Shaking she pushed herself to her feet. Hands before her like a ghoul, she stood in the uncomfortable light, mouth agape. Archie looked up at her, helpless in the face of her fear; he did not know how to calm her. He needed a doctor.

She began to rock, one foot to the other. Breathing deeply she began to chant frantically, head twitching.

'Dinner time, she is gone, not there. The house. I call. Empty. 'Rosalind, Rosalind...' she is gone. Where Percy? Where? Where?'

Archie watched, his forehead creased.

The widow continued, 'where, where? She is gone... she is not... where? The river!'

The last word sounded low within the widow's chest, grating like stone.

'Run to... the river... Percy get a light,' the voice, even deeper now, rose in tension as the widow's hands shook more violently.

Rosalind began to pace the small room.

'Where is she? Where is she? There... the reed bed,' a hand pointed out, eyes wide staring at the port hole at which the foamy ocean lapped.

'No, no, no... I am too late. Rosalind. I am here.' She fell to her knees and motioned with her arms, grasping.

'Cold, cold, no heart beat, she is dead.' Laying herself down, 'come back, come back... Ah!'

Crying out the widow rose in a leap to her feet.

'She is dead. I killed her. She is dead!'

Archie jumped up and strode over to the widow, taking her in his arms he pleaded, 'Rosalind, please, please stop this. Calm yourself, please...' but the widow pulled away, screaming in his face.

Backing up against the wall of the room her fingers gripped the edge of her dress' neckline. Face blanched from yelling, neck strained to bursting, her fingers began to pull and tear. Archie stepped back, his heart pounding, unable to stop the scene unfolding before him. The widow screamed and tore until all her garments were strewn across the floor, last to land was her widow's veil.

There before him stood the atrophied body of a gentleman: sloped shoulders, the remains of muscular definition twitching in agitation; a flat chest, sunken from age, heaving with emotion; the mutilated remains of a penis between withered legs. Archie gasped, the men's eyes met.

'It was a lie. It was all a lie,' Edward was repeating, the horror of confession painted over his face.

'She died, she left me...she left me. I am alone, I am alone!'

The man, so strong moments before as to break from Archie's grasp now crumpled, naked to the floor.

'A lie, she is gone, she is lost to me. I have nothing, I have nothing. I tried to save her, I tried to keep her safe. Gone, gone, gone.' He began to moan and rock on his knees.

Archie was frozen still, watching in horror as the poet crooned his confession, the deception of a quarter century.

'The river took my baby, it took my Rosalind...'

Rosalind Barrington was dead. Edward Barrington was alone.

Archie leaned over and vomited onto the cabin decking.

The River Finniss, Australia 1888

Edward threw himself up from the soggy soil, propelled by desperation, the light dimming around him.

'Bring me candles,' he screamed behind him, 'Bring them quickly'. He surged forward through the shallows. Thick reeds whipped at his legs and lower torso, their sharp slaps marking his skin through his trousers, he did not notice.

'Rosalind!' he cried his voice booming into the dusk. A flock of water fowl took to the sky in fear of his echoing cries, the blood red of dusk bleeding colour from the heat of the day. 'Rosalind!' His boots filled with water, sinking deeper now into the mud, sucking on his limbs with every move he made. Edward felt his strength fading, wild fear drove him on. Then he saw it. Up ahead a white silk scarf hung from a reed, waving to him in the evening breeze. He raced forward, the heaviness of his body forgotten. Grabbing the scarf, be brought it momentarily to his lips, before scanning the waters wildly. He could see nothing; the surface a milky film bobbing only to the current.

'Where are you?' he whimpered.

'Sir!' Percy spoke from behind him, holding a lantern towards some reeds. Edward snapped his head around. A few paces down from him, a narrow line of reeds had been bent over, out in the river the rowboat rocked on the current. Edward rushed at the spot throwing his body into the currents.

'Rosalind!' his anguished cries tore from his throat.

Still he could not see her. He propelled himself through the river, stroking for the rowboat and pulled himself up on its side. Empty. Head first, he plunged into the water, diving down, hands searching wildly. His lungs screamed for air, his heart pounded in his ears. Beaten he surfaced, but only for a moment before diving down once again. His hands sunk into the murky depths, the riverbed mud, gluey from years of sediment, pulling him under. He struggled free. About to resurface for more air, the edge of something silky caressed his hand. Striking out he found soft flesh, cold to match the water, but solid in shape. He pushed himself forward, hands groping around the limp shape before him. Launching off the bottom Edward's head broke the surface just in time, his lungs opening as his mouth found air. After his face came his arms, dragging up the heavy body of Rosalind.

'Ahhh,' Edward let out one self-indulgent cry as his body took her dead weight, added to by the soaking muddy water in her once white nightgown.

'Heat, candles, water. Get the doctor. Get George!' he screamed at Percy, waiting on the shore.

Edward pulled Rosalind's body. But having no inertia of her own, his own body weary, he stumbled back down into the river. Splashing up again to the surface, Edward felt the warmth of tears burning his eyes. Unbearable fear fixing around his soul, turning his legs to lead. But he had to get her out; he had to get her safe. With one final effort he pressed his feet into the mud and, Rosalind's body laying over his own, slid on his bottom up the riverbank. On the grass he laid her out beside him. Her face ash white in the fast fading light, rolled to one side. He wiped the tangles of hair from across her face, out of her eyes.

'Rosalind?' he whispered, pressing his hand to her chest.

Cold dampness rose to his skin, her thin ribs like ice sticks pressing against his hope. Nothing beat within. Gently he took her chin and turned her face to his. Pulling himself up to her side he cupped her body with his own hoping to give her some warmth. Knowing he was too late.

'Rosalind,' he whispered into her ear, 'Rosalind, please. I cannot, I cannot do this alone. Please.'

Edward carried Rosalind's damp body into their bedroom. There he lay her down and curled up beside her. He did not leave the bed, no one came to check on him.

Time passed.

Edward woke, Rosalind felt cold beside him. Instinctively he curled around her, pulling her close, to warm her... then he remembered. He jerked up, her body limp in his arms. His mouth opened wide in a gaping, soundless howl. The muscles of his chest and neck strained in unbearable anguish, his throat silent and raw. Tears dripping onto white lace.

Time held no meaning. His chest rose and fell. For a while his stomach growled its hunger but soon went quiet. Rain pattered on the roof, sun shone through the window, Edward remained in darkness.

Balun knocked on the door. Edward ignored him.

The police came. He could not face them. He could not voice the truth.

George came. He was horrified. George left.

The scent of burial smoke, a fire of dried river reeds filled the air.

Sunlight cast shadows across Hathrone as Edward walked out into the crisp, dew filled air. Taking a shovel from the shed he began to dig. Sometime after the sun had reached its highest point, he returned inside to her body and removed her clothes, white night gown chastely buttoned. He bathed her and himself in their small bath pot. Carrying her body back to the bed, he towelled her dry, gently, carefully, without haste. He lay down beside her, naked, hand resting on her bare stomach. A cool breeze blew through the open house. Edward watched his arm hairs rise, goose pimples appearing. Rosalind's skin remain smooth. A cry choked up in his throat. He buried his head into the flesh of her side.

Edward rose dressed himself in his finest suit. Opening Rosalind's cupboard he searched until he found her wedding dress and veil. He pressed the fabric to his nose, breathing in the scent of her. Carefully, he dressed her and carried her out into the yard. The sun was low as he stepped into the grave, Rosalind's body in his arms. There he lay her down as gently as he could, pulling the white, lace veil across her face, arranging her limbs as if in sleep. He then sank down on his knees and wrapped his body around her as if she were doing just that, merely sleeping, and held her in his arms one last time. Sobbing, barely in control, he climbed out of the grave and took up the shovel. Below him she looked so alone, so colourless.

He glanced around frantically and spied her roses growing tall and strong. He strode over and pulled off every flower with his bare hands. Thorns tore into his flesh but Edward did not feel their edges, nor notice the slippery blood that oozed down his shovel as he filled in her grave. The earth was silent as he worked; the usual insects of the summer evening, cries of birds nesting, mute. The only sound was the scraping of the shovel and flop of dirt hitting petal, silk and skin.

Her smell began to fade from the sheets. In passionate desperation, Edward flung open her closet and thrust his face into her dresses. Sucking in her scent he wailed himself horse. Sleep finally found him underneath a pile of her clothes.

Clarity.

After an unknown time of dazed sorrow and confusion, *clarity*. Edward knew what he had to do. Filled with the sudden energy of determination, he strode to the kitchen and took up his largest chopping knife. Blade in hand he went to the bedroom mirror and pressed the knife to his throat. There he stood, eyes blazing, body quaking with grief and fear and…

The knife clattered on the floor. Edward fell to his knees.

'Coward!' he screamed at his reflection. 'Useless coward!' He could not endure this emptiness, this hole within his chest; he was too weak to escape. Crawling to the pile of Rosalind's clothes, he buried himself within their gentle folds. Slowly, he began to calm, a new solution forming in his mind

He was ready. Taking up the knife, he cut off all his clothes, slowly, ceremonially. In the watery reflection of the mirror, under the light of a pale moon, naked, fragile, eyes shimmering with tears, Edward took hold of his part. Kneeling down he made the preliminary incisions, carefully. The pain was hot and sharp, but he did not flinch from his task. Edward would be free of all of himself. Cutting through the soft skin of his scrotum caused such pain he passed out momentarily, the blood was profuse but it did not stop him. It only took a flick of the wrist to remove his shaft.

Edward was on the floor in a pool of blood when Mary found him. If it were not for her knowledge of herbs, he may have been spared the pain of the following years.

Edward dressed in a loose fitting mauve dress. He found the black laced dress Rosalind had worn the night they met and, tearing the black lace lining, fashioned a widow's veil. A scarf over his hair, blush along his check bones and he was ready to face the world. Mary, eyes red rimmed and down cast, poured him tea at the verandah table. Silent. There were no words to speak.

Edward Barrington was dead.

Epilogue

41

Even in shadow, there will always be hope.
-Ted Cannon

Adelaide, Australia 2019

I stood, leaning against my hire car: Toyota corolla, red with black feature lines. Good air-con. The warm breeze of early March blew gently through my hair, rustling the dried gum leaves overhead. The gardens on the suburban street were dry: brown lawns, yellowed bushes, wilted and shrivelled leaves. It had been a hot summer. The rains had not yet begun, still the eucalyptus stood tall and resilient. The dry scent of dust and grass and sun and gums swirled around me. I breathed it in deeply, the smell of home.

Just down the street a low brick fence topped with wrought iron feature poles bordered my childhood home. Rendered brick, low green verandah, white window frames. The bushes along the front facing were larger than I remembered, wilder. It must have been a while since mum trimmed them. Or was that one of dad's tasks? Had they been free to grow since he left? Perhaps Shane didn't like gardening.

Shane. My biological father. That still sounded so wrong, like something from a midday soapie, not from my own life. I rolled my neck, trying to release the tension that sat along my shoulders reaching it's fingers up towards my skull, and looked up at the bright blue sky. Closer to the sun. A few wispy clouds floated aimlessly across the arch of the world. I sent it out to him. My love. My heart. He was still my dad, him and only him.

But Shane was my father, and dating my mother. And it was time that I acted like a grown up.

It was time to visit my mum.

It had been an intense few months since Taj and I had read the letters of George Harbot, begging Barrington to tell the truth of what happened to Rosalind. Throughout my conversation with Lord Hargraves as he read the missing pages of Archie's journal my heart had pounded so hard the sound filled my ears. The truth: the body by the river was Rosalind Barrington. It was she who had died that fateful day in 1888, not Edward. Accident? Suicide? Barrington himself did not know. Or could not accept the truth. Standing beside her cooling corpse he had confessed it all to George who tried to reason with him, but never betrayed his truth. Nor did Archie.

Edward could not live without Rosalind, had to be with her. So he became her. Faked his disappearance and took her identity. For the remainder of his life, he lived the lie. A lie with consequences to the lives of so many: to Archie, Clara, Grace, Audrey and Jen. To Balun, Allambee, Percy and Mary. To Deb and Andy. To me. All the threads joined by one man's choice, one man's deception. One man's sorrow.

After that I was rarely in one place for more than a few nights. First there was Adelaide with the police, to share what I had found. Then to Sydney and my professor, to turn my discovery into my thesis. While I worked on my final chapter drafts the police announced their investigation into the mystery body on the Finniss River had been concluded. That 'new evidence' from a young researcher had come to light and after careful cross referencing with their counterparts in the UK they could officially name the mystery woman as Rosalind Barrington.

That's when the interview offers started: the 7:30 report, Foreign Correspondent, BBC radio and the Morning Show. The world was bursting with curiosity. People wanted to know it all. The sadness, the scandal, the gory details of the mutilation. Between editing my thesis and talking to reporters about my discovery I had barely a moment to think of anything other than Edward and Rosalind Barrington.

I caught a few moments of an exposé with Lord David Hargraves. Rosalind's body had been returned to England, and David had generously allowed for her to be buried at Harrowbow, to rest eternally beside her husband. United in death. He stood humbly beside the fresh turned earth and spoke of the dark secret his family kept, 'for our privacy. And for that of people past, who can no longer speak to their actions and choices.' I smirked to myself, remembering

David's lament that Harrowbow attracted no fresh attention to garner revenue. *Well played*, I acknowledged. *Well played indeed.*

And then, as suddenly as it began, the whirlwind stopped and the world turned its face to the next scandal, the next reality TV show, the next piece of celebrity gossip. I handed in my thesis draft and booked a flight to Adelaide for the uni break.

My pocket buzzed. I stuffed my hand between the denim folds of my jeans and extracted my mobile phone. A wry smile curved my lips as I read the number.

'Hi Taj,' I answered brightly.

'Long time no see,' Taj said. I could hear the joviality behind the words. It made me smile even wider, my tummy a riot of champagne bubbles.

'Long time,' I agreed.

'Smooth flight?'

'Yeah, got in about an hour ago.'

'So you are there now? I'm not interrupting am I?'

'No, no, I've just pulled up. Was taking a moment to... gather my nerves.' I could feel the encouraging nod over the mobile network, felt my shoulders relax.

'You'll be fine, Ellie, really. She's your mum after all. It's time, don't you think?'

'Yes,' I said. 'It is.'

'And Shane?'

'I will meet him, in time. My dad always said good came out of a challenge. It's time to live that message.'

'Hmmm,' Taj agreed. 'So what next? Back to Sydney?'

'Actually, I have a few weeks off now for the term break. I was thinking I might stick around in SA...'

'It will be good to have time with your mum, now that you are reconnecting.'

The bubbles in my tummy went instantly flat. I swallowed, gathering myself, glad we weren't face to face. I'd been hoping Taj would...

'Still, can't spend all your time in the city,' Taj continued, a sly tone creeping into his voice. 'Everyone needs some real holiday time.'

A joyous laugh escaped my lips, excitement and relief crashing along my limbs. I breathed deeply, steadying my voice.

'Any suggestions?' I asked coyly.

'Well... see I have some time off too. Lucky coincidence...' he began.

I suppressed a giggle at the thinly veiled lie. 'Was thinking of going up river camping for a few days, maybe a week or so. Would be great to have some company. Would be great if that company was you.'

'Taj,' I said, teasingly. 'Are you asking me to come away with you? Up river. Just you and me alone?'

'I can't think of anyone else I'd want to take away with me, Ellie,' he said simply.

Throughout my hectic few months of fame I'd had no time for me whatsoever.

But now, I had time. Nothing but time.

'Yes,' I breathed into the phone. 'Yes Taj, I will come up river with you. I can't think of anyone else I'd rather be with.'

I felt his smile. It matched my own.

Appendix

The Fall

The Fall
By Edward Barrington

Silence. Cold. Dry and brittle. Adrift in an ocean of darkness.
I reach for colour, bright and warm. Rejection another shade of black.
I create escape. In browns and greys and maroons.
But black returns. Always returns. Dark waters swirling.

White, wet snow reveals a light. Anchor. A gleaming emerald of green
and fawn.
I approach. Hesitant step.
Head too high to see horizon's future. Gently glowing golden aura.
Red. Billows of red surround me. Beneath the red tinge we vow.
Offered honestly. Freely.
Slithering, slippery mud peeks between the auburn.
Reveals the lie.

Black start. Black Heart.
But then: pinks and pearls. Copper and light, sun. Blues hues and
greens and violets.
Tipping the currents in every shade. Emotion filled. Black concealed.

Cracking bright golden light shatters emerald mists.
Dark and cold seeps. Slowly, slowly. Silently creeping.
Faster, faster. Pressing out the forest and gold and fawn, white.
The hope.
Cobalt water flows, toward the future.

Life bringer, sustainer, hope returner.

Darkness paused. Shades muted. Hold. Hold. Hope. Shimmering
opalescence.
Transparent winds whisper: distances past, journeys to come. Faceless.
Nameless.
The breezes pass. Across the world. Alone.
Beneath the currents of the sky I remain, passed by.
Deserted. Colours bleed.

Trapped beneath the mirror surface, danger lurks. Hidden. Unseen.
Waiting.
Thick rivulets course down.
Suction pulls, dragging down, down, down. I fight, I flail. I sink. Cased
in the cold wet dark.

Without I cannot be. Without I will remain. Nothing. Empty. Floating.
All to give, nothing to take. To wait, to hope, to feel, relief to fall.
To fall
To fall

To sink beneath.

No scarlet haze to blur my eyes. No emerald green and fawn.
White cloud mist rain light.
White. No darkness either, to conceal. All revealed.
White. And alone, beneath the currents I wait.
The waters travel forward. The winds pass over. And on and on and
on.
I wait. Stagnant. Transparent. Unmoving.
I cannot move.

The hope is gone, but the river flows. Bubbles. Froths.
Isolation a shadow I can't see,
Shrouded in nothingness.
My eyes are closed. Nothing to see, to feel, to taste.
Just time. Time. Time.
Nothing to fight for. Nothing is left.
* * *

I wait.
For the inevitable.

Drifting

Bibliography

Bibliography
World war 1
https://www.britannica.com/list/timeline-of-world-war-i
https://www.nationalarchives.gov.uk/education/greatwar/g2/backgroundcs1.htm
McLeay Mission
https://guides.slsa.sa.gov.au/Aboriginal_Missions/PointMcLeay
https://www.findandconnect.gov.au/guide/sa/SE01329
Industrial Revolution
https://en.wikipedia.org/wiki/Industrial_Revolution
The Orient Steamliner
https://www.theshipslist.com/ships/lines/orient.shtml
Regent's Park
https://www.regentsparklit.org.uk/authors_o_s.htm#rowe
History of London
https://en.wikipedia.org/wiki/History_of_London_(1900%E2%80%931939)
Bristol
https://www.flickr.com/photos/brizzlebornandbred/4018454647

Thank you

I would like to thank so many people for their support and encouragement in writing this novel.

To my dear friends and family who read drafts filled with run-on-sentences and typos, and then re-read my polished drafts, you are all amazing.

To my wonderful husband, for bringing me cups of coffee, giving me neck massages and talking through plot ideas late into the night, I could not have done this without you.

To Jazzy-Pud, for your constant purrs of love that remind me that all is right with the world.

And finally, to all of you who read this novel, thank you for giving me the opportunity to share my first work with you. I hope you enjoyed the journey.

Kind regards,

Lelita Baldock

Printed in Great Britain
by Amazon

43946752R00144